P9-DZN-686

Grimgar of Fantasy and Ash

level.7 - The Rainbow on the Other Side

Written by: **Ao Jyumonji**

Illustrations by: **Eiri Shirai**

As they got closer, he gradually understood.
The lights were no illusion. He could see a number of
buildings clearly. It wasn't large enough to be called a
town. A small village, maybe.

Yume was being unusually nice to Ranta.

Actually, Haruhiro wasn't sure when or how it happened,

but Yume was letting him rest his head in her lap.

That was so incredibly unusual, he doubted his eyes.

Grimgar
of
Fantasy
and
Ash

GRIMGAR OF FANTASY AND ASH, LEVEL. 7

Copyright © 2015 Ao Jyumonji
Illustrations by Eiri Shirai

First published in Japan in 2015 by
OVERLAP Inc., Ltd., Tokyo.
English translation rights arranged with
OVERLAP Inc., Ltd., Tokyo.

Seven Seas books may be purchased in bulk for promotional,
educational, or business use. Please contact your local
bookseller or the Macmillan Corporate and Premium Sales
Department at 1-800-221-7945, extension 5442, or by
e-mail at MacmillanSpecialMarkets@macmillan.com.

Follow Seven Seas Entertainment online at
sevenseasentertainment.com.
Experience J-Novel Club books online at j-novel.club.

TRANSLATION: Sean McCann
J-NOVEL EDITOR: Emily Sorensen
COVER DESIGN: Nicky Lim
INTERIOR LAYOUT & DESIGN: Clay Gardner
COPY EDITOR: Michelle Danner-Groves, Lora Gray
PROOFREADER: Jade Gardner
LIGHT NOVEL EDITOR: Nibedita Sen
EDITOR-IN-CHIEF: Adam Arnold
PUBLISHER: Jason DeAngelis

ISBN: 978-1-626928-40-4
Printed in Canada
First Printing: July 2018
10 9 8 7 6 5 4 3 2 1

Grimgar of Fantasy and Ash

level. 7 — The Rainbow on the Other Side

Presented by
AO JYUMONJI

Illustrated by
EIRI SHIRAI

Table ᴏꜰ Contents

Characters

YUME

*Airheaded soothing-type.
Speaks an iffy sort of Kansai dialect?*

CLASS:
Hunter

HARUHIRO

*Sleepy eyes.
Passive-type. Provisional leader.*

CLASS:
Thief

SHIHORU

*Shy and withdrawn.
Hard worker with little presence.*

CLASS:
Mage

RANTA

*Selfish, flaky joker.
#1 most unpopular.*

CLASS:
Dread
Knight

MERRY

*Cool beauty. Has more experience
as a volunteer soldier and is a little
more of an adult.*

CLASS:
Priest

KUZAKU

*The new guy. Hard to tell if
he's motivated or not.*

CLASS:
Paladin

Other Characters

Team Renji

Renji—CLASS: Warrior
Head of Team Renji. Wild beast-type. Dangerous.

Ron—CLASS: Paladin
The Team's No. 2.

Sassa—CLASS: Thief
Flashy woman. Probably an M.

Adachi—CLASS: Mage
Wears glasses.

Chibi—CLASS: Priest
Mascot.

Team Tokimune (Tokkis)

Tokimune—CLASS: Paladin
Handsome. Friendly optimist.

Inui—CLASS: Hunter
Looks middle-aged. Has middle school syndrome, maybe?

Tada—CLASS: Priest
Fighting priest. Real show-off. Kind of a serious headcase.

Mimori—CLASS: Mage
Ex-warrior mage. Nickname is "Giantess."

Anna-san—CLASS: Priest
Blonde-haired, blue-eyed, self-proclaimed pretty girl.

Kikkawa—CLASS: Warrior
*Good at getting by in the world. Enlisted
at the same time as Haruhiro and the others.*

MOGUZO
Bear-type. A somewhat slow, but reliable, bear. They relied on him too much.
CLASS: Warrior

MANATO
Kept the party together. Was a good guy. (Past tense)
CLASS: Priest

SOMA
Started the Day Breakers Clan. Seems to have some objective.
CLASS: Samurai

CHOCO
Did Haruhiro know her? Fell at the orcish keep.
CLASS: Thief

1 | The Blurry Ridge

G REMLINS CHANTED all around them.

"Nafushuperah, toburoh, furagurashurah, purapurapuryoh."

"Anabushoh, fakanakanah, barauarafurenyoh, kurakoshoh."

"Kachabyuryohoh, kyabashah, chapah, ryubaryaburyah, hoko-shoh."

Blue light leaked out from hole upon hole upon hole. How many gremlins lived here in these flats? Hundreds? Thousands? Tens of thousands, maybe?

Those creatures that looked like a bat combined with a goblin were fundamentally harmless. Even knowing that, they were a little scary. If something went wrong and they attacked, the party wouldn't stand a chance.

After they made it through the Gremlin Flats, they came to the Egg Storage.

The layout of the place was simple. Along the single path was a series of oblong rooms where the gremlins laid their eggs. The party had no interest in the eggs, so they kept going down the path, ignoring the rooms.

We can just keep going, right? Haruhiro thought.

Haruhiro looked to Ranta, Kuzaku, Yume, Shihoru, and Merry again and again, making sure they were still there, as he asked himself if they should go on or turn back. Ask as he might, he never reached an answer. He had no clue what he ought to do.

The dominatrix, Lala, and her servant, Nono, were up ahead, moving at a careful but confident pace. Nono carried a lantern, its light illuminating Lala's bold and extreme appearance.

Honestly, she didn't have to accentuate her womanly charms and expose herself as much as she did, barely hiding the parts she absolutely couldn't show in public. It wasn't like Haruhiro wanted to see those. But... he couldn't help looking. Did she just like to show off? Maybe she was aiming for every reaction she could possibly get from showing off like that.

Nono, who was white-haired and wore a black mask that covered the bottom of his face, was silent. In fact, Haruhiro had yet to hear him speak. Whenever they took a break, he served as Lala's chair. That was, well...

They were an odd couple, to put it lightly.

They were capable, though. Terrifyingly so. Reliable, too. But was it okay to rely on them? That was somewhat iffy. It felt like if the party trusted them too much, they would be taken for suckers and suffer for it.

Eventually, the group came to the end of the Egg Storage.

From there, it was a single straight path that gently curved to the right before taking a sharp turn in that direction.

It came to a T junction.

Haruhiro felt a sense of déjà vu. It was nearly identical to the entrance of the Egg Storage in the Wonder Hole. The T junctions there eventually met up again, whether you went left or right, and the Wonder Hole had been on the other side.

Can we make it back through here, maybe?

For a moment, he thought that. But naturally, that wasn't the case.

Lala and Nono went right at the T junction. Another curve, and then, as expected, the path split. They turned right, then continued. The tight, twisted path with its low ceiling seemed to go on forever.

The two paths were similar, but this one wasn't quite like the entrance in the Wonder Hole. Where exactly would they come out? Could Haruhiro and the others go back home?

"We're near the exit," Lala told them in a whisper.

Now that she mentioned it, the air was flowing slightly. The temperature had dropped a little. When Nono covered the lantern, it was suddenly pitch black. No sign of light up ahead.

"Is it night...?" Ranta whispered, gulping.

There was the sound of someone sighing. Footsteps. The rustling of clothes. The clinking of armor. Breathing.

Nono didn't lift the lantern cover. Only a small amount of light leaked out from the gaps in it.

Lala stopped, making some gesture to Nono. Haruhiro and

the party stopped, too. It seemed Lala intended to have Nono go investigate the situation by himself.

Nono knew how to use Sneaking. As a thief himself, Haruhiro recognized it. Nono used it at a fairly high level, too.

Nono left the lantern with Lala, then melted into the darkness. He made not a single sound and soon vanished from sight. It was probably around five minutes later when Nono finally returned.

Nono moved in close to Lala and whispered something in her ear, but Haruhiro couldn't pick up his voice. Lala nodded once, then gave the lantern back to Nono and began walking. Haruhiro and the others had no choice but to follow.

With the lantern still covered, it remained completely dark, but they were clearly approaching the outside.

Just a little longer, Haruhiro told himself. *We're almost there.*

"Mrrowr..." Yume let out a strange sound.

The outside was damp, locked in a cold darkness. There were noises, but from what?

Ou, ou, ou...

The sound steadily repeated—was it the cry of some animal? There was a continuous high-pitched sound, too. Was it the beating of some insect's wings?

A third sound, like the rapid clicking of someone's tongue, joined in. It was creepy, and it made him uncomfortable.

"Where is this place...?" Kuzaku whispered weakly.

Someone started sobbing. It had to be Shihoru.

"It's okay," Merry said, trying to encourage her, but her voice shook.

"Night..." Haruhiro had a sudden thought. "Could this be the place? The Night Realm?"

Lala and Nono were the ones who had discovered the Gremlin Flats accessible from the Wonder Hole were connected to another world in addition to the Dusk Realm. No morning or night ever came to the Dusk Realm, but in this other world, there was only night; the day never came. That was why it was called the Night Realm.

"Wait, if that's true..." Ranta did a little dance. "...we can get back, don'tcha think?!"

"Possibly," Lala snorted. "Possibly not. This place is dangerous in its own ways. We've barely explored it ourselves."

Haruhiro rubbed his belly. His stomach hurt. Intensely. Even the jubilant Ranta fell silent.

At any moment, some unknown creature might appear from the darkness to attack them.

"Well, on that note, we'll be going," Lala said briskly.

Then Lala and Nono moved away. It took Haruhiro a moment to understand what she meant.

"...Huh?! That's—whoa, whoa, whoa, hold on?!" he yelped.

"What?" Lala asked.

"No, you're going—huh? What does that mean... Huh? Huh...? Just the two of you? By yourselves?" he stuttered.

"We have no clue what's up ahead, after all," she told him.

"No, w-we have no idea either, obviously, but... But, still..."

"When in an unfamiliar place, experience tells us that we move best on our own. That's how we've always worked, and I intend to keep it that way."

"No, b-but..."

"Don't...!" Ranta got down and performed a kowtow. "Don't leave meeeee! Please, please! Seriously, seriously! I'm begging you! Don't leave me here!"

Even Haruhiro, who was well aware of what kind of human—or piece of trash—Ranta was, was appalled by the display. He couldn't not be.

How is he not embarrassed by himself? He's too shameless. And hold on, what's with this "me" stuff? He only ever thinks about himself. He's still horrible, the worst...

"Bye." Lala might have waved to them, or maybe she didn't. Either way, suddenly they couldn't see her anymore.

The dominatrix and her servant were gone.

"Wh-what...now?" Kuzaku asked in a whisper.

Oh, crap. This is bad, thought Haruhiro. *I can't believe how dark it is. I can't see anything. It's solid darkness.*

Haruhiro was trapped inside some dark mass. He couldn't move, couldn't escape. This was the end.

—No. No, that wasn't true. It was all an illusion.

"R-right, first thing's first, we need light." Haruhiro rummaged through his bag and pulled out a lantern. Once it was lit, he felt a little calmer.

Yume had pulled out her own lantern and was trying to light it.

Haruhiro stopped her. "We only need one. Just mine, for now. I want to conserve oil."

"Ohhh. Yeah, that makes sense, huh?"

"Damn that woman." Ranta punched the ground, grinding his teeth. "I'll never forgive her."

"Don't cry, man," Haruhiro said.

"I-I'm not crying! You're stupid! Stupid, stupid Haruhiro! Urgh..."

Merry hugged Shihoru tight. Shihoru looked like she would collapse at any moment if she didn't.

Haruhiro took a deep breath, forcing himself to relax. *I need to keep it together. I'm the leader. I need to support everyone. Need to pull them along. I won't let anyone die. We're going to survive. We'll all get through this alive.*

"Let's move," he said. "Take it a bit at a time. Things will work out. I'll make them work out. I'm, well, all of us are here. Just be careful not to make too much noise. If you sense anything coming, let me know right away. We'll take things cautiously and... Yeah. Okay. Let's go."

I'm rambling. Even I know that. What am I thinking? What should I be thinking about? I don't know. But, staying here is bad, right? Or maybe I just don't want to stay here? It might be that I'm just scared to stay put. But, I mean, Lala and Nono took off immediately. Yeah. We can't stay here.

Haruhiro and the others had their backs to a rock wall. The hole that led to the Egg Storage opened up out of it.

Lala and Nono had vanished off to the left. There was a gradual downwards slope in front of them.

The ground was uneven. Rocky. Right, forward, or straight?

He didn't hesitate long. Haruhiro decided to go after Lala

and Nono. They probably couldn't catch up, but those two had gone left. It would be a little safer than going right. Maybe.

While checking their footing, they proceeded carefully along the rock wall to their left. They walked as if crossing a narrow bridge.

Is this too slow? Should we hurry? No, what good will rushing do? It would help if it would just get brighter. Does morning come in this world?

Shihoru sobbed convulsively.

"Oh, cut it out, would you?" Ranta clicked his tongue. "—Ow!"

"Shut up, you dummy!" It sounded like Yume had hit Ranta.

If I open my mouth, I feel like I'll start whining, Haruhiro thought. *Time. How much time has passed? I can't even imagine. How long do we need to walk? Should we rest? Are my comrades tired? Should I ask? Are they hungry? Thirsty? We need water. Food, too. What do we do? How can we get those? Is everyone going to survive? Is that a realistic goal in this situation?*

At some point, Shihoru stopped crying. The rock wall had been at almost a 90-degree angle before, but it was much less steep now. Haruhiro could probably climb it now, but he didn't feel like climbing.

Off to the right, there was darkness, darkness, endless darkness. Even holding the lantern out in that direction, he couldn't see a thing.

The animal cries, the batting of wings, the clicking. They all continued, coming from here and there periodically.

Suddenly, the wind blew against them.

"Hold on." Haruhiro raised one hand for his comrades to stop.

He inched forward. The ground in front of him soon disappeared. They had reached a cliff.

How high was it? Crouching down, he lowered the lantern as far as he could. He couldn't see the bottom, it was too far down.

He listened closely. Was that... water? Was there a river down there?

If there was a river, there was water. That said, they couldn't make it down the cliff. They certainly couldn't jump off, either.

He picked up a stone and threw it over the edge. After a few seconds, there was a splashing sound. It didn't seem like dozens of meters; it had to be around ten.

"There's water down there," Haruhiro said.

But he got no reaction. Not even from Ranta. Everyone must have been exhausted, both in body and soul.

"We'll continue along the edge of the cliff here and look for a way down," Haruhiro said. "If we can just get water..."

"Yeah," Kuzaku responded briefly.

"Shihoru, you okay?" Haruhiro asked. Shihoru silently nodded.

She didn't seem okay. That concerned him, but if they could find drinking water, even Shihoru would start to feel safer. But, was the river water potable? Not as it was, probably. But, if they boiled it? They would have to start a fire.

They would have to be careful not to fall off the cliff, too. He didn't think anyone was *that* stupid, but just in case.

A strong, damp wind blew along the cliff. It was unpleasantly cold. If they didn't find a way to warm themselves eventually, they'd start shivering.

After some time, a fog rolled in. The ground was no longer rocky. It seemed like something grasslike grew on top of the dirt. It wasn't green, though, but white. Was it really grass?

"Whoa!" Ranta suddenly jumped. "Wh-wh-wha...?!"

"What?" Haruhiro asked.

"I-I just stepped on something! Nothing alive, I think, but— Ahh!" Ranta picked something up. It was a white object. "Look at this! Bones!"

Shihoru shrieked.

"What're you pickin' 'em up for?" Yume asked.

"You're unbelievable," Merry muttered.

With that concentrated attack from the girls, Ranta got defensive. He started waving the white object around. "What're you scared of some stupid bones for? You stupid women! What's there to be afraid of? I'm totally fine. Because *I'm* me!"

"What kind of bones are they?" Haruhiro asked, squinting at them.

A hand. It looked like a hand. It hadn't fallen apart after the blasphemous treatment Ranta had given it, so there had to be flesh or something else holding it together.

"Hmm?" Ranta brought his face close and inspected it. "Size-wise, it could be human... but the fingers are too long. Yeah, too long. Wait, there're too many of them. Like, eight? Hmm?"

Kuzaku crouched down next to Ranta. The rest of the bones were there, hidden by tufts of the long, white grasslike stuff.

"Yeah, doesn't look human," Kuzaku agreed. "Some other creature, I guess."

Yume, Shihoru, and Merry backed away. Haruhiro moved over to Ranta and Kuzaku, and crouched down.

It's a skeleton, Haruhiro thought. *It's wearing some sort of metal armor. Two arms, two legs. A tail, too, so it's probably not human. No head anywhere to be seen. Maybe it never had one to begin with? Or some animal took off with it? Looks like it's lying face down. That long, thin object looks like a sword. The round one, that's a shield, maybe? This white, grasslike stuff is wrapped around it.*

Kuzaku grabbed the edge of the shield and pulled. The white, grasslike stuff snapped as he did. "Think I could use it?"

"A paladin without a shield's about as useful as a maggot, after all," Ranta said. "Take it." Ranta chucked the skeletal hand aside and picked up the sword. "This one's no good. It's rusted like crazy."

Haruhiro frowned after the hand Ranta had thrown away, then looked down at the body. It could very well have been a woman or a man, but Haruhiro was going to assume he had been male, for convenience's sake.

The man was armed, so that probably meant he'd been a sentient being from this world. How much time had passed since he died? It seemed unlikely that it had only been a few days. So, a few months? Or maybe a year?

A few years? Or decades?

"Ranta, turn him face up," Haruhiro ordered.

"Hell. No. Why should I listen to you? Go die."

"I'll do it." Kuzaku lifted the man up and turned him over. "There we go."

Haruhiro examined the man now that he was facing upwards. The head had definitely been cut off. Haruhiro could see what looked like the neck bones.

There were box-shaped containers attached to the man's belt. Haruhiro opened one and took out the contents. It was black, hard, and round. A coin? There were also what looked to be seeds and a rusty dagger. He frowned and continued to investigate.

Was that...a key? It was certainly some sort of tool. It hung from a chain around the man's neck.

That's a pretty chain, thought Haruhiro. *It looks like it might be gold. It couldn't possibly be pure, though.*

When he brushed the dirt off the front of the armor, he realized there was some sort of pattern carved there. Writing, probably. The same sort of characters were etched on the coin-like object, too.

Back in Grimgar, he had heard orcs had their own language, while the undead used one that closely resembled elves', dwarves', and humans'. Whatever race this man had been probably was intelligent, on the same level as Haruhiro and the others. Or close at least.

"Haru-kun." Yume pulled on Haruhiro's cloak. "Y'know, Yume's thinkin' she might be hearin' a rustlin' noise."

Ranta started and looked around the area. Merry and Shihoru

huddled close together, holding their breath. Kuzaku held the man's shield at the ready, crouching on one knee with a hand on the hilt of his longsword.

Haruhiro quickly threw the man's possessions into his bag. He listened closely.

Rustle. Rustle. Rustle. Rustle. Rustle.

He definitely heard something. From the opposite direction of the cliff. Should they watch for it? Or flee? Haruhiro decided instantly. It was a compromise between the two; they'd retreat while staying on watch.

"Let's stay on guard as we move forward," he ordered. "Ranta, Kuzaku—" He waved his hands to get people in formation.

Haruhiro took point. Merry, Yume, and Shihoru formed one column behind him, while Ranta and Kuzaku stayed beside them but opposite the cliff. Haruhiro glanced at the lantern. Was carrying a light here saying "Please, come after us?" But if they put it out, they would be in total darkness. There was the risk they'd fall off the cliff, too.

Haruhiro and the others began to move.

Rustle, rustle, rustle.

He could still hear it. Was it coming after them? It didn't seem far off. Within ten meters? No, probably less. Too close.

He felt compelled to see whatever it was with his own eyes. Would that be a good idea? Yes. No. He couldn't decide.

While remaining careful of the cliff, he listened closely to the sound for any sign of change.

This is driving me crazy. I don't want to do it anymore, he thought over and over, at least once every few minutes. When the doubt was at its worst, he thought it every few seconds.

He wanted to throw everything away and run. But where could he go?

The lantern's fire's getting weak. The moment he thought it, the light was gone.

"Whaaaaa?! Parupiro, come on! I can't see, you moron! You scum!" Ranta screamed.

"The oil just ran out, okay? Uh, well, we'll have to use Yume's lantern to—"

"Hold on," Merry said in a stifled voice. "The sky."

Haruhiro looked off into the distance, beyond the cliff. She was right. There was something off about the sky.

"Is it...morning?" Haruhiro asked slowly.

There was a ridge in the distance burning faintly. It was red, or orange rather. It was strange. Normally, when the sun rose in the morning, the darkness gradually faded from the edge of the sky. It turned blue or purple, then slowly grew redder. It never looked like this, like the sky had caught fire.

He knew there were worlds like the Dusk Realm. If this world's sky changed in strange ways, that wasn't going to surprise him at this point.

Well, at least it doesn't seem to be Grimgar or the Dusk Realm. The realization hit him hard.

"Huh?"

Haruhiro craned his neck. He didn't hear the rustling anymore. Had it gone away? Or was it laying low? Either way, he figured it would be a good idea to get away from this spot while they had the chance. Haruhiro signaled for them to set off.

That was when it happened.

"Mrrow!" Yume made a strange noise and collapsed. No. She hadn't collapsed. She'd been knocked down. There was something on top of Yume. "Something" was the only way Haruhiro could describe it. He couldn't see.

"Ohhhhhh?!" Ranta was trying to pull that something off Yume.

"Damn, it's too dark!" Kuzaku shouted.

"Yume! Yume! Yume!" Haruhiro shouted his comrade's name as he rushed toward the thing. Flustered, he nearly lost his footing and fell off the cliff. He panicked.

He could hear punching, hitting. Yume was screaming and sobbing.

"It took off!" Ranta shouted.

Suddenly, there was a light. From a candle. A portable candlestick. It was Shihoru.

Shihoru sat down next to Yume. "Yume! Hang in there!"

"The enemy! That bastard! Where is he?! Dammit!" Ranta swung his sword around.

"What was that?!" Kuzaku kept his shield at the ready, shoulders heaving with heavy breaths.

Yume had fallen over, clutching at her throat. Blood. The blood. Her neck. It'd gotten her neck. Blood. So much blood.

Kuh. Fuh. Fuh. Hah. Kuh. Fuh. Hah. Yume's breathing was strained, shallow, and ragged.

Haruhiro was stunned. *No way. Don't do this to me. You're kidding. What the hell? Tell me it's a lie, somebody. Please, tell me it's a lie. No. This is wrong. It's a lie. It can't be real. Right? I mean, it makes no sense. This makes no sense.*

"Ahhhhhhhhhhhhhhhhhhhhhhhhhhhh!" Haruhiro screamed.

His level head. His sense of duty. His responsibility, self-control, reason. His very ability to think. All of those were blasted away.

Haruhiro didn't even cling to Yume. He just stood there and screamed. He knew one thing: he couldn't take this anymore. He had totally snapped.

It's over. Just let it end. No! I can't let it end, but what can I do? There's nothing I can do, is there? It's hopeless, isn't it? Yume's gonna die, isn't she?

"O light...!" Merry touched her fingers to her forehead, making a pentagram, then touched her middle finger to her brow to complete the hexagram. Then, rushing over, she brought her palm to Yume's throat. "May Lumiaris's divine protection be upon you! Sacrament!"

What? Haruhiro thought numbly. *What are you doing? Have you gone nuts? It's hopeless. I mean, light magic doesn't work in the Dusk Realm! Sure, this isn't the Dusk Realm, but it's not Grimgar, so Lumiaris's power shouldn't reach here! And—*

No doubt Merry knew that. Was she unable to give up, even knowing that? Had she decided to bet on one thin thread of hope?

"Ahh... Hah..." Yume blinked repeatedly. "Huh...?"

Her body was wreathed in a dim light.

Merry gritted her teeth. Her entire body was shuddering.

This can't be real, Haruhiro thought, stunned. *Really? No lie?*

"Your wounds!" Shihoru's eyes went wide. "Yume! Your wounds are closing!"

Ranta stopped swinging his sword and stood there, staring blankly at Yume.

"Haha!" Kuzaku laughed like a crazy man. "Ahaha! Hahahahaha! Wahahaha!"

Haruhiro wanted to laugh along. How could he not? What could he do except laugh? But he cried instead.

Yume still hadn't gotten up. Merry's healing wasn't done. Sacrament took a surprisingly long time.

Haruhiro got down on all fours next to Yume. Merry finally pulled her hand back and fell onto her backside. She panted, looking spent.

Yume looked at her, then smiled softly. "Thank you, Merry-chan. Huh? Haru-kun, what're you cryin'—"

"Yume!" Haruhiro hugged Yume without thinking about it. "Thank goodness! Thank goodness, Yume! Thank... Sorry! I thought you were a goner!"

"Ohhh," said Yume. "If you squeeze tight like that, Haru-kun, you'll get blood on you, y'know?"

"Who cares?!" he screamed.

"Okay. But, still, when you're squeezin' her tight like this, Yume, she's happy, but it hurts a little, y'know?"

"S-s-s-s-sorry!" When Haruhiro tried to let go and jump back, someone whacked him hard on the back of the head. "Ow?! Huh?! R-Ranta?! What was that for?!"

"For nothing, you damn idiot!" Ranta glared at him, trying to intimidate him.

Seriously, what was that about? Was he a moron? Was he total scum?

"Sorry to interrupt," Kuzaku said hesitantly. "But don't you think it'd be a good idea to get away from here? I mean, we did let the thing from earlier get away."

"Ah!" Haruhiro wiped his face with both hands. *He's right. I completely lost myself there. I need to do some serious reflecting on that, but it can wait. For now, I should do what Kuzaku suggested.*

"Y-Yume, can you stand?!" Haruhiro exclaimed. "Merry, how about you? Oh, right, someone get a lantern out! Okay, let's go!"

Before they set out, he looked once more at the distant ridge, still burning orange.

Was the sun coming up?

He couldn't imagine that was the case.

2 | Please

I**T SEEMED HIGHLY LIKELY** their unknown assailant had scaled the cliff to attack Yume. Haruhiro and the party kept a cautious distance from the cliff as they pressed onward.

They knew that because light magic had worked, the power of the god of light Lumiaris extended to this world. However, from what Merry told them, when she cast Sacrament, it had been far more draining than usual. It had also taken a long time for Yume's wounds to heal. Haruhiro found both those facts strange. Sacrament was supposed to be a spell that instantly healed all wounds.

They tried having Ranta summon his demon to see what would happen, and Zodiac-kun came just as it was supposed to. It looked like a person with a purple sheet over its head, with two hole-like eyes and a gash-like mouth. It carried a blade in its right hand and something like a club in its left. It had legs, although it sort of floated along. But Zodiac-kun arrived at a third of its usual size.

The power of the dark god Skullhell reached this world, too. However, perhaps because of distance or perhaps because of something else entirely, Lumiaris and Skullhell could only provide about a third of their usual protection.

Well, whether it was a third or a quarter, it was still a step up from nothing. Thanks to that, Yume had survived. Praise be to Lumiaris.

While they were able to use light magic now, they still couldn't afford to relax. Haruhiro watched carefully for any presences. It was exhausting. Whenever it became so hard that he thought he might break, his mind flashed back to Yume on the brink of death. He never wanted to experience that again. What was a little struggle now compared to that? He had to tough it out. If he could, that meant he wasn't at his limit yet.

No matter how much time passed, the sky grew no lighter. The sun in this world was incredibly shy, it seemed. In the end, the sun never rose, and the flame-like light he'd glimpsed coming from beyond the distant ridge burned out. When night finally came, the world became pitch dark, making him realize it had been relatively bright in the middle of the day.

Everyone was silent. Occasionally Ranta would say something stupid, as if he had just remembered that was a thing he did, but it never developed into a conversation. Whenever someone stopped walking, they took a break.

The morning that he couldn't think of as "morning" came, and then a night that was deeper than the one before. Haruhiro's hopes had been misplaced when he waited for morning to come.

Still, whenever the flames on the ridge burned out, he felt his chest tighten with helplessness.

They were volunteer soldiers, albeit not very good ones, so they all had been carrying emergency rations and water with them. Their supplies quickly ran out.

Ranta would occasionally summon Zodiac-kun and chat with the demon. He might have been trying to distract himself. Haruhiro began to doubt his own sanity. If he saw lights ahead of them, he thought they were a dream or illusion. Things that couldn't be real.

Occasionally, here and there, lights like distant bonfires would flicker in and out. They didn't seem natural. If they weren't illusions, they were probably being lit by intelligent life forms. Was there a connection between those life forms and the ambush that had nearly killed Yume? He couldn't possibly know.

The ground sloped gently downward. How far was it to one of the lights? A kilometer or so?

As they got closer, he gradually understood. The lights were no illusion. He could see buildings clearly and even noticed a watchtower-like structure. The lights *were* from bonfires and lamps. There were fires hanging from the eaves of buildings and up in the watchtower. There were maybe twenty of them.

The place wasn't large enough to be called a town. A small village, maybe.

The problem was the residents. He called them residents, but they weren't people.

"What should we do?" Haruhiro asked hesitantly.

"Man, what do you mean, 'what'?" Ranta sighed. "What are we gonna do?"

"Keehe... Don't ask, you runny piece of crap, Ranta... Worry and agonize over it...until you die... Ehehehe."

"Don't joke like that, Zodiac-kun," Ranta said. "Not now. It's kind of depressing and just too much."

"Don't worry... Kehe, kehehe..."

"Well, I'm not, you know?" Ranta said defensively. "I understand it's just your dark sense of humor, okay?"

"Kehehehe... That a misunderstanding... Zodiac-kun always serious... Ehe..."

"Seriously?! For real?! And why did you say that like you have a heavy accent?!"

"Ranta-kun sure is energetic, huh?" Kuzaku muttered.

Who was it that said, "If you have energy, you can do anything"? Haruhiro didn't think you could do *anything* if you had energy. But without energy, there were a lot of things you couldn't do. So it wasn't such a bad thing that Ranta was getting his energy back. But it was noisy and annoying.

"We shouldn't approach carelessly," Shihoru said hesitantly.

"She's right," Merry agreed. "We don't know what's lying in wait, after all."

"But it makes you wanna find out what's goin' on in there." Yume's stomach groaned loudly. "Oof. Yume, she's gettin' hungry."

Of course she is, Haruhiro thought.

Honestly, their hunger and thirst were all reaching dangerous levels. They needed more water and provisions soon, or they were finished.

"I'll go scout it out," Haruhiro said. "You all stay here."

"We're counting on you, thief." Ranta slapped Haruhiro on the shoulder.

That irritated him, but Haruhiro held himself back, leaning in close to whisper in Ranta's ear. "If anything happens, I'm counting on you to handle the rest."

"S-sure... Well, if it comes to that. C-come back, okay, you moron? In one piece."

"It's creepy when you act like that," Haruhiro muttered.

Haruhiro instantly shifted into a fresh frame of mind. First, he eliminated his presence—Hide. Second, he moved with his presence eliminated—Swing. Third, he utilized all his senses to detect the presences of others—Sense.

In other words, he used Stealth.

He imagined himself slipping underground without a sound, moving through the earth like a mole. At the same time, he would stick his eyes and ears above the surface, looking and listening. Sensing.

He heard a sound.

Clang, clang! It was the sound of something hard being beaten.

The closest light was the bonfire on top of the watchtower. There was a moat around twenty-five meters from it. The moat looked about two meters across. Its depth was unknown, but it probably wasn't shallow.

There was a humanoid creature sitting up in the watchtower. Its torso was strangely large, its head small. That small head was wrapped in something like cloth. Was that a bow and quiver of arrows slung over its back? The creature was clearly a lookout. The residents of the small village were protecting themselves against intrusion with the moat, and they had a lookout posted. They weren't going to get in there after all.

No, it was too soon to make that call. Haruhiro turned left, advancing toward where the river seemed to be. He soon ran into a cliff.

He called it a cliff, but it was only two or three meters to the bottom. It wouldn't be impossible to make his way down. At the bottom was a riverbed, and a river flowing just past it. It looked like the village was drawing water from the river into their moat.

When he looked from the river over to the moat, he noticed another watchtower. There was another bonfire atop it and a lookout. But this lookout was much smaller than the first one. It had a roly-poly body, only about as large as a human child. Still, its head was wrapped with cloth, just like the first. It also seemed to use a bow and arrow.

Haruhiro decided to designate this Watchtower B and the first one Watchtower A. He turned back to Watchtower A, proceeding in the opposite direction.

The moat eventually began to curve. He could see the buildings more clearly. They were all one floor, and there were no more than ten or so of them. Eventually he came to another a third watchtower, now Watchtower C. Watchtower C was big and sturdy, clearly part of a gate. There was a bridge extending out from that open gate, made of wood and solidly built. The bridge over the moat looked strong enough to bear the weight of a carriage.

There was a lookout on Watchtower C, too. This one wasn't sitting. It was standing. Unlike the lookouts at Watchtower A or B, this one had a strangely long and lanky physique.

There was something weird about those arms. Too many joints? It looked like it had two, maybe three elbows. Like the other lookouts, its head was wrapped with cloth, but it protruded from it at the very ends. There was also a tail. The lookout on Watchtower C had a tail.

At the very least, he could say the lookouts at Watchtower A and B and the one at Watchtower C were of different races. If Haruhiro used his common sense, there was only one possible conclusion.

Was the lookout at Watchtower C the same race as the skeletal remains Ranta had found? It *did* have a tail, after all. The corpse had had eight fingers, too. What about the lookout? That remained to be seen.

The lookout at Watchtower C suddenly looked his way.

Have I been noticed? Haruhiro held his breath and remained still. If he panicked and tried to flee, that would make things worse.

The lookout took out the bow that had been slung over its back, nocking an arrow. It drew back on the bowstring.

Oh, crap, he thought. *I want to run away. I have to run away. No. Hold on. It's not clear that I've been found. Besides, if it fires, it won't be too late to run. Probably.*

The lookout loosed up on the bowstring. It spun the un-nocked arrow around. Then, as if to say, *Must have been my imagination,* it tilted its head to the side.

Yeah, that's right. It was just your imagination. Haruhiro took a small breath, then he began moving.

That lookout was bad news. It was sharp. Had he made a noise? Haruhiro didn't think so. Besides, there was a constant clanging at regular intervals, so he should have been fine with making a little noise. Still, the lookout had detected *something.* He decided it was best to be careful.

He continued scouting. Passing by the bridge, he followed the curve of the moat. After confirming a Watchtower D and E, he came upon a cliff. The riverbed was below.

This village was in a warped circle, surrounded by the moat and river.

To enter the village, they would have to cross the bridge, get over the moat, or swim along the river to reach the riverbed on the village's side.

It would be dangerous to swim in the darkness. They could very well drown. They could probably manage to swim across the moat but scaling the wall on the other side would prove troublesome.

That meant crossing the bridge was their only option. Of course, if he tried to walk across openly, he'd probably be sniped by the lookout. Could they remove the lookout with Yume's bow or Shihoru's magic? But then what? Force their way in? Just the six of them? There were at least four other lookouts armed with bows and no guarantee that there weren't more.

Could they win? Was this even a win-or-lose situation? It didn't feel like it. Haruhiro and the party's goal was to obtain water and food, that was all. If the party could show they weren't hostile somehow, would the residents let them in? Then Haruhiro and his party could trade their possessions or money, whatever it took, for food and potable water. Was that possible?

Haruhiro took the same path back the way he had come, observing the village across the moat as he went.

He spotted a number of the residents. He was surprised. They weren't people. No, there were some that weren't humanoid. That was the better way to put it.

The most intensely different residents had six insect-like arms, with furball-like lower bodies. They had their heads wrapped in something, too. All the residents here seemed a little too diverse.

When Haruhiro returned to his comrades and gave them the short version of what he'd seen, Ranta thumped his chest, snorting excitedly. "Leave it to me. I've got an idea."

"Kehe... I have a good feeling about this... Kehehehe... It feels like Ranta's heading for the eternal slumber..."

"That doesn't sound like a good feeling to me at all, you know?" Ranta shot back. "I've said this before, but if I get sent off to my eternal rest, you're gonna disappear too, got it, Zodiac-kun?"

"O dread knight... Ehe... Let us be embraced by Lord Skullhell together... Ehehe..."

"I-I'm thinking it's a bit early for that, yeah? Listen, um, I've got lots I still want to do, like playing with some boobies, and— Wait, what are you making me say?!"

"Nobody's making you say anything." Haruhiro massaged his brow with his fingers.

"You just wanted to say 'boobies'," Yume said, and Haruhiro thought she was probably right.

"You're the worst." Merry practically spat the words at him.

Shihoru said something awfully harsh under her breath. "I hope Zodiac-kun's right about *that* prediction..."

Ranta was undeterred. "Hmph! Don't think you mediocre people can hurt me with that level of petty slander. Just you watch. Soon enough, you'll be getting down on your knees and begging me for forgiveness. I'll play with your tits then. No complaints allowed. Oh, just the girls, I mean, of course."

"You've got one hell of a tough heart, Ranta-kun," Kuzaku said.

"Damn straight I do, Kuzacky. My heart's made out of diamond, okay? Now, all of you, follow me. I'll teach you the one true way to handle this."

It wasn't like Haruhiro had a better idea. If it was a bust, they would be right back where they started. He decided to let Ranta handle it. They all moved close to the bridge.

Ranta put on his helmet, lowered his visor, and then told Haruhiro and the others, "You wait here," with a self-important tone.

"What're you planning to do?" Haruhiro asked.

"It'll be fine, just shut up. If I'm right about this—"

"Kehe... This is you, Ranta... You must be wrong... Kehe... Kehehe..."

"We'll find out soon, okay?" Ranta said. He started walking.

No way, thought Haruhiro. *To be on the safe side, he had the rest of their comrades get ready to flee. You're going? You're seriously going there? That's crazy, you know that? Are you that desperate?*

But Ranta walked with an awful lot of confidence. He even started humming as he went. Had he finally snapped?

The others could only hold their breath and watch in silence. Ranta had gotten pretty close to the bridge. The lookout of Watchtower C noticed him, drew its bow, and nocked an arrow. Even that moron Ranta had to get chills when he saw that.

Ranta cringed but didn't stop.

Seriously? thought Haruhiro. *No, man, it's coming for you. The arrow. It's gonna come flying.*

"Okay, okay," Ranta called, waving his hand. They had no idea what he was thinking.

He would cross the bridge soon. Finally, he stepped onto it.

The lookout lowered its bow.

"No way," Haruhiro said, mouth hanging open.

"Welcome, welcome," Ranta called before crossing the bridge, laughing.

What good is saying "welcome", man? Haruhiro thought indignantly. *Like, why are you okay? I don't get it.*

When Ranta had crossed over to the bridge without incident, he looked up to the lookout of Watchtower C.

"Oh. Me. My. Friend. Friends? Comrades. Together. I bring them. Here. Now. You? Okay?"

The lookout tilted its head to the side. It didn't seem like it understood. Well, Haruhiro didn't blame him.

"Good." Ranta gave a thumbs-up. "Okay. My. Comrades. Together. Now. Okay, okay."

Then, leaving the clearly flummoxed lookout behind, Ranta came back to Haruhiro and the others in high spirits.

"There! How'd you like that?! I was right, huh?! Bow down before me! Worship me! Also, women, let me touch your boobs!"

"I'm never letting you touch them," Shihoru said, covering herself with both arms.

"Ranta, you'd probably end up hurtin' them if you did." Yume occasionally said things like that, things that were slightly weird. Maybe she just didn't understand... Haruhiro wished she were more aware, but it was hard to caution her about it.

"But why?" Merry tilted her head to the side. "They seem pretty blatantly wary of outsiders."

"It's a mystery, for sure." Kuzaku couldn't accept it, either.

"Could it be—" Just as Haruhiro was about to say it, Ranta cut him off.

"You moron! It's *my* job to give the answer! *I* had the flash of inspiration! Don't *you* steal my thunder, Parupirorin!"

"Ehe... Your face... You hid your face... That's why they let you in... Ehehe..."

"Zodiac-kun?! Why'd you tell them?! I wanted to be the one to say it, you know?!" Ranta shouted.

Like the five lookouts, the residents Haruhiro had seen had all hidden their faces with some kind of cloth. Haruhiro had thought it strange, which was why it caught his attention.

"Covering your face is the condition for entering the village," Haruhiro theorized. That was fine, but risking life and limb to test the idea? That was reckless.

Was it okay to let it slide because it turned out fine in the end? He worried over that. He was the leader. What should he do? He had an idea.

"Ranta." Haruhiro rounded on him with a serious attitude. "It worked out, so it's fine. But what would you have done if it hadn't? What would have happened? Did you think about that, even a little?"

"Huh? I don't have time to think about that stuff, moron. Besides, I'll have you know, Ranta-sama is never wrong."

"You could have been in serious trouble. That's all I'm trying to say."

"H-hey, it's my life, I can do what I want with it, okay? I'm a free man, you know."

"Don't say that in front of our comrades," said Haruhiro. "If anything happened to you, everyone—even me—we wouldn't be okay with that."

"Shut uuuuuup! S-s-s-s-s-stop that, you're embarrassing me! I-I get it, okay?!"

"Then promise you'll be more careful."

"F-fine, I just have to do it, right? I-I'll promise! There, that ought to be good enough!"

"You won't do it again, right?" Haruhiro asked.

"I-I won't!"

"Good." Haruhiro quickly turned his back to Ranta.

Don't laugh, he told himself now. I can't crack up now. I just pulled off the "Passionate Leader" role. Still, Ranta's surprisingly weak to this stuff. It's hilarious. No, that's no good. If I think about how hilarious it is, I'm gonna end up laughing.

Haruhiro cleared his throat, then directed everyone to cover their faces with something. Yume stared off into space, while Merry and Kuzaku looked at him dubiously. Shihoru looked down at the ground, suppressing a laugh. She saw right through his act.

Kuzaku, like Ranta, covered his face with his helmet. Haruhiro covered his head with his cloak. It was worn and full of holes, so if he positioned it right, he could see. Yume, Shihoru, and Merry worked with towels and the like to fashion masks. As for Zodiac-kun, the demon's face seemed to be already hidden. But it was questionable whether the residents would see it that way. There was no way to know, so they had the demon vanish for now.

Now their odd-looking group was ready. Haruhiro wasn't confident about it, but the lookout at Watchtower C let him and the party cross the bridge without even readying its bow. They really would let them into the village if they covered their faces.

There were fourteen buildings inside the moat. They were of varying sizes, but all were single-floor buildings. There was a plaza in the center of the village, with something that resembled a well. The massive humanoid creature sitting next to the well had to be a guard. It held a big hammer, with a bow and arrows slung over its back. Its face was hidden by its helmet.

They identified the source of the clanging. There were five

buildings facing the central plaza. One of them had a large over-hang supported by pillars. Beneath that roof were coals and a large oven-like contraption.

It was a furnace. There was an anvil, too, and another humanoid creature. Its naked torso was frighteningly swollen, and its back was crooked. Its butt stuck out, and it had astoundingly short legs. The creature fixed a bar of iron to the anvil and beat it. That was the source of the clanging.

"They have a blacksmith," Haruhiro murmured.

The weapons and armor forged or repaired by that bizarre smith hung from the wall of the building or leaned against it.

The smith had something like bandages wrapped around its face. But crimson eyes, so deep and bright it looked like it was weeping blood, and a mouth full of hard, gapless mortar-like teeth, were both exposed.

There wasn't just a smithy. The other four buildings facing the plaza had their own selection of goods on display, either under similar eaves or inside the building.

The building next to the smithy carried what looked like clothing and bags. Completed products were displayed on shelves or stacked on the table. Sitting next to the table was something shaped like a flattened egg. It had two arms sticking out of it, and it wore a hat. Haruhiro thought it might actually be the owner of the shop.

Across the plaza was another building, or rather a shed. That shed had had a wall removed, or never built one there in the first place. Either way, the inside of it was clearly visible.

The wall of the shed was completely covered with bags with holes in them, elaborate masks and veils, and what looked like helmets. In the center sat a thin, emaciated humanoid creature. It looked almost like a dried, dead tree. The owner of the mask shop had six arms, and its more than thirty fingers were interlaced in complicated patterns in front of its chest. The face covering it wore befitted such a shop owner: a shining golden helmet, as intricate as an art piece.

Next to the mask shop was another building just as structurally similar as the clothing and bag shop. However, it was about twice the size. It was clear at a glance that it was a grocer's. The meat of four-legged beasts and birds stripped of their skin hung from the ceiling, while bundles of some plant were left on a shelf, along with what looked like berries. Already-cooked dumplings and fried skewers caught Haruhiro's attention.

In front of the store was a creature best described as a man-sized crab. It stirred the contents of a pot being heated over a stove with a ladle. The giant crab also wore a mask, but its two eye stalks were sticking out completely, so it was questionable whether its face was actually hidden.

The building next to the grocer's had miscellaneous goods scattered around, displayed in a variety of ways. It might have been a general store. Haruhiro didn't see anyone running the place, but it might have been inside.

"What do you think?" Ranta snorted, puffing up his chest with pride. "Quite the village, huh?"

"What are you acting proud for?" Shihoru showered Ranta

with a look of seething hatred. Even with her face hidden, it was easy to imagine her expression.

"It's gotta be 'cause he's an idiot," Yume said, sighing with exasperation.

Merry looked around restlessly. "We're being ignored?"

"Um..." Kuzaku waved to the well guard. "H-hey there."

The giant guard adjusted its grip on its giant hammer. Kuzaku gulped and took a half step backward, but that tightening was the only reaction the guard gave. It offered no response; it didn't even look in Kuzaku's direction.

Definitely ignored.

There were some residents taking a leisurely stroll nearby, but they didn't give Haruhiro and the others a second glance. Merry was right. They were being completely ignored.

Haruhiro crossed his arms, "Hmm," he groaned. *What to do?*

"Don't just groan." Ranta kicked the ground with his heel. "Do something, leader. It's times like this that I let a loser like you be the leader."

"You think you can get away with talking to me like that, Ranta?"

"If you don't like it, then do something to shut me up."

Hm, Backstab or Spider? If I wanted to snuff Ranta out for good, which skill would be better?

For a moment, Haruhiro seriously considered it, but he had more important things to deal with than the piece of trash. There was water and food right there. They had to get some, no matter what.

Haruhiro cleared his throat before approaching the well. The well's guard didn't move, but remained silently huge. Even seated, its head was higher than Kuzaku's, and *he* was 190 centimeters tall. It was scary.

Even so, Haruhiro worked up his courage and walked forward. The well was only five meters away. Then four meters. Three meters. Another step and he'd be within the guard's reach. If the guard felt like it, it could kill Haruhiro in a single blow as it rose.

Haruhiro struggled to breathe. He felt like his stomach might jump out of his mouth. Well, not really. He'd be shocked if that happened.

When he shook off his fear and took that next step forward, the guard suddenly half rose from its seat.

"Eek!"

"Meowha?!"

"Huh?!"

There were screams, but not from Haruhiro. From the girls. Haruhiro was scared so stiff, he couldn't even utter a sound.

O-o-o-o-oh, crap! A-am I... Am I gonna die?

"I-I-I'll give you a decent burial. Maybe," Ranta whispered.

"Come on, let's at least do that much for him," Kuzaku retorted.

Wait, wait, wait? Before you bury me, isn't there something you should do first?!

"P-please." Haruhiro put his hands up. His body moved on its own.

Come on, "Please"? Really?! I'm not Ranta.

Even on the verge of tears, Haruhiro kept his left hand in

the air while using his right to point back and forth between the well and his own throat. "W-water. I want drink. Water. Throat, dry. Um, we are travelers. Water, want. You...understand? Water, water! Could you...let us drink some? Water. Water!"

The guard remained half-risen, not budging.

It was a bucket well. There were two posts on either side, and a beam went between them. There was a pulley on the beam, and a pail hanging from a rope attached to it.

The firelight from a torch attached to one of the posts illuminated the monsterlike guard. Those arms were definitely thicker than a person. It was way too big. It was crazy. Way too crazy.

"Let us have a drink," Haruhiro said through gritted teeth. He shook his head. *Don't give in. You can't. Lives are at stake here.* "Water! Water please! Please, water! Give us water! Come on, we need water, okay?! Doesn't everyone?! Water!"

The guard moved. In that instant, Haruhiro braced himself for death. But it wasn't the hand holding the hammer that the guard extended. It held its left hand out to Haruhiro. It was like it was asking for something.

"Mo—!" Ranta shouted. "Money, Haruhiro! Money! Pay up! Hurry!"

Oh, shut up, Ranta, I can figure that out without you telling me. Haruhiro hurriedly pulled out silver coins. He was so terrified he thought his heart might give out, but he moved closer to the guard. He laid the silver coins in its hand. The guard brought its left hand up to its face, scrutinizing the coins. Then it dropped them right there.

Haruhiro nearly fainted.

I'm finished, he thought. *I goofed. I done goofed. I goofed bad.*

"The black one!" Shihoru shouted, and Haruhiro was a little proud of himself for immediately understanding what she meant. Though Shihoru was the greatest for coming up with the idea.

"H-h-h-here!" Haruhiro pulled out the black coin the corpse with the tail had carried and showed it to the guard. "Will that do?! Well?! Is this good?!"

The guard extended its left hand again. With quivering hands, Haruhiro placed the black coin in it.

When the guard gripped the black coin, it gestured at him with his chin, saying something that sounded like, "Ua, goh."

What does that mean? "Ua, goh"? Upper jaw? Is that wrong? It's wrong. I think.

"Yahoo!" Ranta rushed over to the well and lowered the pail. "Water, water!"

"No, buddy." Haruhiro felt the blood drain from his face as he looked to the guard.

He's...not mad? It's cool? We can use the well? Apparently, yes. The moment Haruhiro thought that, relief and joy burst from inside him, and the next thing he knew, he was gulping down water directly from the bucket.

"Water is goooooooooooooooooooood," he groaned.

No doubt about it. It was the best water he'd ever had. To think that water could taste so great. What bliss. It made him glad he was born. Glad to be alive.

They took turns drinking from the pail, taking nearly three

or four. But no one said they'd had enough. They could drink as much as they wanted.

Well, there might be an actual limit. So finally, Shihoru, then Merry, Haruhiro, Kuzaku, Yume, and Ranta stopped drinking.

Ranta collapsed to the ground, rolling onto his back. "I-It hurts. I drank too much."

"Oh," Yume crouched down, rubbing her belly. "Yume's never been full of water before. Her belly's all bloaty."

"You got full. On water." Kuzaku held a hand to his mouth.

Come to think of it, Ranta and Kuzaku had both raised their visors. Their faces were visible. Was that okay? The guard wasn't saying anything, so it didn't seem to be a problem. Still, it made Haruhiro uneasy.

"Maybe, if we have that money…" Shihoru glanced toward the grocery store.

"You mean that's the currency here?" Merry was rubbing Yume's back.

Haruhiro looked from the smithy to the clothing and bag store, to the mask store, then the grocer's and the general store. If that was true, and they could figure out how to get more of those coins, they could survive. For the time being, at least.

Grimgar of Fantasy and Ash

3 | The Forbidden Bath

WHEN THE SIX OF THEM pooled all their money, they had one gold, eighty-seven silvers, and sixty-four coppers. When it came to other possessions, all they had were personal effects.

They went around showing these to the proprietors of the plaza stores, but the owners showed no interest and ignored them.

They didn't visit the smithy. It was in the middle of a job, and they didn't want to disturb it. They weren't sure it wouldn't kill them if they did.

They thought the owner of the general store was inside, so they knocked on the door. They knocked three times and got no response, so they gave up.

It seemed like acquiring more of the black coins would be difficult in the village. Their stomachs, previously tricked into thinking they were full thanks to the water, were back to grumbling, and they felt a sense of crisis. They would have to find more of the black coins outside.

Haruhiro clutched his empty stomach as they left the village. They *had* to find black coins. That was the goal. They discussed their plan.

It was dangerous, or rather they thought it was probably dangerous, so they decided not to go too far afield. While making a mental map of the area, with the village at its center, they expanded their range little by little.

First, they crossed the bridge and headed straight. They ran into a forest after about one hundred meters. It was dense with tall, whitish, twisted plants that were probably trees. Making their way through it didn't seem possible. They couldn't keep going that way.

They turned back, traveling around the moat and descending the low cliff. The riverbed was mostly sand. It was strangely warm.

Haruhiro and the others went up to the riverside. The river looked deep, its current swift.

Haruhiro hesitantly dipped his hand into the pure black water. He opened his eyes wide with surprise. "It's lukewarm."

"Seriously?" Ranta took off his shoes and socks, stepping into the river barefoot. "Whoa! You were serious! It's not warm, but it's lukewarm! We could use this in place of a bath!"

"A bath," Shihoru mumbled absently. "I want to take a bath."

"Yeah." Merry looked up into the sky and sighed. "A bath."

Yume let out a silly laugh. "Bathin' would probably feel real good, huh?"

"Yeah." Kuzaku nodded. "Everyone smells pretty awful. Myself included, I'm sure."

"Let's go in!" Ranta gave them a thumbs-up. "Everyone together! I mean, what's the harm? Nothing like getting naked together to build camaraderie, they say! Besides, it's super dark! No one's gonna see much! Gehehehehehehe!"

"That's never gonna fly, and you know it." Haruhiro felt a strong urge to clobber Ranta, but he didn't. "Let's save it for later. We need to find some black coins and get something to eat. A bath can come after that. We'll check that it's safe, and then the guys and girls will take turns."

"Screw you, Haruhiro! I'm against it! Against, against, against! Agaiiiiinst!" Ranta made a whole lot of noise, but the rest of their comrades agreed with Haruhiro.

"Huh?" Yume, who had been splashing in the water along the riverbank, picked something up. "Oh? What's this? It was buried in the sand. It's round and—"

Haruhiro took it from Yume. "It's a black coin."

"There could be more, right?!" Ranta got down on all fours and started to search for black coins with such vigor that it looked like he might take off swimming. "Get searching! All of you! Let me say, though, what's yours is mine, and what's mine is, of course, mine!"

"Save the sleep talk for when you're asleep, man." Even as he grumbled, Haruhiro began hunting for the black coins.

Everyone took the hunt very seriously.

Eventually, the flame-like light from the distant ridge vanished completely, and the area was covered in perfect darkness. They weren't far from the village. But the banging of the blacksmith's hammer had died out long before.

It was night. How long had they been searching for black coins? Haruhiro wasn't entirely sure, but it didn't matter now.

"That was it! We never found another one!" Ranta punched the water.

"I guess it's just not that easy," Kuzaku said and sat down in the riverbed.

"A-anyway," Shihoru squeezed the water out of the hem of her soaked robe. "We should head back, see if we can buy food with that coin."

"That's true." Yume sounded like she might be crying a bit. "Yume's gettin' mighty hungry, and it's been makin' her sad."

"It might buy more than we think, after all." Merry tried to console them, which was unusual for her.

"Yeah, you're right." Ranta hung his head. He didn't have much energy, and it was hard to blame him for that.

"Yeah, let's do that," Haruhiro said languidly, then told himself, *No, that's not good enough.* A leader couldn't afford to let his spirits sink like that. "L-Let's go, guys! It's chow time!"

However, climbing the two-meter cliff on their way back proved a difficult task. They made it back to the bridge on unsteady feet and were shocked by what they found.

Watchtower C was, for all practical purposes, a gate. If they couldn't pass through the gate, they couldn't enter the village. The gate that had been open just a little while earlier was now closed.

"Wh-why?" Haruhiro pressed a fist against his forehead. "Because it's night?"

"Who cares!" Ranta lowered his visor and started to run across the bridge.

"H-hey!" Haruhiro didn't have to stop him.

The lookout at Watchtower C nocked an arrow. When it drew a bead on him, Ranta did more than come to a sudden stop. He launched into an incredible jumping kowtow.

"Sorry! Don't shoot, don't shoot! I'm begging you, don't shoot me!"

It worked in his favor. While the lookout didn't lower its bow, it also didn't fire. Ranta backed away with his head still bowed, eventually making it back to the party.

"You piece of crap! You balding idiot! I nearly died there, dammit!"

"Hey, don't snap at me!" Haruhiro felt dizzy. He felt so weak from hunger it was hard to talk. "We'll have to wait for the gate to open, I guess. Or we could go look for black coins? No, that's not happening. None of us are up for that."

They didn't have the strength, or the willpower, left to move. Haruhiro and the others sat or lay down right where they were. Even as they collapsed, the feeling of starvation relentlessly assaulted them. However, there was nothing to do but sit there and take it. Even if they started nodding off, the intense hunger would inevitably wake them up.

It made them want to lash out. While they fought off the urge, their consciousness grew faint. The shallow slumber that crept up on them was easily broken by aching hunger.

The three girls stuck together, sleeping and then waking back up.

Yume rubbed Shihoru's head. "So hungry," she mumbled. "Hey, Shihoru, she'll only take a little, so can Yume eat you?"

"If you don't mind me eating you, too."

"Ohhh," Yume moaned. "If it means she can have some Shihoru, maybe Yume doesn't mind bein' eaten."

"You want to try eating each other...?" Shihoru mumbled.

"That sounds good. Shihoru, you're lookin' tasty, after all..."

"Um, do you mind if I eat, too?" Merry ventured.

"If you do, then let us eat you, too, Merry," Yume said.

"Sure. Eat me. If it lets me eat, I'll do anything at this point..."

"Hah." Ranta rolled into a ball like some sort of maggot. "What're you damn women talking about? Dammit. I'm jealous. Seriously, seriously..."

Kuzaku was lying on his back with his arms and legs spread out, chanting something. "She shells sea shells by the sea shore... Peter Piper picked a peck of pickled peppers... How much wood could a woodchuck chuck if a woodchuck could chuck wood."

"Well, I guess we're not at our limit yet," Haruhiro said and smiled weakly. "We're not at our limit, or what's a limit, a limit... libit... ribbit... heheh..."

In this world of endless darkness, it was hard to believe morning would come again, but eventually it did.

Even before light peeked out from behind the ridge, there came an ominous bellowing. The lookout at Watchtower C opened the gate from the inside. Immediately afterwards, the distant ridge lit up.

Haruhiro and the others leapt to their feet, rushing to be

the first across the bridge. The blacksmith hadn't gone to work yet, but the pot in the grocer's was already steaming. Haruhiro offered the black coin to the giant crab stirring the pot with a ladle. The giant crab looked back and forth from the coin to Haruhiro and the others with the eyes stuck out from behind its mask.

"Give us something to eat!" Haruhiro immediately began pleading. "We're starving to death! We'll take anything, seriously, anything, so long as it's edible!"

The giant crab took out six bowls made of wood and scooped the contents of the pot—stew or something like it—into them.

Haruhiro and the others said their thanks and then took their bowls. It would have been nice to have spoons, but they didn't need them.

Haruhiro took a sip of the thick, hot, blackish stew. He didn't quite understand the taste. But that didn't matter; it was so good, he could die. When he looked around, everyone else was hungrily wolfing down the food.

We're so happy, Haruhiro thought. *We're happy. We're happy, too happy. It's mind-numbing, like there's glee leaking out through every pore of our bodies. We're too damn happy.*

He slurped the thick broth down in no time. However, he still wasn't done. There were still solid ingredients. Haruhiro poked at the remnants at the bottom of his bowl.

"Ick?!" he cried out in surprise.

Those "ingredients" looked very much like centipedes. *These are bugs, aren't they?*

"Gahahah! A man's food is his castle!" Ranta said something else, incomprehensibly, then boldly tossed those bugs into his mouth. "—Guwaaeh?! Eughhhh?!"

Ranta spat the bugs out. It wasn't surprising; they looked disgusting. It was probably best not to eat them. But the stew wasn't enough. They were still far from being full.

Haruhiro looked at the giant crab. When he did, the giant crab offered him some sort of meat skewer. Faith began to take root in Haruhiro's heart. His god was a giant crab that ran a grocery store.

Even as Haruhiro choked back tears, he took the meat skewer with gratitude. He chomped into it before thinking, *Is this meat safe?* It was cold, hard, and smoked rather than fried, but it wasn't bad. Dry and a little hard to swallow, it released more and more flavor as he chewed it. Now this might keep him feeling full for a while.

The giant crab gave the others smoked meat skewers, too. That meant a black coin was worth at least six bowls of bug soup and six skewers of smoked mystery meat.

With their hunger satisfied, now they wanted water. However, they would probably need another black coin to use the well again. They would do without for now. Maybe they could boil the river water later. While Haruhiro worried about it, Ranta skipped right over to the well, lowered the bucket, pulled up a pail of water, and drank it greedily. The guard didn't move.

Huh? That's okay?

When Ranta was done, Haruhiro hesitantly drank some

water himself. The guard really wasn't going to do anything to him. Was it because they'd paid the day before? If one black coin was good for six bowls of bug stew and six skewers of smoked meat, maybe one black coin had been overpaying for water for six people. Was that why it was letting them drink again today?

Whatever the case, once they all rehydrated themselves, they started to feel more like themselves again. Well, almost.

"Um, Haruhiro-kun." Shihoru raised her hand. "I'd like to take a bath now."

He couldn't bring himself to say, *We have bigger concerns.*

Well, Haruhiro reasoned, *we can think about how to get more black coins while we're bathing. Then, once we're feeling properly refreshed, something will come to mind. Yeah. A bath. Let's take a bath.*

Haruhiro and the party left the village and took the straightest path to the riverbed. They didn't need to be in such a rush, but they couldn't help themselves.

First, they dug a hole near the river. Then they connected the hole to the river with a channel. Once the hole filled with water, they closed off the channel. They decided the girls would go first, then the guys. While the girls bathed, the guys waited off at a distance.

The hole they were using as a tub was a meter and a half across, and about a meter deep. The river water was barely body temperature, but it was way better than cold. They held a lantern to it to test it. It wasn't cloudy, and it didn't smell. Their work went on without complication or interruption, and the lukewarm openair bath was soon complete.

"Well, we'll be off over there," Haruhiro said to the girls.

Haruhiro, Ranta, and Kuzaku left Yume, Shihoru, and Merry behind as they went about twenty meters away from the open-air bath. They settled down by the cliff. Even when the sun rose, or rather the flames rose, this world was still dark. They couldn't see the girls from this distance, so it was far enough.

Still, it was strange. Ranta was oddly quiet.

He had been oddly quiet for a while.

"Well, time to begin the operation, am I right?" Ranta asked.

"I thought so," Haruhiro sighed. How was he going to stop the sleaze ball?

Fortunately, Haruhiro didn't have to do a thing. Kuzaku suddenly held him down.

"Not gonna let you do that."

"Ow! Ow, ow! Wait, dammit, Kuzacky! What're you doing?! Not the joints, man! Seriously, go easy on the joints! That hurts, dammit! Let go of me, you big idiot!"

"Nah, you're pretty strong yourself, Ranta-kun. If I don't go this far, you'll get away."

"You're breaking my arm! My shoulder! You'll burst my organs! What're you gonna do if I die, huh?! You moron!"

"You won't die that easily, Ranta-kun. This is fine."

"It's not fine, it's not fine, it's not fine! It hurts, it hurts, it hurts! I'm dying, I'm dying, I'm dying! Let go, let go, let go!"

"I know you're making it sound worse than it is."

"Dammit, you're too damn uppity, Kuzacky! Can't you show your seniors proper respect?!"

"I do. I actually have a fair bit of respect for you."

"Then let go! I'm gonna see the girls nude! Boobs! I have a disease that'll kill me if I don't see some boobs! Seriously, man, I'm not lying here!"

"Well, there goes some of that respect," Kuzaku told him. "That was a little much."

Ranta doesn't deserve any respect, thought Haruhiro. *Still, Kuzaku sure was quick to act. Is it his thing with Merry? Gotta be. He doesn't want her to be seen. She's his...girlfriend? Lover? Whatever, same difference. He doesn't want to let other men see someone he's in a relationship with. Probably. It's natural to feel that way.*

Haruhiro could certainly understand that much.

I'm still a virgin, though. What about Kuzaku? Do you think they're already doing it? Like, you know, "it"?

Haruhiro sat down on the ground and covered his face with his hands. What was he even thinking about? It was stupid. What did it even matter? He didn't have time for this.

That's right. He really didn't have time for it.

Black coins. How could they find them? They had gotten some from corpses and from the riverbed. Methods that relied on chance. There had to be a better way. They would work for it. Maybe doing some sort of labor for the residents of the village? Would that be possible, even without speaking their language? It didn't seem likely.

Money. The black coins were money. Were they the currency of the village? If they were, then it was a cash economy. But could such a system be practical for one tiny village? There were maybe fifty residents there, at most. Every one of the stores had a wide selection of goods. Wasn't that a little too much for one village of fifty? Did they have other customers? Others like Haruhiro and the party?

"Eek!" They heard someone's voice.

Not just a voice. A scream.

"Hey!" Ranta knocked Kuzaku off him.

Kuzaku quickly jumped to his feet. "Merry-san?!"

Haruhiro started running as soon as he was on his feet. "Merry?! Yume?! Shihoru?!"

"Nu-chah!"

That was Yume's battle cry. She's fighting? Against what? An enemy?

There was a violent splashing.

"Wah...!"

Shihoru? Sounds like she tried to get away, then fell in the river?

"Hah!"

That was Merry. Definitely sounds like she's fighting.

"W-we'll do our best not to see anything!" Haruhiro drew his dagger and sap. But he did kind of think this wasn't the time to worry about what they may or may not see.

He raced over as fast as he could. He could make out vague outlines. Yume and Merry seemed to be moving around with their weapons. They were out of the bath. Where was Shihoru? In the river? Was *that* the enemy?

No. At first, Haruhiro thought the enemy was a lizard. Its posture was low, like it was crawling, but it was fast. It quickly jumped left and right, dodging Yume and Merry's attacks. It was about the size of a person.

Before he could think, Haruhiro moved. He grappled his enemy from behind. Spider.

It wasn't a lizard. This thing was hairy. It didn't matter He went to bury his dagger in the side of its neck, but the enemy struggled wildly.

It leapt, *Boing!* upward on a diagonal. High.

"Whoa!" Haruhiro cried, clinging to the enemy's back.

Oh, crap. The enemy bent backward in midair. It was going to land on its back! With Haruhiro clinging to it, that meant he was going to get smashed into the ground.

When he tried to get away, the enemy wrapped itself around him. There was an unpleasant noise. The impact jarred almost his entire body. He couldn't breathe. His head spun.

The enemy leapt away from Haruhiro. Then immediately attacked. Haruhiro got both of his arms up, trying to protect his neck and face. He had to avoid dying, somehow.

"Gahhh!" Kuzaku jumped at it, trying to hit the enemy with his longsword.

The enemy leapt straight backward, then ran.

"There you are!" Ranta ran over, slashing the enemy.

Nice teamwork, thought Haruhiro, but now was not really the time to be praising his comrades.

He tried to get up and couldn't. Not good. Even turning on his side hurt.

I feel like I'm gonna puke. Pathetic. I was careless. I lost my head.

Why couldn't I stay calm? How embarrassing. What am I, a newbie? That was a rookie mistake. No excuse for it. It hurts.

Kuzaku and Ranta chased the enemy about. Merry and Yume rushed over to him.

"Haru?!" Merry shouted.

"Haru-kun!" Yume cried.

No, that's great. I mean, you two are naked, aren't you? It was too dark to see details, but he still felt bad about it. Haruhiro closed his eyes, figuring it was the least he could do.

"Where's... Shihoru?" he rasped out.

"Meow?! That's right! Shihoru! Where are you, Shihoru?! You okay?!"

"I-I-I'm j-j-just fine," Shihoru responded, which was enough for Haruhiro.

But it was still too early to relax. This wasn't a situation where they could.

"Haru! I'll use my magic now!" Merry cried.

"No, you can't do that. I mean, light magic...gives off light. Before you do that...put some clothes on..."

"Is this really the time to be worrying about that?!" Merry yelled.

I'm sorry. I'm really, really sorry.

"Merry-san, here, clothes!" Kuzaku came back, throwing Merry's clothes at her.

"I don't care!" Merry yelled, but she still threw on what she could quickly. Then she started treating Haruhiro.

"Dammiiiiit!" Ranta shouted. "It got away from us, you idiot!"

"Ranta, don't come over here!" Yume hollered.

"Oh, shut up! Like I'd go out of my way to see your tiny tits!"

"Shihoru's here, too, y'know!"

"Of course, I wanna see hers! I'd love to stare at them, by all means! Gwehehehehe!"

"Jess, yeen, sark, kart, fram..."

"Whoa, whoa, whoa, hold it, hold it, Shihoru! No magic! That's the Thunderstorm spell, isn't it?! If I eat one of those, I'll be toast!"

Haruhiro kept his eyes squeezed tight.

If I open them, I might see all sorts of stuff. I mean, Merry's close. She's close enough I can feel her touching me. I won't look, though. I swear I won't, okay? I feel so ashamed of myself for everything, I want to cry.

Can't we even take a bath in peace? Man, this is tough.

4 | U Naa

LIGHT MAGIC AND DARK MAGIC were both usable. However, their effects and duration had been reduced to about one third of their usual strength, and they took more than double the magic to cast them. Worst of all, doing so was incredibly exhausting on the mind and body.

Protection was so inefficient now, it was practically useless. Even with healing-type spells, seven castings of Cure, four of Heal, or just one of Sacrament were enough to drain Merry's magical power completely.

They decided to have Ranta use Demon Call to summon Zodiac-kun as often as possible. Ranta was a terrible dread knight who couldn't make effective use of his dark magic anyway. Besides, Zodiac-kun was somewhat useful just by being around.

Haruhiro and the party named the village where the well was "Well Village," and the river with the lukewarm water "the Lukewarm River." The cardinal directions were unclear, but going on the theory that the Lukewarm River ran north to south, they decided upstream would be north and downstream would be south. In the daytime, the fire rose, and the eastern sky where the burning ridge was grew a little brighter. It didn't seem like they could cross the Lukewarm River, so for the time being, they would have to search to the west of it.

There was a forest that spread out to the west of Well Village. And to the south? It seemed there were aggressive enemies in the riverbed, so they decided to climb the cliff and try going south from there.

"How far do you figure we're from Well Town?" Kuzaku turned back and looked.

"Like one kilometer?" Yume let out a strange *mnngh* sound as she thought about it. "Somewhere around that?"

"Tch." Ranta clicked his tongue and stamped his feet a few times. "Damn, it's hard to walk like this. It's so squishy! What the hell is with this stuff?! Is it trying to harass me?!"

"Ehehe... Ranta... Your very existence is a form of harassment... Ehe... Eehehehe..."

"Hey, what was that supposed to mean, huh?!"

"B-but, this is kind of exhausting." Shihoru was using her staff to support herself as she walked.

"You okay?" Merry asked. "Shihoru, if you need to, you can hold on to me for support."

"Thanks, Merry. But if I tripped, I'd take you down with me."

"If it happens, it happens." Merry smiled, just a little.

Haruhiro smiled slightly, too.

No, a worthless leader who screwed up has no right to smile. Still, it looks like Merry, Shihoru, and Yume are getting along great now. I couldn't be happier for them.

Merry was a bit contrary when we first met, but I heard she was a cheerful person with a likable personality before. Blessed with good looks, takes her work as a priest seriously, has a good personality—what kind of perfect superwoman is she? As a comrade, and as a friend, I couldn't ask for more. She's pretty much ideal. As a leader, I'm happy. Though I'm sure Kuzaku must be even happier, having a girlfriend like that.

"The area south of Well Village is a swamp." Haruhiro stifled a sigh, squinting. "Looks like it goes on like this for a while."

"It's tough to walk in, sure, but it's not all bad, y'know?" Yume said. "The surface here, it makes sounds. It goes *squick, squick*. So, if somethin's comin', you'll know right away, huh?"

"Dammit, Yume," Ranta complained. "Even with those tiny tits of yours, there you go, saying something useful!"

"Stop callin' them tiny all the time!" Yume screamed.

There is something to what Yume said, thought Haruhiro. *It's easy to stay alert here. For now, I want to expand our range, so let's try going a bit farther.*

With that decided, they went another three hundred meters or so, but at that point the ground wasn't just muddy; there were puddles, and it felt like their feet were going to get stuck. The water was about five centimeters deep at most, but there were soft and hard spots in the bottom, which made it worse.

"Hey, isn't there something buried here?" Haruhiro asked.

"Treasure, huh!" Ranta immediately crouched down and thrust his hands into the mud. "Oh? There is. There's something. This is—"

"Should we shine a light on it?" Yume asked. Haruhiro nodded. "Oof." Yume pulled out a lantern and lit it.

"Here." Ranta brought what he had pulled out up to Yume's lantern. It was a whitish, rod-shaped object.

Haruhiro immediately knew what it was.

"A bone...?"

"There're a whole bunch of them," Ranta said. "Do you think the whole place could be littered with corpses?"

Zodiac-kun cackled. "Uhe... Ranta... You'll turn to bones here, too... Uhehe... Uhehehe..."

"Don't say ominous stuff like that! Dammit, Zodiac-kun!"

"Let's look." Haruhiro, mind made up, nodded. "I'm not keen on it, but it might not just be bones. We might find their stuff, too. There could be black coins. Right now, we need those badly."

There were no objections. Unlike the Lukewarm River, the water here was chilly. When they crouched in it, it could be downright cold. It wasn't easy work, but compared to starvation and dehydration, it was nothing.

And eventually...

"Ahah!" Shihoru gulped as she lifted something up. "A black coin!"

"Oh, ho!" Ranta slapped Shihoru on the back. "Nice! Well done, Shihoru!"

"Don't take advantage of the situation to touch me."

"No way?! You're snapping at me now?! Seriously?! It's not the time for that, is it?! Aren't you happy?!"

"Kehehe... Ranta... Your existence ruins everything... Kehehehe..."

"If my very existence is the problem, there's no room for fixing that, you know?! Just saying!" Ranta yelled.

The discoveries continued. There were more than black coins. They found two short, un-rusted swords, one longsword, one metallic, masklike thing, and four black coins.

"Hmm." Ranta scrutinized the longsword before handing it to Kuzaku. "You hold onto this one, Kuzacky. It looks pretty good, and we can probably use it with a bit of sharpening, but it's too plain for me. A bit too long, too. Besides, my Lightning Sword Dolphin's numbing effect hasn't run out yet."

"...Thanks."

"The short swords go to Haruhiro," Ranta went on.

"Kehe... Ranta's acting all important... Die, you blowhard... Kehehe..."

"Could you stop dissing me all the time, like it's the natural thing to do?!"

"Hmm," Haruhiro said, examining the short swords. "Nah, I think one's enough for me. How about you take the other one, Yume? The slightly bigger one is about the size of your machete."

"Meow. Now that you mention it, it is. Well then, maybe Yume'll take it."

"How about the mask?" Merry tried putting it on. "Oh. A perfect fit."

It was shaped to look like some sort of creature, but not one Haruhiro recognized. If he had to put a name to it, it might have been an ape. It was kind of silly, with a funny-looking shape to it.

"I-It suits you. Really," Shihoru said, struggling to keep her voice level.

"Bwah!" Ranta burst out laughing and pointed at Merry. "It does, it does! It's the best! A masterpiece! That one goes to Merry! Decided!"

"I-I don't want it!" Merry took the mask off, trying to hand it to someone else, but everyone refused to take it from her. "I really don't want it, okay?! I was just trying it on!"

Haruhiro, for some reason, looked to Kuzaku.

Kuzaku, man, aren't you going to help her? When something like this is happening, really. After all, the two of them were, well... together, you know?

Kuzaku was the first to break eye contact, looking down. It looked like he felt awkward.

Ohh. I see. They haven't told everyone about their relationship. They're hiding it? That's why, even at times like this, it's hard for him to stand up for her.

It's fine, Kazuku. No need to hide. Why not just open up about it already? If you'd just do that, I'd feel a lot better about it, too.

But now's not really the time to announce it. If they suddenly went, "Hey, guys, guess what?", no one would know how to react.

Even as Haruhiro thought about that, Yume offered to take the mask.

"In that case, maybe Yume'll take it? It'd be easier havin' a mask when we go back to Well Village. This one's not cute, but maybe when she gets used to it, she'll start thinkin' it's cute."

"Um, about these black coins..." Shihoru picked up one of the four black coins resting in the palm of her hand and showed it to the rest of the group. "There's a slight difference in their sizes. This one is big, but the other three are much smaller. And it looks like the letters written on them are slightly different."

"Whoo." Yume held the lantern up closer. "You're right. That one is much bigger, huh?"

Haruhiro compared the one Shihoru held up to the three. "You think the valuation is different? Like silver and copper? But the material's the same here. What were the first two we found like? I don't remember."

"Come on, you should at least remember that much." Ranta snorted. "Well, not like I do!"

"Kehehe... Because your head's empty... Kehe... Kehehe... You'll be embraced by Skullhell soon..." Zodiac-kun suddenly lowered its voice. "It won't be long now... Kehehehehe..."

"Hey, Haruhiro." Ranta gestured with his chin.

"Yeah." Haruhiro bent his knee, lowering his center of gravity. "I know."

Were all dread knights' demons like this? Haruhiro, being a thief, didn't really know, but Zodiac-kun was capricious. They couldn't rely on the thing. It was only useful because, when danger was approaching, it warned them. Sometimes.

Haruhiro didn't have to give the orders; his comrades were already on alert. He hesitated for a moment. Should he have Yume put out the lantern? No, if she put it out now, they'd barely be able to see anything until their eyes adjusted to the darkness. That would be bad.

He listened carefully. There it was. A noise, a splashing sound. From the west. *Splash. Splash.* It was getting louder. Something was walking through the water.

It was closing in.

Haruhiro looked to Kuzaku, pointing to the west. Kuzaku nodded, then lowered the visor of his helm, turning to face that direction.

It happened immediately after that.

The thing started running. Yume turned the lantern in its direction.

They saw it. A black beast. Huge. With shining yellow eyes. Four of them.

Was it a dog? A wolf? No, nothing like that. It was big enough to be a tiger or lion. Maybe bigger.

It charged them. Kuzaku tried to stop it with his shield, but it was no use. It sent Kuzaku flying.

"Gwah!"

"This is bad!" Ranta took a swing with his Lightning Sword Dolphin. The beast didn't dodge. Incredibly, it deflected the blow with its forehead.

For an instant, it seemed to get zapped, but the beast shrugged it off.

Ranta leapt backward. "Damn, how hardheaded is that thing?!"

"Ohm, rel, ect, del, brem, darsh." Shihoru wrapped herself in an Armor Shadow. It nullified all attacks, or, failing that, blunted them for a while. It was the sort of cool-headed decision they had come to expect from Shihoru.

"Kuzaku?!" Merry screamed, but there was an immediate "'Kay!" followed by the sound of someone getting up in a pool of water. Kuzaku seemed all right.

The beast moved its head languidly, looking at each of them. Its shoulders were one to two meters off the ground, its torso about three meters long. It was huge, and more than a little intimidating, but it wasn't ten times their size or anything like that. But its jaws... If it chomped down on one of them, it could bite through an arm, a leg, or even a neck like it was nothing. Kuzaku was lucky to be all right after being tackled by that thing.

Yume crouched low, breathing heavily. She had her machete drawn, but she didn't have her bow at the ready. Arrows weren't going to do anything against an enemy like this. They were already in close quarters combat. Honestly, they were *too* close. If they turned to run, the beast would pounce on them, no doubt about that. And that would be the end of it. It would kill them easily.

The beast hadn't made a single cry or growl. Every time its tail slapped the water lightly, Haruhiro's heart jumped. If it roared, he'd probably die of shock.

What *was* it anyway? Had they wandered into this beast's territory? Was it trying to drive Haruhiro and the others off? But wouldn't it have tried to intimidate them first? Then were they prey? Was the beast hunting them to satisfy its appetite?

He wanted to run away. *The footing here is bad, it's dark, that thing looks fast, and it'd be pretty hard to escape without casualties. We have to fight it, don't we?*

If it was looking to eat them, they only had to hurt it a little. If they made the beast think they were too much effort, it would back down.

That's the sense I get. I just hope it's true.

"We're doing this!" Haruhiro tensed himself, shouting the order as powerfully as he could. "Don't bunch together! Surround it while not getting in front of it!"

When Haruhiro and the party went to move, so did the beast. It was large but incredibly light on its feet.

The beast pounced at Ranta.

"Whoa!"

Ranta hadn't let his guard down. He seemed to be trying to dodge it while beguiling the beast with his bizarre footwork. It was probably his dread knight fighting skill, Missing.

On more solid ground, he might have succeeded. Unfortunately, he didn't quite pull it off. While Ranta got out of the way of the beast, he tripped and plowed into a pool of water.

"Gwah?!"

"Keep trying, Ranta... Kehe... Fwehehe..."

"Ranta-kun!" Kuzaku tried to hit the beast with Punishment. The paladin's Punishment was similar to a warrior's Rage Blow, but they tightened their defense with their shield while swinging down with their sword. That difference saved Kuzaku. The beast dodged and then swung out with its front leg.

A beast punch. It was a hook. Kuzaku blocked it with his shield, but he couldn't withstand the impact. Kuzaku was knocked over.

"Jess, yeen, sark, kart, fram, dart!" Shihoru slammed the beast with a Thunderstorm spell. Thin streaks of lightning caught the beast. It let out a groan, its entire body shaking, but it didn't fall. It shook its head, turning toward Shihoru.

"Chuwang!" Yume let out a weird cry as she charged headlong toward the beast.

Merry was trying to thrust at it with her short staff.

The beast roared, spinning in place and successfully knocking both Yume and Merry away. They landed in the water.

"Dammit, don't take me lightly! O Darkness, O Lord of Vice!" Ranta took a knee, with the tip of his sword pointed toward the beast. "Blood Venom!"

No good ever came of Ranta using dark magic. Even when a bizarre and terrifying aura fired out of Ranta's body and enveloped the beast, Haruhiro still had a bad feeling about whatever was happening. The effectiveness of dark magic was already reduced in this place. Why would anyone go out of their way to use it?

However, the beast stumbled. It recovered quickly, but something was clearly wrong with it.

Blood Venom. It was a spell that used Skullhell's miasma to weaken the body, or at least that's what Haruhiro remembered about it. Certainly, the beast looked like it was suddenly ill or weak.

Now he had an opening. He would save praising Ranta for later. Or rather, he would avoid praising the trash at all. Ranta being Ranta, he was guaranteed to get even more conceited.

Haruhiro would be lying if he said he wasn't scared. But he was confident he would succeed. No matter how fierce it was, their enemy was a four-legged beast.

He leapt at it from behind, clinging to its back. He stabbed his dagger into its neck with all his might. He stabbed the hell out of it.

The beast thrashed. It twisted, flailing its front and rear paws violently as it tried to throw him off. But because of its structure, neither its front nor rear paws could reach its back. Or so Haruhiro thought, but then one of its claws sank deep into Haruhiro's right thigh and tore it apart.

"Gwah?!"

It hurt so much that Haruhiro easily let himself be thrown off. Worse, he let go of his dagger which was still embedded in the beast. And to top it all off, he fell face first into a pool of water, leaving him unable to see anything or breathe.

This is bad, isn't it? Like, I'm gonna die.

"Jess, yeen, sark, fram, dart!"

If Shihoru hadn't cast her Lightning spell, Haruhiro might have.

"Nngahh!" That one *definitely* hurt the beast. With that awful cry, its massive body fell over sideways, kicking up a large amount of muddy water. Haruhiro couldn't see it, but he could hear it perfectly.

The dagger. It was the dagger.

Haruhiro's dagger had still been jammed into the beast's neck, and that was where Shihoru had aimed her Lightning at.

"Ehe... Now... Ehehehe..." Zodiac-kun spurred them on.

"You don't need to tell us!" Ranta screamed.

"Yeah!" Kuzaku shouted.

Sensing their time to strike, Ranta and Kuzaku assaulted the beast. As Haruhiro wiped his face and got up, he thought, *We can do this.*

The beast took off.

That was fast.

Well, the world was harsh for everyone. If it'd stuck around any longer, it would have been too late. It had to make instant decisions, or it would never survive. The beast completely vanished in no time.

"Anyone injured?" Haruhiro asked, raising his hand. "Other than me."

"My back hurts a bit," Kuzaku said, "but that's about it."

"Yume's doin' great."

"I am, too," said Shihoru. "Thanks to all of you."

"I'm totally invincible, after all!" Ranta bragged.

"Don't worry... Kehe... It'll be sometime tomorrow... You'll die instantly... Kehehe..."

"Listen, Zodiac-kun! Could you not say that like it's a prophecy?!"

"Haru, let me see." Merry rushed over and crouched next to him, laying Haruhiro's left leg over her knee. "This is pretty bad. Don't be so reckless."

"I wasn't *trying* to be reckless. I was just...too optimistic, I guess. I'm sorry about this."

"Were you trying to make up for before?" Merry asked him in a whisper.

Honestly, that might have been part of it. When they'd been ambushed in the riverbed, Haruhiro had been the only one hurt, and he'd had to have Merry heal him. This time, he wanted to do something impressive and show off his good side.

Could he say he *hadn't* been trying to do that? Probably he had that sort of ulterior motive in the corner of his mind.

Still, he was the leader, cheap thief or not. He wasn't the type who dragged his team along by showing off how capable he was, or who displayed a whole lot of leadership. But once in a while, he had to try. If he didn't make them think, *Hey, he's better at this than we thought* every once in a while, he'd find it hard to go on.

Besides, if Ranta started looking down on him, it'd cause all sorts of trouble. That, and piss him off.

It wasn't limited to Ranta, though; it went for all of them. He would rather have their respect.

Haruhiro looked away, answering, "Maybe a little," in a quiet voice.

"I respect you, Haru, and I'm grateful to you," Merry said even quieter. "Everyone does. Know that much."

"I know that, kind of."

"Well, that's fine, then. Let me heal you."

"Right." Haruhiro closed his eyes.

I don't want to see Merry up close like this, he thought. *I don't want her being so kind to me. I like it, but it's painful, I guess you could say. I really am grateful for it, though.*

Haruhiro had been wounded, in multiple ways. Merry healed him, but he'd lost his favorite dagger. The short sword they'd found while searching through the mud wasn't usable as it was. He could sharpen it himself, but he didn't have a whetstone. And he really wanted a proper smith to do the job.

He decided to call the area with the pools of water and their submerged remains "Corpse Swamp."

They could probably still get more black coins and items in Corpse Swamp, but there were dangerous animals living here, like that four-eyed beast. They'd have to be very careful as they went about their work. If they let their guard down, they'd be killed and eaten for certain.

Since they had gotten a hold of one large black coin and three small ones, they decided to return to Well Village for now. Not only was Corpse Swamp already cold, they were also soaked. They felt cold all the way down to their bones. They wanted to warm themselves by a campfire, eat, and drink.

Haruhiro and the party hid their faces before crossing the bridge. Once inside Well Village, they felt deeply relieved. Beneath that relief, though, the gloominess of the village, and the bizarreness of its residents whose language they didn't speak, threatened to overwhelm them.

There were just too many obstacles. Were they going to be able to secure basic necessities? Could they live here? Could they stand to live here? They wanted to go home. To Grimgar. Was there a way back? If there wasn't...

What if we can never go home? What then? What should we do?

"Hey." Ranta pointed at the blacksmith. "Look. There's someone there, yeah?"

The blacksmith with the massive upper body and bloody eyes was banging away at the anvil.

Someone was standing in front of it.

"Someone, yeah, but..." Kuzaku shook his head. "Well, yeah, it's someone."

Was it a customer? It could be a Well Village resident, but Haruhiro didn't recognize it. If he'd seen them even once before, he'd remember.

It was tall, easily twice Haruhiro's height. It looked like, well, a scarecrow. If it hadn't moved with swaying steps, occasionally crouching down to inspect the blacksmith's wares, he might have thought, *Oh, what's a scarecrow doing over there?*

Scarecrows, though, didn't move, so it wasn't really a scarecrow. It had long, thin arms with hands that had ten or more wirelike fingers. It was wearing something like a raincoat over its head. There was something like a mask on its face, too.

"Y'think it's a customer?" Yume asked quietly.

"A customer." Shihoru repeated, shuddering. "Is it dragging something behind it?"

"A corpse?" Merry covered her mouth with her hands.

Haruhiro let out a deep breath. *Let's calm down. All right. Keep a clear head. It's okay.*

Well Village was a safe place, or it was supposed to be, right? He thought so. Even if they met a dangerous-looking creature here, if they just acted like normal, or ignored it, nothing would happen. Probably. Or was Haruhiro just assuming that to be true? Could he be completely wrong? What basis did he have to think that? It felt like there might be none.

The corpse. Like Merry said, it was probably a corpse. Scarecrow-san was dragging what could only be a humanoid corpse behind it. Now that he noticed it, it seemed like there was a beast slung over its right shoulder.

Scarecrow-san abruptly picked up a massive sword and turned to face the blacksmith, saying, "U naa?"

"U naa?" It had a throaty voice that was difficult to hear, but that was what it sounded like to Haruhiro.

The blacksmith stopped pounding, held up three fingers on its left hand, then held up eight. "Son zaa."

The blacksmith didn't have five fingers on each hand; it had eight.

"Ouun daa," Scarecrow-san said, shaking its head.

"Bowna dee," the blacksmith responded.

"Giha," Scarecrow-san put the massive sword back where it had gotten it from.

"Zeh naa."

The blacksmith looked dissatisfied, waving its left hand, then returned to swinging its hammer. Scarecrow-san had tried to buy that sword, but they hadn't been able to come to an agreement on price or something. Scarecrow-san left the blacksmith, now heading to the grocer's.

"'U naa,'" Yume said, tilting her head to the side questioningly. She was currently wearing the apelike mask. "Does that mean 'How much' or somethin'?"

"Hey, don't say what I was gonna say, not when you have such tiny tits!" Ranta yelled.

"Don't call them tiny, stupid Ranta!"

"If it does mean that," Shihoru said nodding slightly, "it could make shopping easier."

"U naa." Merry repeated it to herself a few times. "It's worth trying, I think."

"That sounds good," Kuzaku said.

Haruhiro silently agreed. *It's good, Merry's "U naa." It was kind of cute. Yeah. But, I mean, so what? I need to stop being so weirdly conscious of everything Merry does. I can't let it continue. It's not good to be thinking like this.*

It looked like Scarecrow-san had bought itself a bowl of bug stew. It brought its mouth to the bowl, gulping it down. It polished it off in one go, crunching the bugs with gusto.

"Did it start when we lost that person?" Haruhiro said aloud. "Was that when I became afraid to try things?"

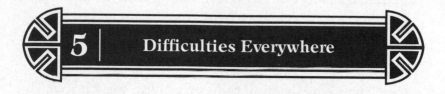

5 | Difficulties Everywhere

"*U NAA?*" = "*How much?*"
"*Faa noo*" = "*Hello*" / "*Zee naa*" = "*Goodbye.*"
 A=1 Muu=2 Son=3 Jo=4 Do=5 Kua=6 Shi=7 Zaa=8 Zama=9 Zamu=10 Zan=11 Zaji=12

Yume and Ranta had tried saying various things to the blacksmith and the giant crab grocer, and they were relatively certain about all those phrases.

The numbers were a bit complicated. Haruhiro and the others were used to base-ten math, probably because they had ten fingers. The residents of Well Village, however, had varying numbers of fingers. So those with eight fingers used base-eight, and those who had twelve fingers used base-twelve. Or at least, that was how it seemed to work. If they pointed at their fingers and asked "U naa?" the shopkeeper would hold up fingers to show them the price. However, if they didn't know how many fingers the shopkeeper had, it could lead to misunderstandings.

There were three sizes of black coin. The ones they had thought were bigger were actually medium-sized, and the small ones were just slightly smaller than them. The grocer had been kind enough to let them see one of the big coins. It was noticeably bigger than the medium-sized coins, thick with silver lines running through it.

The big coins were called "rou," medium-sized coins were called "ruma," and the small coins were called "wen." It seemed rou were fairly valuable, so most trading was done in ruma and wen. How many wen were there to a ruma? That was a bit troublesome, as there didn't seem to be any set value. Rather, it varied from store to store, or rather person to person.

For the blacksmith and grocer, eight wen equaled one ruma. However, at the clothing-and-bag shop, twelve wen equaled one ruma. And at the mask shop, five wen equaled one ruma. That being the case, when the blacksmith said, "Son zaa"—which was three followed by eight—and held up three fingers, followed by eight fingers, what it meant was three times eight, which was twenty-four wen, or three ruma.

If the clothing-and-bag seller said "Jo zaji"—four followed by twelve—and held up four fingers, then all twelve of its fingers, that meant four times twelve, which was forty-eight wen or four ruma.

It was a bizarre situation where, depending on the stores, the difference between three ruma and four ruma was almost double the amount in wen. But this was completely normal in Well Village.

The coin they had found on the body and the one they had found in the riverbed were both medium-sized coins. The giant crab grocer was rather loose about prices. If they paid it one ruma, it would let the six of them eat until they were full. As for well water, after the one ruma they'd paid the first time, they hadn't been asked to pay again. It was probably not a per-use fee, but a one-time payment for the right to access the well.

Uh huh, yeah, that's not plausible at all. There are humans who use base-27 on Earth right now. There have been humans who've used base 60 in history, and a whole lot of others. It's far more plausible that they'll have decided on a common mathematical base for the sake of communication, and it won't necessarily have been based on fingers.

They worked up their courage to ask the blacksmith the cost to have a short sword sharpened. It indicated three wen. Ranta did everything he could to haggle that price down, but it was no good. Having no other choice, they ignored Ranta's vehement protesting and paid three wen to get it done.

At this point, the party's fortune was one ruma. It was just enough to get everyone fed. They negotiated with the crab grocer, asking for as much of anything but insect stew they could get, and then ate until they were full.

The blacksmith finished sharpening the short sword in the meantime. It was excellent work, but by the time he'd finished, night had come. The gate was now closed, and they weren't getting back outside short of breaking it down.

They didn't feel like finding a random place to lie down and sleep, so they decided to walk around Well Village. Incidentally, Scarecrow-san hadn't left yet. They saw him lying down near Watchtower A.

In addition to the blacksmith, clothing-and-bag shop, mask shop, grocer, and general store that lined the central plaza, the village had nine other buildings. The largest of them was on the other side of the plaza. It was made of piled stones and incredibly had glass windows, although they were cloudy. Light leaked out of the windows, indicating someone might live there. They didn't feel like trying to drop in for a visit.

To the left—or rather north—of the plaza, there were four buildings. And to the south, there were also four buildings. These were all shacks of wood or mud, with straw thatched or wooden shingle roofs. The party could probably build a simple shack like one of these, but they lacked the materials to do it.

They passed a number of residents. Some were humanoids, and some were not, but all of them hid their faces. The party tried greeting them with a "Faa noo," but they were ignored.

There was a wharf set up on the section of riverbed inside the moat. However, it had aged badly and was rotting in places. There were no boats.

Maybe they could bathe safely if they used the riverbed inside Well Village. It was an idea, but they weren't sure they'd be allowed to just start digging. They were newcomers and outsiders, after all. They didn't want to do anything to offend the residents. If they were going to try it, they agreed it would be after they had a better sense of their situation.

They decided to camp out in an empty lot so as not to disturb any of the residents. It was cold, but if they wrapped themselves in their cloaks, they would manage to get to sleep.

The girls huddled close together to share warmth. The guys were jealous, but there was no way they were going to snuggle like that. It was better to tough it out. For as long as they could think that way, they managed to do it.

It wasn't long before Ranta started snoring loudly. The girls were whispering among themselves. Judging by how Kuzaku was tossing and turning, he couldn't sleep either. Of course, he couldn't; Ranta was the weird one here.

Haruhiro came close to striking up a conversation with Kuzaku several times, but he always stopped short. Eventually the girls grew quiet, and Kuzaku stopped tossing and turning.

I should sleep, I'm gonna sleep, come on, sleep. Haruhiro tried to will himself to sleep, but the more he did, the less sleepy he felt. He could only think about meaningless nonsense and lie there discouraged by the hopelessness of their situation.

This is no good, he thought. *I need to make choices. There are things I can think about and things I can't. Review what we did today. Take note of what I've learned. And then think about what we'll do tomorrow. Just tomorrow. It's better to forget everything beyond that. I mean, even if I think about it, I have no idea what's gonna happen. No, I guess I know some of it. We're going to die someday. That's one certainty. We're going to die, no matter what. Well, doesn't that make it all kind of meaningless? Sooner or later, I'll die. My comrades will die. I wonder how. Will it hurt? Will it be scary?*

Manato. Moguzo. What was it like? Did you think, "No, I don't want to die," or something like that? Will I be able to die at least satisfied? If I died right now, I know I'd have regrets. I don't want to die yet. I don't want to see any more dead faces. It's best not to think about this. It's too horrifying. What did we do yesterday and today? What will we do tomorrow? If I focus on that, the time will go by, and—

"Boweeeeeeeeeeeeeeeeeeeeeh!"

"Whuh?!" Haruhiro jumped to his feet and looked around.

It looked like his comrades had woken up, too.

Yume rubbed her eyes. "That's gonna give someone a heart attack," she said.

"Was it a rooster?" Shihoru was holding her chest.

"That surprised me," Merry whispered.

"Nngh!" Ranta stretched. "Well, that's a refreshing sound to wake up to!"

"How?" Kuzaku grumbled.

You can say that again, thought Haruhiro.

Looking around, they saw up on top of the bar the well bucket hung from, there was a brownish chicken-like creature. But it couldn't be a chicken; it was much too big for that.

"Boweeeeeeeeeeeeeeeeeeeeeh!"

The ominous bellowing was coming from that creature. What a terrible way to wake up.

"My whole body aches." Kuzaku rolled his shoulders and hit himself on his lower back.

"Well, let's give it our all again today." Haruhiro tried to encourage them out of a sense of duty, but his voice sounded incredibly weak.

"We're still going without breakfast, though!" Ranta said, then let out a cackling laugh.

"That's fine," Yume said, puffing her cheeks up under her mask. "Just think of it as goin' on a diet."

"If you lose any more boobflesh from those tiny tits of yours, what're you gonna do?" Ranta asked.

"Yume's boobs haven't changed that much!"

"Well, let me touch 'em, I'll check for you!"

"Being a little too direct there, aren't you?" Kuzaku looked creeped out. "With your demands, and your desires."

"I'm starving here!" Ranta yelled at Kuzaku. "I'll take tiny tits, or whatever I can get! I just wanna squeeze something! With all the danger we're in, my urges are running high! Ohhhhhhhhhhhhhhh! I wanna procreate!"

"You're way too dangerous, man." Haruhiro was worried about Ranta.

"If only he'd die," Shihoru said. She was probably at least half-serious.

"Because it's morning?" Merry's response was a mystery, but she might have still been half asleep.

"Ranta." Yume backed away while still sitting. "You're *super* unpleasant."

The way she said it was so serious that even a piece of trash like Ranta must have felt a little hurt.

Ranta mimed putting something off to the side. "Okay, putting that joke out of the way, let's move on."

"You think you can play it off like that?" Shihoru wasn't having it.

"Yeah, I think I can! Do me a favor and let me!"

"Why should we do you any favors?" Haruhiro sighed. "Anyway, going without breakfast is gonna be tough. We'll need to earn at least three ruma today so this doesn't happen again."

"Okay, Parupiro, give us a detailed explanation of how we're gonna earn enough to avoid a repeat of this. I'll hear you out. You'd better be grateful."

It wasn't like Haruhiro had some incredible plan. "We search Corpse Swamp for black coins and other things of value. And remain alert for four-eyed beasts and other such creatures while we do it."

Ranta cried out, "Booooring!" and was vehemently against it, but the rest of the party was in favor. They left Well Village and headed back to Corpse Swamp.

It was good to stay on guard, but what could they do if another four-eyed beast showed up? There could be other, unknown threats, too. Could they deal with them? There was plenty to worry about, but this was the most reliable way they had to earn money at the moment. They had to do it.

That day they found one ruma, five wen, a rusted sword, and a spear tip. Fortunately, the four-eyed beast never showed up.

When they returned to Well Village, they brought the blacksmith the sword, the spear tip, and their loot from the day before: Yume's short sword and Kuzaku's sword. The blacksmith raised four fingers. That apparently meant it would pay four wen for all of it together. Most likely, it was going to use them as scrap metal, so it probably valued them at one wen apiece.

They agonized over it for a bit, but the blacksmith wasn't the type to negotiate, and carrying weapons they weren't going to use was just extra weight. They sold them, and with the additional four wen their fortune totaled one ruma and nine wen. They could feed everyone on eight wen or one ruma, so they had more than enough for two meals. They could eat before going to sleep, then eat again in the morning!

It felt good going out to work on a full stomach. Hunger always put them on edge.

Let's make more tomorrow than we did today, Haruhiro thought. *Our target's three ruma.*

The four-eyed beast was scary, but he didn't sense it anywhere nearby. Yume, Merry, and Haruhiro found one ruma, two wen, and two swords in quick succession. Things were going smoothly.

"Hm?" Ranta pulled something long up out of the pool of water. "What's this?"

"Myeeeek!" Yume jumped backward. "It's slitherin' around!"

"Ohh?! Y-you're right! It's moving?!" Ranta went to throw it away. However, the thing wrapped itself around Ranta's right arm and wouldn't let go. "Wh-wh-wh-what?! I-I-I-Is it a snake?!"

"Ah." Kuzaku looked down. "Th-there's one on my leg, too."

When they looked over, there was indeed something long coiling around Kuzaku's left leg.

Was it a snake? Was it dangerous? Venomous? How would they know?

"D-don't move, Kuzaku," Haruhiro stammered. "No, maybe you should move...?"

"Which is it?!"

"Gwahhhhhhhhhhhh!" Ranta desperately tried to shake the snakelike thing off him, but he couldn't manage it. "What the hell, what the hell, what the hell is this thing?! It's scary, scary, scary!"

"Ah!" Shihoru froze solid. "Th-the-there could be l-l-l-l-lots of them r-r-right beneath us..."

"Huh...?" Merry lifted her short staff as if it were heavy. Why would she do that?

There was a snakelike thing wrapped around it, too.

"C-c-c-c-calm down." Haruhiro took a deep breath. "I-I-It's not like they're attacking us. It doesn't look like they're gonna, either. It's fine. I'm sure. P-probably."

"Kehe..." Zodiac-kun had been right next to Ranta only moment ago, but now was far away from them. "To believe without proof...is folly... Kehehe..."

"Zodiac-kun's trying to bail on me?! That's a seriously bad sign!" Ranta tried to pull the snakelike thing off him using his left hand. However, there was no sign he was going to get it off. "Nnnngh! H-h-help me! Someone, help me! Save me, you idiots!"

"Noooooooooo!" Merry was swinging her short staff around wildly. Even with that, the snakelike thing still held on tight.

"Uwahhhhhhhhhhhh." Kuzaku was stumbling.

What? It wasn't just his left leg? No, there was a snakelike thing on his right leg, too. There were two, three more of them, crawling up Kuzaku's legs and trying to ensnare him.

"O-Ohm, rel, ect, del, brem, darsh." Shihoru cast Armor Shadow to wrap a shadow elemental around herself. It might have been the rational thing to do. However, to be honest, Haruhiro wasn't entirely okay with her doing it.

"H-Haru-kun?!" Yume looked hurriedly to Haruhiro.

No, don't ask me, was a thing he wanted to, but couldn't say. Haruhiro was the leader.

Right. I'm the leader. But, leader or not, there are things I can't do, and things I don't know. Still, if I don't do something, things are going to get bad, yeah?

"L-Let's get out of the water!" Haruhiro called. "That's the first thing! I-It'd be kind of awkward trying to deal with them here!"

Yume and Shihoru took off running. Ranta and Merry followed suit, waving arms and staffs around as they did. Haruhiro pulled Kuzaku by the arm as he ran.

While they were running, Ranta screamed out. It sounded like he'd been bitten.

"Y-you okay, Ranta?!" Haruhiro shouted.

"Moron! There's no way I'm okay! Go die! Dammit, it hurts!"

He's screaming, and he's still moving, so he's probably fine, thought Haruhiro.

With a bit of luck, they got out of Corpse Swamp, and the snakelike things backed off. They were relieved for only a moment, though. Ranta suddenly collapsed and started convulsing.

"Gweh... guhguhguhguhguhguhguhguhguh, oughhhhhhhh, gurbbbbbbbb..."

"Ranta?!" Yume pulled Ranta's helmet off. "Yikes?!"

It was bad. Ranta foamed at the mouth. Poisoned. The snake-like things must have been venomous.

Merry immediately cast Purify to eliminate the poison, but Ranta still lay there limply.

"Urgh... I can't believe myself. I nearly got killed there. Damn it all..."

"Ehehe... Why didn't you... just get embraced by Skullhell... Ehe... Ehehe..."

"C'mon, Zodiac-kun, don't you bully him at a time like this! Or else bam! Bam! You're gonna get a smackin'!" Yume was being unusually nice to Ranta.

Actually, Haruhiro wasn't sure when or how it happened, but Yume was letting him rest his head in her lap. That was so incredibly unusual, he doubted his eyes.

"Hold on... Is the poison even gone? I feel like I'm gonna die... Sorry, Yume, let me rest like this a little longer..." Ranta moaned.

"Huh? Well, sure, Yume doesn't mind."

"For another hour."

"Isn't that a little long?"

"Fine, just thirty minutes then."

"Meow."

"Geh heh... You fell for it... Ranta tricked you... Geh heh heh..."

"Huh? Did he?"

"I-I did not!" Ranta shouted. "What're you talking about, Zodiac-kun? I-I'm seriously, seriously feeling awful! L-Like, I've got nausea, a headache, and a stomachache, okay? I'm not making this up!"

"That's soundin' super fake! You're actin' pretty energetic, too!" Yume cried.

Ranta was forcefully evicted from Yume's lap. It didn't matter, but they were in a bind now. Their guaranteed method for acquiring black coins in Corpse Swamp came with not just the threat of the four-eyed beast, but now poisonous swamp snakes. It could hardly be called reliable anymore.

"So? What're you gonna do now, Parupiro?"

When Ranta asked him that, in that grumpy tone, Haruhiro nearly snapped.

What do you mean, "What am I gonna do?" You're pushing this off on me? At least ask, "What are we gonna do?" We've got to start talking it over!

Haruhiro thoroughly chewed Ranta out in his head, which helped calm him down. Even if he snapped at that stupid piece of trash, it wasn't like he was going to have a change of heart. Snapping would only tire him out. It was a waste of perfectly good anger.

"Maybe we could try going into the forest..." Haruhiro began.

The rest of them accepted the idea with surprising ease.

Is it okay? he wondered. *Isn't everyone else not thinking enough about all this?* He couldn't help feeling it, but they just couldn't find the energy to think about it. Haruhiro felt the same way sometimes. That said, he couldn't just do nothing. If they didn't do something, anything, they wouldn't survive.

For now, they decided to go into the forest closest to Well

Village's bridge. It was harder than they expected. The twisted, whitish trees grew so densely that finding a gap big enough for one of them to pass through was hard. Were they going to have to cut them down as they went?

Kuzaku was a little hopeful. "If it's like this, there're probably no large beasts or anything."

Shihoru was not. "There could still be snakes or something like them."

"Shihoru—" Haruhiro started to say, then shook his head.

"Huh? What is it?"

"N-no, nothing. You're right. There could be snakes. Venomous ones..."

"H-how about we turn back?" Ranta was scared.

Serves you right, thought Haruhiro. But he wasn't any keen about dealing with venomous snakes himself. He wouldn't want to get bitten.

"Be careful," Merry cautioned them. "I can only cast Purify as many times as I can cast Heal."

Yume said, "Hey, hey," pointing off to the west. "Waaaaay over there, y'see, it's far off, but there's somethin' shinin' over there, maybe?"

"Shining?" Haruhiro squinted his eyes and looked. "Hey, you're right."

What it was, he couldn't say, but there was something like a light beyond the trees.

"Think we can get there?" Kuzaku asked in a whisper. "Make it all that way, before night comes?"

"Hard to tell how far it is, after all," Ranta said, uncharacter-istically timid.

Incidentally, Zodiac-kun hadn't come into the woods with them. It seemed like the demon might get caught on branches, so it had declined. If he didn't have Zodiac-kun with him, Ranta was just a piece of trash, worth less than crap.

Shihoru hesitantly suggested, "Should we go back?"

Haruhiro looked to Kuzaku, Yume, and Merry. Not only did none of them say anything, they didn't do anything that would express an opinion.

"Yeah," Ranta said. He was the only one to agree with Shihoru.

This wasn't good, not good at all. Haruhiro wanted to change it but had no idea how.

For now, at least, he wanted time to think. But even if he thought, would he find an answer? He wanted time. No, he wanted to run away. It might not have been just Haruhiro, either; maybe they all felt that way.

This is no good, Haruhiro thought. *It's not gonna work out. Not like this. No two ways about it, this is no good. Still...*

"How about we head back for now?" Haruhiro proposed.

He'd gone ahead and said it. As leader, he needed to straighten them out, chastise, or encourage them. He knew that, but he couldn't do it. He was beyond hopeless. His strength had left him.

Are we gonna be able to go on like this, from here on out?

6 | What is Living?

WHETHER THEY COULD GO ON OR NOT, they had to keep trying.

In addition to the one wen they already had, they had another one ruma and two wen from Corpse Swamp, plus two wen they'd gotten by selling another two swords to the blacksmith as scrap metal. One ruma and five wen now. They were a bit short of the two ruma they needed for two meals, but if they negotiated with the giant crab, they might be able to work something out. The grocer had been fairly reasonable already.

Haruhiro didn't know what time it was, so he looked at the ridge in the distance to judge the strength of the flames. They had to tell him if night was coming or not. Otherwise, he had to rely on his stomach and his intuition. How did the people of Well Village keep track of time? They might tell him if he asked, but it wasn't exactly a question that could get asked through gestures and an extremely limited vocabulary.

Though they had eaten, there was still time before night. They had to do something; sitting on the ground in silence would be difficult in its own right. Shihoru was staying awfully quiet, and Haruhiro wanted to do something about it. He didn't know what, though.

"Bingoooo!" Yume suddenly let out a shout and jumped up. "Listen, Yume, she had an idea. How about startin' a campfire?"

The forest was keeping them out, and it wouldn't be easy to get inside, but they could find dry wood there. They would gather it and make a campfire right outside Well Village. It'd warm them up. When night got close, they could hurry back inside the village. And if they missed the gate? Well, it shouldn't be too dangerous next to the village, so they could sleep around the fire.

Unanimous agreement. *All right, let's do it.*

They left the village and headed to the forest. They gathered fallen branches at the edge. Yume identified the ones that were properly dry, putting the half-dried ones off to the side.

They set up a little ways from the bridge. They put the thickest branches on the bottom, then piled thinner ones on top. If they did that, the thick ones on the bottom would burn like charcoal.

Yume was good with campfires. That was to be expected from a hunter. Once Yume had a brilliant fire going, she kept an eye on it, throwing on more branches and blowing into it to make it stronger. They left the half-dried branches near the fire; eventually they would dry out, and they'd be able to use them.

"That's warm..." Ranta sat with his knees up against his chest, sticking his hands out toward the fire. "Seriously, seriously warm.

It's damn soothing. Fire's the best, greatest thing in all of history. Oh, the conveniences of civilization..."

"Um, Ranta." Kuzaku was sitting cross-legged. "Are you crying?"

"I am not. It's not tears, it's snot."

"Snot comes out of your eyes, huh?" Shihoru sat close, almost too close, to the fire. "Gross."

"Shove off! When a guy's enjoying himself, don't go dissing him and ruining it!"

Merry crouched down, putting her palms toward the fire and closing her eyes. Her lips loosened a little. She looked comfortable.

"If only we could catch some fish." Yume sat between Shihoru and Merry with her legs in a v-shape, looking into the fire she started. "Then we could cook 'em and eat 'em."

"Fishing, huh." Haruhiro sat in front of the fire, like everyone else. "You think there's fish in the Lukewarm River? I mean, it's lukewarm..."

"Well, it wouldn't be weird if there were," Ranta said, snorting. "Like, there could be man-eating fish. Don't you think?"

"If we started a fire in the riverbed," Merry started to say, "it might keep enemies away, and then we could bathe in peace."

"No, we'd be able to be seen then." Kuzaku looked down for some reason. "That's bad, isn't it?"

"Oh." Merry hung her head. "That's right."

"I wouldn't mind." Ranta flared his nostrils. "I'm generally okay with nudity. Like, is it anything to really worry about? Whether you're seen, or not, it doesn't matter. If it means you can take a bath, you better be ready to make some sacrifices. In fact, go ahead and show off. I don't care if you see me, so all of you guys should let me see you. It's fair. That's neatly resolved, huh? Let's go do it right now."

"Why don't you go by yourself?" Shihoru said coldly.

But I want to take a bath, thought Haruhiro. *Like Kuzaku was saying, a campfire would keep everything lit, but isn't there some way we could make it safe? Maybe we should dig out a hole to use as a tub at the riverside inside Well Village. I mean, it's not like the residents are guaranteed to get angry. They might overlook it. They might not even care. Maybe I'll try asking the grocer, the blacksmith, or the well guard. Though I might have trouble explaining what bathing is.*

Haruhiro didn't have the energy to fight off the sleepiness sneaking up on him. He lay down and went to sleep. And if a wild beast attacked them? Well, he'd deal with that if it happened. It was a bad, haphazard way of thinking, but he was tired, and the fire was warm.

Please. Just for today. Just for today, don'—

"...ro-kun... ruhiro-kun... Hey, Haruhiro-kun."

Shihoru was shaking him awake.

"Huh...? What's up?" Haruhiro sat up, looking toward the ridge in the distance. "Huh? Is night not over yet?"

"Look." Shihoru pointed toward the bridge.

"Whaa?!" To say Haruhiro was shocked by what he saw would be an understatement.

There was something in front of the bridge.

At first, he thought it might be a horse. But wasn't it awfully hairy and too big for that? The horselike creature was pulling a cart. Or rather, a wagon. It was covered, so Haruhiro couldn't tell what was in it.

There was a humanoid-creature crouching next to the wagon. *That creature, it reminds me of someone,* thought Haruhiro. It had a terrifyingly muscular upper body but extremely short legs.

The blacksmith. It had the exact same body structure as Well Village's blacksmith. Maybe the one who owned the wagon and the blacksmith were the same race?

It wore a hood low over its eyes and had something like a pipe in his mouth that gave off smoke.

Everyone but Haruhiro and Shihoru were still asleep. The campfire had gone out. The wagon had lantern-like lights hanging from it, so it was a little bright.

"How long has he been there?" Haruhiro asked in a whisper.

"Um..." Shihoru leaned in close. She must have been scared. "I woke to the sound of the cart approaching. It looked like it came out of the forest."

"Out of the forest? A big cart like that was able to get through?"

"Off in the distance." Shihoru gestured northwest with her chin. "There must be a road or something. The cart came from there, after all."

"A road, huh... So? How long ago was that?"

"I couldn't say. I thought I was having a strange dream at first."

"Yeah, that makes sense. I understand. You wouldn't expect something like that to come out of nowhere."

"So, the cart stopped there. That...person got out. Then, after a little bit, I woke you."

"Who do you think they are?"

Eventually, the giant chicken of Well Town cried, *Bo-weeeeeeeeeeeeeeeeeh,* and the rest of their comrades woke. There was a confused uproar about the wagon, but that made the wagon's owner look in their direction. They all shut their mouths and tensed.

"Y-y-you wanna fight, bud?" Ranta said in an incredibly tiny voice.

Maybe it heard him. When the wagon owner stood up, Ranta performed a kowtow.

If it comes down to it, let's offer Ranta up as a sacrifice, thought Haruhiro.

Unfortunately, it wasn't necessary. When the lookout of Watchtower C opened the gate, the wagon's owner got back into the wagon. The hairy horse-creature shook its head, and then began pulling the wagon. The wagon moved forward.

Could it cross that bridge? It could, but barely. It wasn't just a matter of width. The bridge was only just strong enough to support it, and every time the wagon's wheels turned, the planks screamed.

Once the wagon was across the bridge safely, Haruhiro had the strange urge to burst into applause. Not that he was going to.

Haruhiro and the others hid their faces and followed the wagon into Well Village. The wagon stopped in front of the blacksmith. As they perhaps should have expected, the wagon's owner and the blacksmith started chatting like close friends.

"Those two dudes, they've gotta be brothers, right?" Ranta started to panic, frantically explaining himself. "Wh-when I said, 'those two dudes,' it just came out that way! I-I totally didn't mean to be disrespectful! Let me tell you, I respect them! Seriously!"

"Like I care," Haruhiro sighed. "But they do look like brothers, or relatives at least. Do you think the cargo has something to do with the blacksmith?"

"Looks like they've started unloading," Kuzaku said.

It wasn't just the wagon's owner; the blacksmith helped, too. They removed the cover from the wagon. The owner got into the back of the wagon and started passing the cargo to the blacksmith. The blacksmith carried it beneath the smithy's overhanging roof, laying it all on the ground.

"Hey, guys." Ranta raised his thumb and pointed to the blacksmith's shop. "How's about giving them a hand? It might get us better prices in the future, you know?"

"What a blatant ulterior motive." Yume sounded exasperated, but it wasn't a bad idea, especially coming from Ranta.

"Okay," Haruhiro said, nodding. "Let's help. Just us guys, for now. If we're not careful, they might get mad and try to beat us to death. Yume, Shihoru, and Merry, you all stay here."

Haruhiro's concerns were almost realized. The blacksmith raised his hammer, trying to chase them off, but when Ranta performed a kowtow and desperately tried to explain, the blacksmith seemed to understand. Though it looked at them doubtfully, the blacksmith let them help with the unloading.

The cargo was charcoal. Haruhiro had heard back in Alterna that a blacksmith's work required coke or charcoal. Coke had to be processed with coal, but charcoal could be used as is to produce high temperatures. It could be used for other work as well, like purifying water.

It seemed the wagon's owner didn't just deliver it but also made the charcoal. There were sturdy-looking axes in the wagon that Haruhiro figured were meant for felling trees; the wagon's owner was likely a woodcutter, and therefore a charcoal burner.

When the unloading was complete, the charcoal burner started helping the blacksmith. The charcoal burner seemed to enjoy it, but the blacksmith complained about everything he did. From the way they were acting, it was almost as if the blacksmith was the charcoal burner's older brother. Maybe the charcoal burner had aspired to become a blacksmith like his big brother, but he hadn't had the talent, so he'd become a charcoal burner instead. At least then, he could help in the smithy. Well, these were Haruhiro's thoughts, anyway, but it was just a wild idea.

Perhaps as a way of paying them for their help, the blacksmith demanded to see the party's weapons. He and his little brother worked on them together. The party was grateful for that.

Then the blacksmith pulled out a sword. It was a beautiful great sword that shone blue with complicated designs carved into the blade. Fine details were etched on the hilt and pommel, too. The blacksmith had Kuzaku hold it.

The moment he did—

"Oh!" Kuzaku cried out in surprise.

It was light. He took a fighting stance, swung once, and then shuddered with excitement.

"This thing's crazy. Absolutely crazy, no joke. Even a guy like me can tell that. This is an incredible sword."

The blacksmith took the sword back, showed them a large coin, then raised five fingers, followed by eight fingers. Forty large coins. In other words, forty rou. Haruhiro thought, if he compared it with Grimgar's standards, it would be around forty gold. But it might have been more; the large coins seemed really valuable. In any event, he knew it was expensive. It might have been the blacksmith's most expensive item, or at least among the top.

Later, while they ate a meager meal at the grocer's, the charcoal burner's wagon started to move. The wagon went at the same speed as a person walking. They tried going along with it, intending to back off if the charcoal burner looked upset. That wasn't necessary, though, since it looked like he didn't mind.

When the wagon crossed the bridge, it went north for a while, then turned west. Shihoru had been right. There was a road through the forest. The trees had been cleared from it, and wagon tracks were well worn into the ground.

The wagon went along at a good pace. The road meandered a little, but it stayed mostly straight.

They heard birds or some other animal. Eventually, Yume noticed the wagon making a strange noise. There were bell-like objects hanging from the coachman's seat. They made a low, heavy ringing sound. Was there some reason behind them? Like warding off beasts?

They came into an open area. There was a little shack like a mountain hut, and next to it a kiln with a roof and a charcoal shed. There was a stable, too. A great amount of firewood was piled up. It looked like this was where the charcoal was made.

The charcoal burner parked his wagon and went into the hut.

Haruhiro and the others walked around the site, then tried going into the forest. Here, many of the trees had been cut down, making it easier to walk through.

In addition to the road to Well Village, there was another road leading off in a different direction. The wagon tracks were worn deep in this one, too. Haruhiro wondered where the road led. Were there villages other than Well Village?

When they returned to the charcoal burning site, the charcoal burner was sitting in front of his hut smoking. He seemed relaxed and didn't even look at Haruhiro and the others.

The hairy horse was loose, off to the side eating grass. If that thing kicked them, they'd die instantly. Even a swipe of its tail would probably do some damage. It was best not to approach it carelessly.

"It feels like our world just expanded a bit," said Shihoru.

"Yeah." Kuzaku nodded in agreement.

"Not that it'll make us any money." Ranta crouched down, pulling out some of the grass and twirling it around his fingers. "Oh, yeah, forgot to summon Zodiac-kun. Oh, well."

"There's more to life than money, isn't there?" Yume hung her head. "Yume *is* hungry, though."

"Want to head back?" Merry hesitantly suggested.

Haruhiro was grateful for the suggestion. They had come out here on a whim, but it was hard to say if they'd gained much for it. He didn't want to say they'd hadn't, but the truth was something close to that. He didn't want to go back empty-handed, but what else could they do?

"Let's go back," Haruhiro said, trying to make it a strong declaration. Everyone looked at him funny, so he added a "...maybe?" muddying the waters.

How lame, he thought.

He really was lame. He had always been so, but he felt especially bad lately. Manato would have led them better and more intelligently. Tokimune would have pulled everyone along with his easygoing cheer.

Haruhiro? He could only do things his own way. What was his own way, though? What should he do?

Now that they'd been thrown into this ridiculous situation, his flaws were so much more apparent. He was so flawed that, honestly, it depressed him, and he was at a total loss for what to do.

He wanted someone to rely on. Desperately. He couldn't cast his duty aside. He knew that, but he wanted to abandon it. To throw it away and flee.

They followed the road back through the forest to Well Town. What should he do now? What did he notice, and what did he have to do about it? Haruhiro needed to think about that, but his thoughts were dominated by dissatisfaction, discontent, and displeasure, as well as unease, fear, and despair.

Maybe he should open up and tell them. What if he said,

Right now, this is how things are, and I'm the leader but I'm not acting like much of one and I'm sorry. He could apologize like that. If he did, he might feel better.

Haruhiro would probably be the only one who felt better. What would his comrades think? Ranta would snap at him for sure.

Like he cared about Ranta.

Would the girls sympathize with him? He could use some sympathy. He wanted them to spoil him a little. He wanted to be freed from the tension, the pressure.

The road was wide and easy to walk along, but they were in near total darkness, so Yume carried a lantern. Haruhiro looked back. He saw Yume's face, and then Shihoru walking beside her, His eyes were drawn to...a certain part of her anatomy. He immediately turned back around.

Oh, crap. He had been thinking something weird there. No, it hadn't been a thought. It had been an impulse. Flustered, Haruhiro was disgusted with himself.

He had felt a sudden lust, and for some reason it had been for Shihoru. Maybe because her breasts had caught his eye? No, the cause and effect didn't matter. What mattered was he had felt it. On top of that, his lower half was now in a state he found hard to describe.

Oh, no, oh, no, oh, no, oh, no, oh, no, oh, no...

Haruhiro, like anyone, had a sex drive. However, he felt his wasn't all that strong, and he preferred things in moderation. He thought he did, for the most part. *I'm a young man, I can't help it,* was *not* something he wanted to think.

I'm a young man, so I really can't help it.

Not that it consoled me at all, okay? What's wrong with you, Haruhiro? You're going crazy. You're tired. You really want to turn into some sex-crazed animal? At a time like this? Stoooooooop...

He did his best to hold off the urge to clutch his head and scream.

"—Meow?" Yume made a strange sound. "Just maybe, you know, there might be something out there?"

"Something? What do you mean?" Ranta gulped. "What is it?"

"S-s-stop." Haruhiro raised his hand, but everyone had already come to a halt. "Yume, where is it?"

"That way, maybe?" Yume pointed behind them to the right. "There's a sound. A presence, maybe?"

Kuzaku let out a deep breath, drew his sword, and readied his shield. "Should I fall back?"

"Um—er—" Haruhiro shook his head to clear it. "Kuzaku, you go in the direction Yume indicated. Ranta, you'll be...on Kuzaku's left. I'll be on his right. Merry, protect Shihoru. Yume, cover the rear."

His comrades fell into formation in no time. He was the only one a little slow. Haruhiro couldn't help feeling that way. His decisions, his actions, they were slow.

I'm not hard anymore, right? He was exasperated with himself for suddenly thinking that. *What's wrong with me? This isn't the time.*

For a while, he held his breath and stayed still. Nothing happened. He didn't hear anything, either.

"You sure you didn't imagine it?" Ranta asked quietly.

"Maaaaybe?" Yume didn't deny the possibility.

"We'll stay on guard for now," Haruhiro looked around. *Nothing here,* he thought. He was about to do an about face, saying, "Back to Well Village."

Then, there was a series of *kohh* sounds. Something flashed in here and there. They were closing in on them.

Creatures, but not very big ones. More than one or two. Five of them, maybe six.

Kohh. Kohh. Kohh.

Was that them barking? Howling?

"Incoming!" Haruhiro yelled. They already knew.

Immediately, Kuzaku used Bash and sent something flying with his shield.

"Monkeys?!" Ranta swung his Lightning Sword Dolphin around. He didn't hit anything.

Monkeys. They were like monkeys, with bodies covered in black or brown fur and tails. They kicked off from the ground with their front and rear legs to leap at them, but they didn't run like other four-legged beasts. They grabbed trees and brushed branches out of their way with their front legs. Their faces, though, were less monkey-ish and more doglike. They could be called inuzarus, or dog-monkeys.

Haruhiro knocked an inuzaru away with the sap in his right hand. He tried to kick another one, but it dodged. The first inuzaru leapt at him again. He lowered himself and took aim with his short sword, but it dodged.

"They're quick little buggers! Leap Out!" Ranta launched

himself forward, drawing a sharp figure-8 with his Lightning Sword Dolphin. "Followed by Slice!"

The inuzaru Ranta sliced up let out a dying *Kohhhh* and collapsed.

Ranta lifted his Lightning Sword Dolphin aloft. "How's that?! I'm awesome!"

Yes, yes, we get it, now stop wasting time and keep fighting, was what Haruhiro wanted to say, but before he could, the inuzarus howled and began retreating.

"You think you can run away, huh?!" Ranta was about to go after them, but immediately stopped. "Well, we'll just say they were terrified of me. I'm the ultimate dread, after all! By the way, the 'ultimate' there is about how I'm the ultimate dread knight, not how I'm ultimately powerful. Though, I'm that, too! Gahahahaha!"

"I-Is everyone okay?" Haruhiro looked to each of his comrades. "You all are, right?"

"Yep." Kuzaku lowered his sword.

"Meow." Yume's response was as incomprehensible as ever, but he took it to mean she was fine.

"That surprised me..." Shihoru let out a deep sigh.

"Do you think any more are coming?" Merry still held her short staff at the ready.

Thankfully, it looked like no one was hurt.

Ranta walked up to the inuzaru's body. It wasn't dead yet. It had cuts all over and trembled, on the verge of breathing its last. Without a moment's hesitation, Ranta stomped on the back of the inuzaru's neck and crushed it, killing the creature.

Haruhiro thought, *Is that really okay?* But it might have actually been kinder to finish it quickly, rather than letting its suffering drag out.

Ranta crouched down, looking the inuzaru over before turning to Haruhiro. "So, this thing, y'think it's edible?"

Ranta didn't call himself "the ultimate dread" for nothing. It was a self-proclaimed title, but the things he thought up *were* dreadful.

The rest of their comrades didn't give him a favorable response. Killing animals and eating them. It might seem cruel at times, but it was natural. But with some things, you just couldn't do that. They would never consider eating a goblin if they killed one.

The inuzarus were monkey-like, though. They felt the same aversion to it as they would with a goblin—the same sense of the taboo. However, they were hungry, and they had no money to buy food.

"Think you can butcher it?" Haruhiro asked Yume, with a kind of determination hidden in his heart.

Yume looked incredibly unhappy about the idea. "It's not impossible, no. Yume, she doesn't really wanna do it, but she can."

"Skin it, and take out the organs, huh?" Ranta put an arm around Yume's shoulder, acting way too chummy. "Should be a cinch, Yume. I know you can do it! Go for it!"

"Hands off, dummy!" Yume brushed Ranta's arm away. "Yume doesn't wanna do it after all!"

"I'm not really up for eating it," Shihoru said. She gagged, then bent over.

"Yeah." Merry covered her mouth with her hands.

"If you tell me to eat it, I will," Kuzaku said hesitantly.

Kuzaku, you're a good man.

It wasn't like it was human meat. It was from some monkey-like animal, that was all. Even if it tasted bad, it was better than starving. If they could eat it, they had to eat it.

"I'll help, Yume." Haruhiro looked Yume straight in the eye. "Do you think you can at least try for me? If you can't, just tell me how to do it, and I'll do it."

In the end, Yume didn't refuse.

Haruhiro carried the inuzaru's corpse off, preparing a campfire next to Well Village's bridge. When the fire was ready, they began butchering it. Once she decided to do something, Yume was reliable. Haruhiro only had to lift it, turn it over, and hold it still for her. Yume did the rest. She offered part of the kill to the White God Elhit, then started cooking the meat she had put neatly onto skewers.

When the meat was cooked, everyone dug in.

While they chewed and swallowed, Ranta moved his head from side to side.

"Well, tastes pretty normal," he decided. "Not that bad, not that good. Be better with a little salt, maybe."

"Murrgh," Yume frowned. "Maybe it's not that tasty."

7 | The Future Project

NASTY OR NOT, it was edible at least.

Yume had learned the hunting skill Pit Trap. There were other trap skills, like Foothold Trap and Snare Trap, but Yume didn't know either of those. Besides, Foothold Trap required specialized equipment. Her master had shown her Snare Trap once, and she thought she might be able to build one herself. She decided to try it. If they set up traps near the road to the charcoal burning site, they might snag another inuzaru.

The poisonous swamp snakes were scary. The four-eyed beast merited caution, too. But for now, Corpse Swamp was the only place where they could make an income.

If there were snakes, they would move elsewhere, and if they heard the footfalls of the four-eyed beast, they would flee. With those agreements in place, Haruhiro and the others decided to continue searching for black coins in Corpse Swamp.

Haruhiro couldn't afford to be dispirited, even though there were countless things that could make him feel that way and he was never far from falling into self-loathing.

There was no helping it. It was always like this, so he was getting somewhat used to it. Haruhiro had found some tricks for recovering from it, too. If he gave up and decided this was just the way things were, he could accept it.

Haruhiro never had, and never would have, aptitude as a leader. He had no desire to be one. But he had to do it. He had no choice but to do it, and so he did. That was why it was hard, and why the stress built up.

Haruhiro was no saint. He was a mediocre person. It was only natural he might go a little crazy and lust after his comrades.

It wasn't like he wasn't trying to improve. He wanted to be a better leader, for his comrades and for himself. But it wasn't so simple. Progress wasn't steady. It was one step forward, two steps back. Another step forward, another step back. That was fine. If he didn't tell himself that, he couldn't go on.

One day, when they went to Corpse Swamp, there were several four-eyed beasts lurking around. They had no choice but to turn back.

Another day, they changed spots several times, but they kept running into the poisonous swamp snakes. In the end, Kuzaku and Yume were both bitten, giving them a terrible time.

When the inuzarus got caught in their traps, they usually broke free and escaped. Still, Yume was getting better at trap-making because they managed to catch them a bit more often now. They figured out how to cook them, too. If they bled the inuzarus quickly, seasoned the meat with strong herbs, and flavored it with salt, they were pretty tasty.

The grocer sold salt, but a tiny bag cost one whole ruma. It was pricey, so they were careful with how they used it.

In Well Village, they would see visitors here and there, though not every day. They were of many races, but all of them covered their faces, well aware of the village rule. Perhaps it wasn't only Well Village that did this; perhaps it was a rule that held true across this world, or at least across this region.

Visitors primarily came to trade, but some came to sell. Others came to buy, and a few to do both. The ingredients at the grocer's were gathered by people from Well Village or else brought in by hunters like Scarecrow-san.

The residents of the stone building still hadn't shown themselves. Haruhiro and his party more or less recognized all the others.

The lookouts on the five watch towers and the guard at the well worked in shifts. There were nine of them in total, as far as Haruhiro could tell. They could apparently eat at the grocer's without paying.

Apart from those nine, the blacksmith and everyone else had to pay to eat. Furthermore, Well Village residents only ate once, maybe twice, a day.

Due to their limited finances, Haruhiro and the party did the same.

They couldn't hold anything resembling a proper conversation with the residents. Thanks to that, they hadn't been able to get permission—and it had taken some courage to just go ahead and try—but they managed to bathe safely at the riverside in Well Village. When they had gotten carried away and tried to pitch a campfire there, the well guard had come over and put it out without letting them try to explain. That, apparently, was against the rules.

It was cold and unpleasant sleeping without a fire. It made sleeping outside Well Village preferable.

By the time they were spending their nineteenth night in this world, their money had exceeded four ruma, and they had developed something of a daily routine.

Four ruma was worth four meals, two days' worth of food. It was no great amount of money, but even a little gave them some degree of comfort. For the moment, Haruhiro was holding all of it as shared property, but when they saved up more, he intended to give everyone their own share. Then he could buy small things as he pleased. They all could. Little dreams would open up to them.

"Man," Ranta said, rolling over in bed, "we can't go on like this forever. I mean, I'm tired of digging through the mud."

"It doesn't matter if you're tired of it," Shihoru said. She huddled by the fire with Yume and Merry.

The three of them had bathed before Well Village's gate shut for the day. They seemed strangely...radiant, and Haruhiro couldn't stand looking at them directly. When he looked too long, he got kind of aroused. But curbing his baser desires was Haruhiro's specialty.

Well, maybe not? Maybe not...

How did Ranta and Kuzaku handle it? Did Kuzaku occasionally sneak off and do you-know-what with Merry? If that was going on, even Haruhiro would notice. Were they holding themselves back, then? They didn't have to. There was already little enough to enjoy; a little fun would do them good.

But clapping Kuzaku on the shoulder with a smile, telling him they could go at it all they want... That seemed wrong, somehow. Haruhiro certainly could never do it.

Lying on his back, Kuzaku sniffled a little. He apparently had a cold. "Feels like our efficiency is dropping. We haven't cleaned the place out yet, but it's looking like we'll need to go into the poisonous snake-infested areas, or the ones where the four-eyed beasts always show up."

"How's about goin' a little further out next time?" Yume had her cheek up against Shihoru's chest and was hugging Merry.

Damn, Haruhiro was jealous. *No, no, no, no, no.*

"There was a road past the charcoal burner's place." Merry seemed a little tired. She looked drowsy.

"I've been curious about that, too, actually." Haruhiro stared into the fire. *O flames, bring me to my senses. Please,* he prayed. "Like, is there another village out that way? Or maybe a bigger town? Although I'm not sure it matters to us."

"That's our number one candidate," Ranta declared with a click of his tongue. "Or we could cross Corpse Swamp and head south. Heading downstream along the Lukewarm River's an option, too. There was something in the riverbed, but if we put our minds to it, we can deal with whatever it is."

Haruhiro kept staring into the fire, never looking away. "But it's not like we have anything to go on."

"Are you stupid, Parupiro?" Ranta said scornfully. "It's a brand-new world, damn it. Of course, we don't have anything to go on."

"Yeah, but you don't think things through enough."

"Call me bold and fearless," Ranta declared. "You know how it is. Figuring all that out is the task at hand. But we do have another task to accomplish, don't we? An important one."

"I don't want to hear it." Shihoru plugged her ears. "It can't be anything good."

Haruhiro looked over at Shihoru, then instantly regretted it. Yume had her face practically buried in Shihoru's chest, while Merry leaned against Yume, her eyes half closed. He wanted to punish himself for carelessly thinking, *Hey, share some of that warmth with me.*

"I'm saying, we could end up living here forever." Ranta took on a serious tone, completely out of character for him. "We've gotta be ready for that, you know?"

"Hey, now." Haruhiro struggled to find a response. "What are you saying?"

"It's a fact, and you know it," Ranta replied. "I'm not wrong, am I?"

"Hope is—"

"—not lost yet, right? Come on, Parupirorin. Don't start talking like some hot-blooded hero. You've never been that positive and optimistic. We have to face facts. We may never make it home. So, we've gotta live here until we drop dead."

Merry took a deep breath, held it, and then gently exhaled. She gazed absently into the fire. Shihoru started to open her mouth but said nothing. Yume let out a weird groan.

"You say we may never make it back home," Kuzaku said, sitting up. "But where is home? Grimgar?"

"Huh?" Ranta cocked an eyebrow and glared at Kuzaku. "What's that supposed to mean, Kuzacky?"

"Nah, was just thinking about it. It seems like we weren't always in Grimgar, after all."

"Sure, but we don't remember anything from before," Ranta said.

"Well, yeah."

"Don't talk about stupid stuff," Ranta shot back. "Besides, the issue I'm bringing up now has nothing to do with that. Get a clue, you damn moron."

"You didn't have to go that far."

"You looking for a fight, pal?! I'll take you on!"

"Quit it," Merry sighed. It stopped them.

Normally that would be Haruhiro's job, but his mind was elsewhere.

"We're looking for a way back to our original world," Shima had whispered to him.

Back, Haruhiro thought. *Back to our original world. What did that mean, anyway?*

Haruhiro touched the receiver hanging around his neck underneath his clothes. With everything that had happened, it wouldn't be strange for Soma to contact them. Secretly, he hoped he would. But the receiver had shown no signs of vibrating. Maybe it didn't work across worlds.

Haruhiro shook his head. No use dwelling on it. They were here. Here, and nowhere else. They were in another world, not Grimgar, nor the Dusk Realm.

They might end up spending their whole lives here. The possibility had, of course, crossed his mind before.

"Ranta," Haruhiro said, "I knew that without you telling me. It's entirely possible, I know that much. But so what? Even if we prepare for that, nothing will change, you know? What we have to do won't change. It'll all be the same."

"Are you stupid? There's no way it's the same," Ranta snapped. He got up, punching his right fist into his left palm. "We've gotta propagate, damn it! In other words, baby-making! Ba-by-ma-king!"

"Whaaaaaaaaaaa?" Shihoru managed as she held Yume tight.

"You—" Haruhiro was at a loss for words.

Merry shook her head as if to say, *Unbelievable.*

Yume looked dumbfounded.

"The thing about Ranta-kun is," Kuzaku muttered, "no matter what happens, he's always Ranta-kun."

"So, with that decided!" Ranta hopped up, looking around at all of them. "Let's decide on couples! We conveniently have three guys and three girls! Three pairs, and if you each pump out about ten brats, we'll have a population of thirty-six in no time! How's that?! As for me—Well, this is just, you know, part of the project to leave behind descendants. I won't be picky, but, if I *had* to choose, I want—"

"I refuse," Shihoru said, raising her hand.

Without missing a beat, Merry did likewise. "Absolutely."

Yume stuck out her tongue. "Yume says no waaaay!"

"Heeey, come on." Ranta stuck his left hand on his hip, waggling his right index finger and tut-tutting them. "There's no refusing here. This is a project for our future. Don't be selfish. Guys and girls can't make babies without one another, so you're gonna cooperate whether you want to or not. It's your duty, damn it."

"Don't try to push this project forward on your own, man," Haruhiro muttered.

"Shut up, Parupyuronosuke. I'm doing this because you're hopeless. Oh, I get it! It's not like I think anyone here loves me, okay? There's no helping that. I'll put up with the leftovers. Okay, first up, Kuzacky."

"Huh? Me? What?"

"You have any preferences? Which of the three do you want?"

"Wha—" Kuzaku put a hand on the back of his head, looking down. "Uh..."

There was no need for him to answer. But, honestly, Haruhiro was kind of interested in what he'd say. He knew how Kuzaku felt, but how would he express it in front of the others? Maybe he wouldn't. Maybe he would try to joke his way out of it.

"What's wrong? Hurry the hell up!" Ranta shouted, spittle flying everywhere. "Make it fast! Hurry up! Hurry up! Huuuurryyyyy up!"

"Hmm," Kuzaku considered, crossing his arms and closing his eyes.

He seemed to be taking a long time. Haruhiro glanced at Merry to gauge her response.

Huh? That's not what I expected, thought Haruhiro.

He thought she would be acting awkward, or anxiously waiting for Kuzaku's answer. But she wasn't. Instead Merry held her knees tight with both hands, with an expression like she might start apologizing any second. Why? Did she feel responsible for putting Kuzaku on the spot?

Maybe she did, but that felt off. It wasn't like Merry. But did Haruhiro know Merry well enough to say what was and wasn't like her? It wasn't like he really knows her all that well.

"You're so indecisive!" Ranta stomped his feet. "Make it snappy! For tits, go with Shihoru! For the face, go with Merry! If you're into freaky stuff, go with Yume! That's what it boils down to, right?!"

"Can we bury this guy?" Shihoru asked in a tone so dark it made Haruhiro shudder. "All of us together."

"I vote yes," Merry said. She stood up, wiping all expression from her face.

"Gotta get 'im ready for an easy buryin' first." Yume smiled as she said it, then drew her machete.

"Wait, what?!" Ranta fell on his rump and backed away. "Stop talking about burying me and discussing how to do it, okay?! Let's stop this! Please?! I get it, I'll stop! I'll be more careful in the future! I mean, it was a joke, okay?! You don't have to take it so seriously! I wasn't serious. Forgive me, I'm begging you!"

With Ranta's kowtow, the conversation died. Eventually,

everyone went to sleep. Everyone but Haruhiro. He had a hard time of it. There was a lot floating around in his head.

What about Kuzaku and Merry? he wondered. *Are things going well between them? I mean, they really don't have time for it right now, huh? But if it has to happen, I want them to be happy together.*

He tried to be a good guy, but it made his chest hurt.

What's happiness anyway? I don't even know...

They slept and woke to the morning cry of the giant chicken. A new day had begun.

They crossed the bridge into Well Town and drank from the well. Once they washed their faces at the riverbed, it would be time for an enjoyable breakfast.

At least, that had been the plan, but there was someone at the grocer's already. Of course, early morning customers weren't that unusual or strange, but this one caught their attention.

"That guy," Ranta murmured and pointed at the customer. "Isn't he a little too...human?"

The customer who had just accepted a bowl of bug soup from the grocer had two arms, two legs, one head, and no tail. He stood at about 180 centimeters. Taller than Haruhiro, but shorter than Kuzaku. He wore a wide-brimmed braided hat, made of dry grass woven into a shallow cone, as well as a scarf that covered the lower half of his face. He had an overcoat that went down to his knees. In addition to the ax at his hip, he had a large backpack filled with swords, a crossbow, and other weapons tied to it. He was a walking arsenal.

The customer shifted his scarf aside and brought the bowl to his mouth, turning his face up as he sipped the bug soup. When the broth was gone, he picked up the bugs with his fingers, tossing them into his mouth and chewing them.

There's no way he's human, Haruhiro thought, but it wasn't that strange that a human might like bugs.

The customer said "Ruo keh," and returned his bowl to the grocer before turning toward the group.

"Oh?!" Ranta jumped backward, taking a posture that let him perform a kowtow immediately if need be. That piece of trash should stop calling himself a dread knight and start calling himself a kowtow knight.

Still, Haruhiro understood Ranta's response. The customer's stance was intimidating. Even with all the gear he was carrying, he stood there as if it weren't heavy at all. His center of gravity completely stable, he could move quickly in any direction he pleased. There was no unnecessary tension anywhere in his body.

This guy is good, Haruhiro thought.

Kuzaku brought his hand to the hilt of his sword, then slowly let go of it, exhaling as he did.

"Is..." Shihoru started.

Is what? Haruhiro wanted to ask, but he didn't.

The atmosphere was heavy.

Yume groaned, and Merry tried to say something. That was when it happened.

"You people," the customer said. "Could it be, you're human?"

8 | Their Senior at Life

"MY NAME IS UNJO," the man said in the same language Haruhiro and the others used.

To their surprise, Unjo explained that "night has come thousands of times" since he himself strayed into this world.

Were the days here the same length as those in the other world? They didn't know, but if they assumed they were, two thousand days would be five and a half years. Three thousand would be well over eight years. Unjo had been in this world for over eight years and survived.

"It is hard to believe," Unjo said, in a hoarse voice that had something of a wry, laughing tone to it. "That I'm seeing other humans. It's been so long. So very, very long. Never did I think my eyes would see a human again. Yet now they do."

Haruhiro understood the words. However, his accent was strange, and the word order a little bizarre. Perhaps he hadn't spoken a human language in a long time.

Once he discovered that Unjo was a human, like them, Ranta pelted him with endless questions. "Senior, Senior, Senior, please, teach us! Were you from Alterna, too, Senior?! Were you a volunteer soldier?! How'd you get to this world?! Honestly, what's up with this world?!"

"Alterna," Unjo whispered to himself, then fell silent.

Ranta was going, "Yeah, yeah, Alnerta, that's right, Analta! No, Atarna! No, Alterna! Man, I wanna get back to Alterna! For me, Alterna's the home where my heart is, but how about you, Senior?! Like, if you could go back, would you?! Is there a way back?! If there was, you would have used it by now, yeah?! No, but, you know, if you have a hint or anything, could you maybe tell us, okay?! How about it?!"

Ranta just kept rambling.

Cut it out, you moron, thought Haruhiro. He tried to stop him, but, as usual, Ranta snapped at him when he did.

"Huhh?! I'm not talking to you, pal! I'm asking our senior here! Shut your mouth and go to sleep, dumbass! You've got sleepy eyes, so go sleep forever, you idiot! I hope you go bald and explode, too!"

"Um." Haruhiro ignored the piece of crap and bowed his head apologetically to Unjo. "I'm sorry. Our worthless piece of trash must be bothering you."

"You're trash! Haruhirooo! I hope you go spinning into hell!" Ranta screamed.

"He's talkative." Unjo suddenly reached out and grabbed Ranta by the head.

"Nwah?!" Ranta froze.

Worthless Ranta wore his helmet to hide his face, but Unjo had grabbed hold of his head, helmet and all. He wasn't as tall as Kuzaku, but his hands were much bigger.

"Alterna." Unjo whispered the word once more, pushing down with so much force that it was like he was trying to crush Ranta. "I had forgotten Alterna. Yes. Because I can never return."

"Ow, ow, owww! P-p-please, forgive me, Senior."

"Le—!" Yume took one step forward, gulping. "Let him go! Ranta didn't mean to offend—Okay, maybe he did, but still, he's Yume and everyone's comrade."

"Comrade." Unjo cleared his throat painfully, then released Ranta. "Comrades, huh? Those, I have none of. Not a one."

"Whaaaa!" Ranta spun around and put some distance between himself and Unjo. "I-I-I-I-I'm, I-I'm saved, right?! I—I'm not dead, right?!"

"Unfortunately, yes," Merry said without emotion.

"Did you come all this way," Shihoru asked in a shaky voice, clutching her staff tight, "b-by yourself?"

Unjo didn't answer, pulling up his scarf to cover the lower half of his face. "I cannot return. Nor can you. This is a grave. Mine. And yours."

"Seriously?" Kuzaku exhaled slightly,

Haruhiro felt like hanging his head, but he forced himself to keep it up. If he looked down now, he would never recover. He had to say something. Less to Unjo, and more to the group.

"But, Unjo-san, you're still alive, aren't you?"

Unjo turned to Haruhiro, lifting his braided hat a little. He saw Unjo's eyes.

He's human, Haruhiro thought once again. This was a bona fide human. He was probably much older, quite literally their senior, but he was human. Just like them. He had lived alone in this world, surviving all by himself. How hard must that have been?

It must have been lonely. But, still, Unjo was alive. Unjo might not feel that way, but he was living proof of something.

This place was not a grave.

It might become one someday, but everyone had to die someday. The moment a person died, that place became their grave. But that moment hadn't come for them yet. It was up to Haruhiro and the others, but if they did it right, they could survive.

"It's an honor to meet you," Haruhiro said. "If you don't mind, I'd like to see you again, and learn from you."

"Teaching. From me." Unjo's shoulders rose and fell just once. "To all of you."

"We don't know anything, after all," Haruhiro told him.

"Downstream." Unjo pointed in the direction the Lukewarm River flowed. "They are there. The dead ones. It's a town. A ruin. They are not dead. Yet, they are dead ones."

"What's there?" Haruhiro asked.

"The City of the Dead Ones. Ruins. You are volunteer soldiers." Unjo turned his back on Haruhiro and the others. "It is a good fit. For you people."

Haruhiro wanted to chase after Unjo and ask him more. However, he couldn't. Unjo clearly rejected Haruhiro and the others.

Leave me be, his back seemed to say. Haruhiro felt that was what they should do.

The meeting had probably had as much of an impact on Unjo as it had on them. Considering how long he had lived alone, he might have been even more shocked. If so, he was probably also incredibly confused.

Unjo entered the building made of piled stones. There was light leaking from the windows, as always, so residents had to be inside. Unjo might be acquainted with them.

"The town! Of the dead ones!" Ranta was suddenly upbeat, letting out a corny, malicious laugh. "No one expected this! No! It's just as I anticipated! Our path has been revealed! Yahoooo! I'm so awesome!"

"What are you talking about?!" Yume elbowed Ranta. "It had nothin' to do with you, Ranta! It was all Kampyo-san!"

"You mean Unjo-san," Haruhiro corrected her, sighing. "The City of the Dead Ones, huh?"

"It sounds scary." Shihoru ducked her head, hugging herself and her staff.

"The dead ones." Kuzaku was looking at the stone building.

"'They're not dead,' he said." Merry tilted her head to the side in confusion. "What did he mean? Since he calls them dead ones, I'd expect corpses that still move for some reason, or ghosts of some sort."

When Ranta had been in favor of doing it, it had made Haruhiro want to refuse outright, but Unjo had called them volunteer soldiers. Unjo's past remained a mystery, but perhaps he had also been a volunteer soldier at some point. He might have been looking after Haruhiro and the others as his juniors. He did say it was a good fit for them, after all.

It was a place fit for volunteer soldiers, the City of the Dead Ones.

It made Haruhiro think, *I dunno about this.* But, for some reason, his heart danced. Not because he thought it'd be fun. He wasn't Ranta. He was just a little excited. He couldn't deny that.

Even after coming to this nonsensical world, with no way to get home, and not knowing what will become of us, we're still volunteer soldiers, thought Haruhiro. *Has it become second nature to us now? I don't like it. Give me a break.* Still, even as he thought it, Haruhiro made a decision.

"Let's go check it out."

Haruhiro wasn't alone. Ranta wanted to go, of course, but so did Yume, Shihoru, Merry, and Kuzaku. It seemed, in the end, the volunteer, soldier way of life had seeped into their very bones.

Some of them were proactive, others passive. They had their own attitudes and tendencies, but they had all come to roughly the same conclusion. In fact, not one of them raised an objection.

Digging through the mud had never been the best job for them as volunteer soldiers. But visiting the City of the Dead Ones. That could. Why not check it out?

They got breakfast and then left Well Village. The City of the Dead Ones was downstream of the Lukewarm River, but they decided to follow the river without going down into the riverbed. There was at least one vicious beast living down there, and one that could easily sneak up and attack them. They didn't know what else might be there, or where any attack might come from.

At first, the light on the distant ridge burned faintly, offering little reassurance. When the fire rose, it stopped being completely dark, but it never became so bright as to be "day." The darkness only ever abated slightly, but they had grown used to that. Their sense of the varying levels of darkness seemed to be growing keener. It wasn't bright, but it didn't feel as dark. The midday darkness was a little easier on Haruhiro than it had been before.

He felt like his hearing was improving, too. He had a clear sense of shifts in the air and smells. Without looking, he could determine his comrades' positions, follow their footsteps, and even get a vague sense of how exhausted they were.

Eventually a mist drifted in from the Lukewarm River, covering the entire area.

"Kehe... Kehehe... Kehehehehehehe... Kehe..." Zodiac-kun, who hadn't said a thing since Ranta summoned him back at Well Village, suddenly burst out laughing.

"Wh-what was that about, Zodiac-kun?" Ranta was clearly spooked.

"Ehe... Nothing.... Ehehe... Really... Nothing... Ehehehe..."

"Now you've got me really worried!"

"Kehe... Don't worry... Ranta... It's nothing... Kehehe... You have nothing to worry about..."

"No, see, that's why I worry. Because you say things in a way that makes me worry. It's kind of scary, so could you stop it?

Okay? Hey, Zodiac-kun? Huh? Why're you so quiet? Answer me. Well, Zodiac-kun?"

"Shut up for a minute, Ranta," Haruhiro said. He was trying to sense any presences in the mist-filled darkness ahead of them. "Zodiac-kun is trying to tell us something. Take the hint."

"Yeah, and I was trying to get it out of him, wasn't I?" Ranta demanded.

"Kehehe... As if I'd tell you... Kehehehe..."

"Listen, Zodiac-kun!" Ranta yelled. "Have you forgotten who is in charge here?! I, the dread knight, am the master, and you, the demon, are my servant, okay?!"

"Nuh-uh," said Shihoru.

"That's backward," added Merry.

Yume earnestly piped in, "Maybe, if you were one-five-hundredth as cute as Zodiac-kun."

"A cute Ranta-kun," Kuzaku mused to himself, then let out a little sigh.

"Heyyyyyyyyyy!" Ranta howled. "Don't just say whatever you want about me! If you don't cut it out, I'm gonna give you a thrashing! I'm seriously serious! I'm gonna show you how scary it is when I get serious, and then—"

When Haruhiro stopped and raised a hand, Ranta immediately closed his mouth.

Everyone stopped and held their breaths.

Haruhiro wasn't sure what to do. Because of the mist, he didn't know *what* it was, but there was something up ahead. He thought it might be a building.

Should they go and check it out together? Or should Haruhiro go alone? As a thief, acting alone was easier. Easier, but also scarier.

"I'll be right back," Haruhiro said, fear making him speak more politely than usual.

"Be careful," Merry told him. "Don't do anything reckless."

Thank you, he thought. *Somehow, that gives me the strength to try. Oh, and sorry, Kuzaku.*

No, I've nothing to apologize for. Merry's just concerned about me as a comrade. That's all. Even if that's all it's gotta be, it gives me courage. Where's the harm in that?

Haruhiro moved away, using Sneaking to advance toward the building.

Is anything but me moving? No. Not right now, at least.

The direction of the mist and the wind changed. There was some obstacle blocking the wind.

Haruhiro approached. The building came into view.

It was made of piled stones, but it was collapsing. At one time, it might have looked like a box, but only two-thirds of it were left standing now. Haruhiro didn't see a roof. It might have caved in. Whatever had happened, it was clearly ruined.

It wasn't the only ruined building here. There was another. And another. Here, there, and everywhere. There were lots of them.

Unjo had mentioned ruins. This must be the place. The City of the Dead Ones. This was their destination.

Which meant *they* were here. At the place of ruins, Unjo had said. Unknown beings. The dead ones who weren't dead.

Haruhiro pressed his palm to the first ruined building's wall.

He tried pushing. It didn't budge. Having tested it, he put his back to the wall. He took a breath.

First, I'll try one circuit around this ruined building. If it looks like I can go in—should I even try it? Is that safe? Well, I'll start with a circuit around it.

He looked around, listening closely, before moving. When he had made a half-circuit around the building, scanning for the dead ones, he found an opening.

An entrance? Was there a door here? Not anymore.

He poked his head in halfway. It was too dark to see details, but there was some sort of wreckage scattered around. It looked too dangerous to enter.

They're not here—at least, I don't think so. They aren't, right?

Finishing the circuit, Haruhiro decided to search the next closest building. It was a little bigger than the first one and still had about half of its roof left. There was no door in the opening he found in the wall.

Haruhiro had a bad feeling as he approached. No, not just a feeling. He heard something. Some kind of sound.

What was that?

Squelch. Smack. Chomp. Smack. Hahh. Nnngh. Slurp. Crunch. Crunch. Gulp. Smack. Huff.

He had some idea what those sounds might be. He wouldn't be happy to be proven right, but he had to check.

Why, hello there, Mr. Dead One, he silently greeted the thing in his mind, trying to sound as cheerful as possible as he looked around in the opening.

There it was. He'd found one. The humanoid creature with a tail wasn't far away. It was crouched over and eating something.

Was it an actual dead one? It looked surprisingly normal. What it was doing? That he wasn't sure.

Haruhiro was interested but thought it best to pull back for now. He tried to put his natural caution to good use, but Mr. Tailed Dead One suddenly turned toward him, groaning.

Had he been spotted?

Screaming and running would be a bad plan. He should wait and see how it reacted. Haruhiro made sure he was prepared mentally and physically so he could react quickly if it attacked him. But it might not. It might even be friendly. It wasn't likely, but it was possible.

The tailed dead one picked up a weapon of some sort and stood up. With a thick, curved blade in hand, the tailed dead one started walking.

It came toward him with slow steps. The tailed dead one wore something like chain mail, with a shoulder guard on its right shoulder, gauntlets, and greaves. It wore a helmet, but its face wasn't hidden.

The eyes... They were white, but they didn't seem to shine. They were just very, very white. Its big mouth was wet with some viscous, slimy liquid.

Haruhiro glanced over at the thing lying where the tailed dead one had been crouched before. He was unsurprised; it didn't shake him badly. He'd been right, that was all.

That thing was another creature. It was probably humanoid, but he'd bet it was no longer alive. Haruhiro didn't look for long.

He couldn't see it all that well in the darkness, but he didn't want to see it anyway.

Oh Mr. Tailed Dead One, were you eating? Did I disturb you? thought Haruhiro. If it would let him off with an apology, he would have taken the opportunity, but the tailed dead one was already picking up speed. This was no time for apologies.

Haruhiro hurriedly pulled his head back, running to hide in the shadow of the neighboring building. Even as he fled, he had to do it quietly, ever so quietly.

"Shaah!" The tailed dead one shrieked.

Where'd he go?! Haruhiro could only guess that was what the shriek meant.

Haruhiro could hear the tailed dead one's footsteps. He moved in time with them.

Maybe I ought to lure it to the others? Worth a shot?

This was the City of the Dead Ones. If that thing was a dead one, it might not be alone. There could be others. But this was the only presence he felt. For now, he didn't sense any more.

Haruhiro had been found already, and, as volunteer soldiers, his group hadn't come for sightseeing or a good time. They had a goal: to hunt. They came to hunt the dead ones, as volunteer soldiers ought to.

The tailed dead one might make for a good test of their skills.

Haruhiro came to a stop. The tailed dead one was closing in. It appeared from around the corner.

When those white eyes caught sight of Haruhiro, it opened its mouth wide. "Kaah!"

It raced toward him.

Good, Haruhiro thought. *Come.*

He ran. He remembered the direction and the rough distance of where he left the group behind. He couldn't screw this up. Haruhiro ran toward them. The enemy was fast, but if Haruhiro ran at his top speed, it would never catch him.

"Haru-kun?!" He heard Yume's voice.

"There's an enemy!" Haruhiro shouted. "I'm bringing it with me!" Then he added, "Just one!"

"Leave it to us!" Kuzaku responded.

There. He could see Kuzaku, coming out with his shield at the ready.

"I'm counting on you!" Haruhiro ran toward Kuzaku.

Immediately after they passed one another, Kuzaku used Block against the tailed dead one's curved sword, then struck out with a Thrust. The tailed dead one pushed on, unconcerned. Kuzaku didn't back down, either. They collided.

"Leap Out!" Ranta quickly jumped beside the tailed dead one and swung his longsword in a figure-eight motion. "Followed by Slice!"

Lightning Sword Dolphin's effect had run out and they'd sold it to the blacksmith, so Ranta was using his old standard, Betrayer Mk. II. The tailed dead one dodged like it was throwing itself to the ground, but Ranta's sword still hit it.

He didn't cut through. It was wearing chain mail.

When the tailed dead one rolled up, Kuzaku closed in on it. "There!" He slammed his longsword into it. Kuzaku had picked up this longsword in Corpse Swamp and had it repaired by the blacksmith.

The tailed dead one took the hard hit to the helmet. It groaned, "Nguoh!" but didn't falter. Without missing a beat, it lifted its curved sword up high and went for the counterattack.

Now, Kuzaku was forced back. "Aww, damn it! I'm so weak!"

"Don't panic!" Haruhiro shouted to Kuzaku, looking at the tailed dead one's back.

Yume and Merry were on standby, defending Shihoru. It was only one enemy, so the formation made sense. There could be reinforcements, after all. They had to be prepared.

If that happened, Haruhiro wanted Yume and Shihoru to respond immediately. Protecting Shihoru was Merry's top priority. Everyone knew what they should be doing.

"Ehe..." Zodiac-kun floated around the battlefield. "Ranta... You're not as good as you brag to be... Ehehe... Finish it already... Ehehehehe..."

"I don't need you to tell me that!" Ranta launched a violent onslaught on the tailed dead one. It was Hatred, followed by a two-strike combo and then diagonal slashes from the top left and right.

The moment Betrayer Mk. II crossed with the tailed dead one's curved sword, he used Reject. The dread knight was at his most valuable when he didn't face his enemies straight on. Where a warrior would lock blades with the enemy, a dread knight wouldn't. He pushed them away or turned the blow aside.

This time, Ranta skillfully pushed it back. At the same time, he fell straight back, though at an incredible speed.

"Exhaust!"

The tailed dead one stumbled a little but managed to brace itself. Ranta kicked off the ground.

This time, he moved forward. Again, at an incredible speed.

"Take this! Leap Out!"

Ranta charged straight into the tailed dead one. It couldn't hope to dodge.

Betrayer Mk. II slammed into the tailed dead one's solar plexus. They thought it pierced through, but it didn't. Ranta was in position to push the tailed dead one down, but instead, he jumped back.

"Dammit!"

"Hashaah!" The tailed dead one leaped to its feet, swinging its curved sword. It seemed more energetic than before.

Kuzaku deflected the curved sword with a loud clang, then tackled the tailed dead one with a shout. The tailed dead one flipped over, but still rose to its feet.

"Shih! Hyahhh!"

"Geez, what is that thing?!" Yume shouted.

"How's this thing supposed to be a dead one?!" Ranta clicked his tongue. "Looks pretty damn lively to me!"

Their attacks didn't seem to be working. The tailed dead one had a black stain on its stomach. Ranta's Betrayer Mk. II had pierced the tailed dead one's chain mail, injuring it. It had taken a blow to the head from Kuzaku's longsword and been tackled. But it was still fighting.

Wasn't it in pain? Did it not feel pain? Because it was in an excited state? Or did pain just not register? Whatever the case may be, they needed to assume it felt no real pain. At least not how they did.

They would have to break its stance, and then pummel it until it just stopped moving.

Long ago, Haruhiro and the others had made trips to the Old City of Damuro to hunt goblins. Their strategy of ganging up on an enemy and pulverizing it had earned them their nickname, the Goblin Slayers. They had to do the same here.

Haruhiro happened to be behind the tailed dead one. It was so distracted by Kuzaku and Ranta, it had forgotten Haruhiro existed.

That wasn't a coincidence. Haruhiro had been moving sneakily to make sure it forgot about him.

Backstab? Spider? No. Haruhiro chose another move. He ran in, keeping his steps as silent as possible. It didn't turn.

Then Haruhiro stepped in hard. He performed a jumping kick. He kicked the tailed dead one in the back with both feet.

"Fungoh!" The tailed dead one pitched forward.

"Now!" Haruhiro shouted, but Ranta was already on the move. Kuzaku wasn't far behind him. Haruhiro joined in, too.

Don't let it stand up. Knock its weapon from its hands. Shut down all resistance. Don't think about slashing, or stabbing, or anything advanced like that. Ignore the fact we're using swords and pummel it.

Of the three of them, Ranta was the most used to this. He used the tip of his sword to peel off the thing's helmet.

Crush its head. Make a bloody mess out of it. Don't move. Stop struggling. You're doing that again? You're gonna do that again? Well, no helping it. We'll have to go all the way.

Kuzaku pressed his shield down on it. "Ahhhhh!"

"Rarrrrrrrrrrrrrrrgh!" Ranta stabbed Betrayer Mk. II into its neck. Then, after Ranta cut it off with brute force, the tailed dead one finally stopped moving.

Inhaling sharply, Haruhiro backed away. He looked around the area. He spotted Yume, Shihoru, and Merry. Merry made the sign of the hexagram, closed her eyes, and then nodded. Apparently, everything was okay.

"Yeahhhhhhhhh!" Ranta lifted Betrayer Mk. II up high, letting out a victory cry. Then he jumped on the tailed dead one's corpse. "Treasure, treasure! Mine, mine, miiiine! If you ain't got nothing, I'll make you pay for it, you worthless dead one! I'll seriously kill you!"

"Come on, man." Haruhiro wanted to say more, but he realized he didn't really have the right to.

The technique Ranta used to strip off the thing's chain mail was impressive. Haruhiro could have called it brilliant, but he didn't want to compliment him.

"Hm?" Ranta picked up something between his fingers. "Hey, hey, hey, hey, heyyyyy?!"

Kuzaku raised his visor, letting out a sigh. "What? Did you find something good?"

"Ta-da!" Ranta proudly displayed it. "Not just something!"

Haruhiro's heart skipped a beat.

This might be love, he thought then shook his head. *Yeah, no.*

There was more than one of Ranta's findings clutched in his hand. There were several of them. Black, and round.

"Wow..." Yume's mouth hung open.

"Huh?" Shihoru managed, still half-doubting what she saw.

"What is it?" Merry tilted her head to the side.

"They're black coins, you silly!" Right now, Ranta was beaming more than he ever had. "Four! Count 'em! Four of them! You're welcome!"

Haruhiro nearly smiled, but he stopped himself. There were things they had to do before they could relax or celebrate. If he didn't force himself to think that way, he would lose all his tension.

Still, four black coins, he thought. *They're medium-sized coins. That's four ruma.*

Haruhiro checked himself; he couldn't start counting chickens before they hatched.

Take it slow and steady, he told himself. *Use methods with certainty.*

He wouldn't celebrate for no reason. He wouldn't get his hopes up just to have them dashed. Haruhiro had to get along with that frail side of himself and keep going.

Grimgar
of
Fantasy and Ash

9 | Confession Etiquette

Though they were all called "dead ones," they came in a multitude of forms.

Kuzaku struck a dead one in the face using Bash. The dead one's head shot back, but its four arms still tried to grab Kuzaku.

Ranta came in from the right, Yume from the left. They charged into a dead one, Betrayer Mk. II and Yume's machete stabbing its flanks.

With the dead one coughing and sputtering, a sharp glint in its two white eyes as it spewed brown mucus from its gash-like mouth, Haruhiro grappled it from behind, stabbing his short sword through its neck.

Slashing wasn't enough to kill a dead one. Or even stop it. The dead ones didn't stop until they were completely dead.

Shouting with exertion, Haruhiro moved his sword as he twisted the dead one's neck. Back and forth, left and right, as hard as he could. It snapped, then ripped off. The strength drained away from the dead one's body. It collapsed.

Haruhiro hurriedly got away from it, losing his balance and landing on his rump. He was about to throw away the dead one's severed head, but he thought better of it. He set it on the ground.

"Aww, yeah! It's looting time!" Ranta declared before assaulting the remains.

Haruhiro always found himself thinking Ranta could be a little less crass about it.

"Haruhiro-kun!" Shihoru pointed into the mist with her staff.

Merry ran up beside her, short staff at the ready.

Kuzaku, through labored breaths, hefted his shield once more. He spun his sword once for exercise.

Another one, huh, thought Haruhiro, rising to his feet with a sigh. "Ranta, how was it?"

"Hold on, damn it!" Ranta let out a vulgar laugh. "Okay, we've got two medium-sized coins and one small one! That's two ruma and one wen! Not half bad, if I do say so myself!"

"If you're done, try gettin' ready to help!" Yume nudged Ranta in the back with her knee.

"Hey, don't kick me, Tiny Tits!"

"Kehe…" Zodiac-kun put in. "Whatever, just hurry… You lowlife… Kehehe…"

"Zodiac-kun! Where do you get off calling me, your summoner and master, a lowlife?!" Ranta screamed.

"It suits you," Haruhiro muttered before looking into the mist.

It was coming. Another pair of white eyes. Another dead one. This dead one was crablike, reminding him of the grocer back in

Well Village. That'd make it harder to fight, but he refused to say that out loud.

"It looks tough, so be careful!" Haruhiro called.

The dead ones came in many forms, but they had things in common. First, there was their eyes. Every dead one had white eyes. It wasn't that they didn't have an iris, but more like their sockets had been filled in with some white liquid. When they died, their eyes returned to normal, so the white had to be part of whatever process turned them into a dead one.

Dead ones also didn't feel pain. Thanks to that, they just kept coming until something destroyed their heart or brain. Or one of them managed to cut their head off.

They were also all cannibals. Dead ones didn't move in groups. They didn't seem to recognize other dead ones as comrades, but rather as enemies or prey.

It had been seven days since they started commuting to and from the City of the Dead Ones. In that time, they had watched the dead ones feeding on a number of occasions. Each time, one dead one had been eating another.

The dead ones attacked each other, and the victor fed on the defeated's flesh and innards. Then they stole any usable equipment and took any black coins the defeated dead one had for themselves.

If all the dead ones were like this, then the City of the Dead Ones was a nice target for Haruhiro and the others. They found themselves continuing as volunteer soldiers in this gloomy and dangerous new world. But the work let them collect the black coins they needed.

There were many types of dead ones, which meant there were vast differences in each one's abilities. So far, they had handled them all, but there were probably dead ones so incredibly strong, they couldn't hope to defeat them. They could very well run into one tomorrow, perhaps today.

There were always risks, but, generally, they didn't need to plan for attacks by multiple dead ones. That was because not only did the dead ones not form groups, they actively targeted one another.

Surprisingly, when a dead one had the choice of attacking the party or another dead one, it usually chose the other dead one. When dead ones were fighting, they had the best advantage. Sure, it was a horrible thing to do, but being a volunteer soldier had always been a dirty job; ethical considerations never factored into things. It wasn't a trade Haruhiro would recommend to anyone who thought of themselves as good or decent.

In any case, the fighting dead ones would ignore them, fully focused on defeating the other and devouring it. In those cases, Haruhiro and the others swarmed the distracted dead ones and killed them both.

Most volunteer soldiers, though they would never say it, would think, *Thanks for the free meal, after such a fight.*

But ones like Haruhiro weren't so insensitive to what they did. They just made excuses about it. Of course, they didn't think what they were doing was okay. *But they had to survive.* That's what they told themselves to assuage the guilt, at least until they got used to it. If they were sickened by what they did, they tended to forget it again by the next day.

With their seventh day of hunting in the City of the Dead Ones finished, they returned to Well Village.

Today they had collected nine ruma and eleven wen. The dead ones' equipment was almost always in incredibly bad shape, and any given piece was usually only worth one wen. They didn't bother bringing any of it back unless they found something particularly good.

Their shared assets exceeded twenty ruma now, and they each accrued several ruma in personal assets since they now found enough to split money between them. Food still cost one ruma for the six of them, but even with two meals a day, they had a fair bit of leeway in their spending now.

Today, while the girls bathed, Ranta started drinking at the grocer's. Because the grocer had alcohol.

There were several varieties that came in jugs. The cheap ones were one wen. Haruhiro didn't think much of the flavor, but Ranta was a fan of it, and he started drinking a lot. It was very likely that the vast majority of Ranta's money was being spent on alcohol.

Haruhiro and Kuzaku decided to ditch the totally-sloshed Ranta and take a bath by themselves, once the girls were finished.

The hole in the riverbed they were using as a bath had been dug where the residents of Well Village were unlikely to look. It had made their hearts race when they first bathed, but it didn't bother them now. They just got naked, and uncovered their faces, too. They kept their helmets and face covers close at hand, just to be safe; if anyone came near, they could cover themselves quickly. It hadn't caused any problems yet, so they assumed it was fine.

The guys didn't care much about being naked together anymore. Even with their eyes adjusted to the darkness, it was still dark. So long as they didn't try too hard, they couldn't really see anything.

First, they washed their hands and faces in the Lukewarm River. For some reason, the grocer's sold soap, which was convenient. They washed the rest of their bodies quickly, and then, finally, sank into the bath.

The water of the Lukewarm River was lower than body temperature; it was, as its name suggested, lukewarm. They would have loved to take a true hot bath, but they were careful. They knew if they started demanding luxuries like that, there would be no end to it.

"Whew." Haruhiro turned his head from side to side and massaged his own shoulders. If he sat with his butt touching the bottom of the bath, the water was just deep enough to come up to his shoulders. He could stretch out his legs, too. However, it was a bit cramped for Kuzaku, what with his bigger body. Being tall wasn't always so great. Haruhiro was still just a tiny bit jealous, though.

"Maaaan." Kuzaku rubbed his face with both hands. "Y'know, today was kinda... I dunno. Today was pretty exhausting."

"Sure was," Haruhiro agreed. "You did good work. You must be tired."

"Oh, no, it must have been way more tiring for you."

"You're the one putting your neck on the line, Kuzaku. I'm just, y'know, hanging out in the back."

"You use your head," Kuzaku contradicted. "That's hard work in its own way. Me, I just do whatever you tell me to. As long as I do that, it all works out. Like, you set things up so that can happen, right?"

"It's because you do such a good job as a tank."

"You serious? I'm doing a good job?"

"You are, man."

"Nah, I've got a long way to go. I'm not that great."

"I'm pretty serious about my compliments, you know," Haruhiro said. "You're being hard on yourself."

"A little, yeah." Kuzaku went quiet. There was an odd pause before he spoke again. "Umm, I don't get the chance to do this often—talk to you alone like this, I mean. Do you mind if I ask something?"

"Huh? Oh, sure," Haruhiro said. "Wh-what?"

"It's about Moguzo."

"Moguzo?" The question had caught him off guard. He hadn't expected to hear Moguzo's name from Kuzaku. *Oh,* that's *what it's about*, Haruhiro thought. *If not that, what would he ask about?*

"Sure," Haruhiro said. "I don't mind. But, Kuzaku... You never, well, you didn't have anything to do with Moguzo, not directly at least."

"Well, no. I know who he was, though."

"Does it bother you?" Haruhiro asked.

"Like, you guys never talk about it. You never compare me to him. At the very least, you never tell me when you do."

"I wouldn't."

"But, y'know, I think about that stuff. Like, there's no way you aren't comparing me to him. I wonder things like, 'Am I doing as well as Moguzo?' Or 'Am I filling the hole he left?' Sorry."

"No. No need to apologize."

"I was just thinking, it's not right to talk about me filling the hole. That's not something I can do. It's not something that can be filled. That's how it is with comrades, isn't it? After all the time I've spent with you guys, I feel that. It's, it's...irreplaceable. Yeah, that's the word. That's what comrades are. This isn't the best way to say it, but just because someone dies, you can't let another guy replace him. It's not that simple. Even if you're forced to do it, it feels wrong, you know? I'm sorry, I'm not really good with words. Like... I can never be Moguzo's replacement. But I want to find a way to protect you all, in a different way than Moguzo did. I'm a paladin, even if I'm not a great one. So, I feel like I've gotta protect you all."

Oh, this is not good, Haruhiro thought. *He splashed water on his face. What the hell, man? Cut that out. You're blindsiding me here. I don't know what to say. I'm not good at this stuff.*

It wasn't that Kuzaku had been gradually getting used to his role and growing as a tank naturally. Sensing a high wall called "Moguzo," he had been facing the enemy and himself, fighting with everything he had. He had a firm sense of purpose, shedding blood for his comrades as he improved with painstaking effort.

Had Haruhiro seen that?

Had Haruhiro understood the struggles Kuzaku went, and was still going, through?

There was no way he could say he had. His mind had been elsewhere. He had a hard enough time taking care of himself, let alone the others. That wasn't an excuse, though. The fact of the matter was, Haruhiro hadn't been giving Kuzaku the credit he deserved.

Sorry for being so hopeless as a leader, for coming up short in so many ways, Haruhiro thought dispiritedly.

It would be easy to bow his head, but what good would come from apologizing like that to Kuzaku? Haruhiro might feel better, but that was probably all. It would be pure self-satisfaction.

"Moguzo was..." Haruhiro started. He pinched his nose and breathed through his mouth.

Oh, damn. I think I'm gonna cry. No, I'm fine. I can hold it in.

"He was an important comrade. I don't think he can be replaced. We can't forget him, and we won't. But still... He died. He's gone. I don't want to say that's why, but now... Kuzaku, you're our party's tank, and I think you're the only one who could be."

"Whoa."

"Huh?"

"Ha ha..." Kuzaku covered his face with his hands. "I'm tearing up here. What a laugh."

"I won't laugh at you."

"Honestly, it'd be better if you would," Kuzaku said. "Man, this is embarrassing."

"No, it's not."

"Could you do me a favor and not tell anyone? Especially Ranta-kun."

"You think I would?"

"Nah, I don't. Just saying it to be safe."

"I won't mention it." For no real reason, Haruhiro used his finger to flick water in Kuzaku's direction.

"Hey!" Kuzaku splashed him back. "What was that for? You're such a kid!"

"No, you are."

"You started it."

"I won't do it again, okay?"

"You swear?"

"I swear, I swear," Haruhiro said, then immediately scooped up some water and dumped it on Kuzaku's head.

"I knew you'd do that!" Kuzaku immediately retaliated.

What the heck are we doing? Haruhiro felt silly and decided he should stop the splash fight, but it took a while before that actually happened. Honestly, what were they doing?

It was fun. It was so stupid, he couldn't help but laugh. Right now, he felt like he could talk about it. About them.

I should ask him directly, Haruhiro thought. He needed to make things clear. Weird as it sounded, he wanted Kuzaku to find happiness.

For the time being, they were stuck here. It would be a year, two years or five years. It could be a decade or longer. They couldn't go on as volunteer soldiers forever, doing nothing but hunting, eating, and sleeping. They needed to have lives outside of that. They could get permission from the Well Village residents to build a house for themselves inside the village. Or, with an eye to the future, they could find jobs other than hunting.

If both sides wanted it, they could become couples. If there ended up being children, they could protect and nurture them together. Hell, it might help motivate them all.

The way things stood, it was still a dream—a wispy figment of his imagination—but it could happen.

"Listen, Kuzaku," Haruhiro said. "You mind if I ask something?"

"Sure. What?"

"It's kind of personal, though."

"Don't hold back. You and me are pals, man. No, sorry, I got carried away there. Acting in such an embarrassing way again..."

"Now it's really hard for me to say...this."

"I know, right?" Kuzaku said. "Sorry, but seriously, you can ask me anything. I don't think I'm hiding anything."

"W-well, then." Haruhiro cleared his throat.

What is this ringing in my ears? I'm ridiculously tense. How do I bring it up? I'm not good at talking about this stuff. But I'm not really good at anything. Oh, well. It's fine being normal. I'll ask him directly. That's the only way.

"H-how are things? With M-M-M...M-Merry?"

He stuttered like crazy. He wanted to do it subtly, like it was no big deal, but in the end, it was impossible. This was the best Haruhiro could manage.

"Uhh..." Kuzaku bit his upper lip with his lower teeth. "What do you mean, how are things?"

"Huh?" Haruhiro faltered. "You know, um... I mean, you know? Kuzaku, you and Merry are... Well, you're, um..."

"What's this about Merry-san and me?"

"H-huh? Y-you're mad?" Haruhiro asked.

"No, I'm not mad."

"You seem sorta upset."

"No, man, I'm not upset, okay?"

"No, no, you totally are. I mean, you look super unhappy."

"That's not it. Ngahh." Kuzaku hit himself on the head with both hands. "Guhh. How do I even explain it? It's not like that. I'm not mad. Besides, what about Merry and me? What are you trying to say? Aghhhh!"

"Wh-whoa, Kuzaku, calm down, man."

"Don't tell me to calm down," Kuzaku snapped.

"You're clearly not calm. You look like you're losing your mind. Wh-why? I mean, you and Merry are going o—"

"I get it! I'll tell you the whole story, okay?" Kuzaku broke in, using large gestures as he spoke. "Look, a lot of stuff happened between Merry-san and me. No, wait, nothing really. I think she's pretty great. Honestly, you know how it goes. I had a thing for her."

"Yeah."

"I mean, she's not just beautiful, she's funny, too. I dunno, she's serious, but there's something kind of, kind of unreliable about her. No, that's not it. What is it? She's cute."

"Yeah, okay I guess."

"I think so," Kuzaku said. "So, well, that's why I fell for her. When I had the chance to talk to her alone, I sort of dropped hints about that."

"Like when we were at the Lonesome Field Outpost?"

"Huh? You noticed?"

"Yeah, kinda."

"Well, I dunno what to say," Kuzaku said. "She's probably the type that gives in if you push a little, you know. Insecure, I guess So, when I said I wanted her advice, she was willing to hear me out. And me and Merry-san, we both joined the group after everyone else. We had that in common, so there was that, too."

"I see."

"It felt like things were going well. Like maybe she's got a soft spot for me. Things are looking good. That's what I thought."

"That's what you thought?"

"That's what I thought. So, of course, I had to go for it."

"Go for what?"

"A confession, of course."

"You confessed to her?"

"Darn straight I did," Kuzaku said firmly. "I mean, I couldn't leave things vague forever. That wouldn't feel good for either of us."

"Is that...how it is?"

"It's different for everyone," Kuzaku said. "For me, if I see a chance and it feels right, I go for it."

"Did you take her aside?" Haruhiro asked.

"Yeah. It was going to be a long talk, after all. That was at the Lonesome Field Outpost."

"That before we went back to Alterna?"

"Yeah. Wait, how'd you know about that? Oh, you weren't in the tent, huh? Were you outside watching, maybe?"

"A little, yeah."

"Urgh. You saw that? How embarrassing. Yeah, it was just

after that. I went and confessed to her. I thought it'd work, too. I got an immediate response."

"Immediate?" Haruhiro asked.

"When it comes to that sort of stuff, she's cut and dry about it. She kept firm boundaries, you know. I was just misunderstanding, you could say, or being overly optimistic. I thought there was a good thing between us."

"And?"

"It went like this." Kuzaku tucked in his chin, shaking his head left and right a little. "'No.'"

"Was that supposed to be your imitation of Merry?" Haruhiro asked.

"Yeah. It's just like her, if I do say so myself. It was a one-word response. Of course, she then explained. It was like, since we're comrades, she could be my friend, but nothing more. She's not interested now. She didn't want the distraction. She was apologetic, and it made me feel bad for putting her in that position. So, I told her, 'Sorry for making this awkward. Please, let's just keep things the way they've been.' And we agreed to do that."

"So then..." Haruhiro said slowly. He finished silently, *The two of them aren't going out?*

Haruhiro noticed he was sinking. The water reached his chin. Then his mouth. Then all the way up to his nose. *Hey, you're going to drown,* he warned himself.

"Haruhiro?" Kuzaku asked, concerned.

Haruhiro hurriedly pushed himself up out of the water, avoiding drowning. "So that's how it was. I... I see. Man, I thought... I dunno, that you two were just keeping quiet about it. I was wrong, huh?"

"I planned to tell you all, if it worked out," Kuzaku said. "It'd be awkward otherwise. Like, if you had people sneaking around behind your back, wouldn't that be unpleasant?"

"I might not be happy about it," Haruhiro said. "You're right."

"It's too bad I didn't get to make my big announcement."

"Well, yeah."

"Are you trying to console me?"

"Kinda?"

"It's fine, man. I'm already over it. I mean, I still love her, and I'd be lying if I said it didn't bother me at all. But we've got bigger concerns."

"Yeah," Haruhiro murmured.

"I can do without romance. For now, at least. I'll leave that to Ranta-kun, though he might be looking for something different."

"In his case, it's more primitive, and childish."

"He's honest with himself," Kuzaku said. "I like that about him."

"I don't like it all that much."

Kuzaku laughed, rubbing his face a few times with his hands. He probably wasn't as over it as he said he was. That said, the guy didn't need to be comforted. Kuzaku was looking forward.

How was Haruhiro, compared to that?

He thought about it. *I don't really know, but, for now, I'm a little relieved...? Why do I feel so relieved right now?*

10 | Plus and Minus

Not only was the City of the Dead Ones larger than Well Village, it was probably larger than Alterna. It must have been a big city before it had been reduced to ruins. Many people must have lived here, more than a few thousand for sure. Perhaps even tens of thousands.

There was a large, castle-like structure in the center of the city. The castle was composed of a main tower surrounded by eight other towers, but three of those had collapsed completely, and another two of them were halfway gone. The main tower was hardly damaged at all but setting foot inside would take a lot of courage. Besides, how would they open those rusty doors? They didn't budge in the slightest from pushing or pulling.

When they circled around the castle, they found two back entrances, but they couldn't convince themselves to go inside. It was too scary.

There were three cobblestone roads leading from the castle,

heading north, south, and west. Each of them had a plaza along the way. These roads and plazas were bizarrely empty; dead ones rarely went near them. They were oddly safe.

On the north side of the city, there were many buildings either half or almost completely destroyed. Furthermore, the closer to the Lukewarm River they were, the heavier the damage was.

To the south, the streets and buildings were largely intact. The Southwest Quarter looked pretty livable, if there weren't dead ones around. There was no chance they would start living there. If they came across a solid building, it was safe to assume there was a dead one inside. It seemed they needed rest, too, and the party occasionally spotted dead ones sleeping in back alleyways or behind rubble. However, dead ones woke up at the slightest disturbance, so it was difficult to attack them in their sleep.

What did the dead ones do inside those buildings? They didn't know, but even if they slept there too, the slightest noise would rouse them. Then they would viciously attack the party. The party didn't want any nasty surprises, so they thought it best to stay out of the buildings in the City of the Dead Ones.

The fog from the Lukewarm River hung thick over the eastern side of the city, making visibility incredibly poor. That was why Haruhiro and the others remained in the western part of the city, hunting dead ones.

The remains of the marketplace in the Northwest Quarter, or what they now called the Warehouse District—what with the remains of large buildings that looked like warehouses—made good targets.

The dead ones had some sort of ranking system or hierarchy. The Northeast Quarter had nothing but weak dead ones. The Northwest Quarter had the next rank of dead ones, followed by the Southeast Quarter, and finally the Southwest Quarter. Their numbers, though, followed the opposite trend. Dead ones were the most plentiful in the Southwest Quarter, with their numbers decreasing as you went from the Southeast Quarter to the Northwest Quarter, and finally to the Northeast Quarter.

For cannibals like the dead ones, more densely populated areas made finding prey easier. That meant there was a lot of competition. It was survival of the fittest; only the strong dead ones survived.

Weak dead ones had their own ways of fighting and surviving, though. If they knew their limits and hunted only prey they could defeat, the lowest level of dead ones would eventually arrive in the Northeast Quarter. There they found weak dead ones like themselves. As they killed and devoured the weak, they grew in confidence and then eventually headed to the Northwest Quarter. If they survived there, they moved on to the Southeast Quarter. Ultimately, they ended up in the Southwest Quarter where the most experienced dead ones gathered, fought, and fed.

Haruhiro and the others did their best to avoid the Southwest Quarter. It was swarming with dead ones, and they fought fiercely. Those dead ones used anything that came to hand as a throwing weapon, and they had a fondness for sneak attacks. They tried take you out with a single blow, then fled if that failed. The *power-ful dead ones* of the Southwest Quarter were crafty.

Of course, there were powerful dead ones so fierce that they were just beyond the others.

Once, they saw a powerful dead one feeding from afar. It looked like a lion on its hind legs, standing about three and a half meters tall. It punched a bearlike dead one, knocking it down with a series of two kicks, then easily lifted the bearlike dead one's massive body up.

The powerful, lionlike dead one effortlessly tore the bearlike dead one in two. It was insanely strong.

Bathing and laughing in a shower of blood, the victorious dead one trembled with unmistakable delight. It was more than just terrifying. If they approached it, it would kill them almost instantly.

The Southwest Quarter of the town was too dangerous. The Southeast Quarter was, too. The dead ones there would sneak up on you through the dense mist, which made them nasty to deal with. There were just too few dead ones in the Northeast Quarter. Therefore, they spent most of their time in the Northwest Quarter.

Honestly, the Northwest Quarter of the City of the Dead Ones couldn't have been more perfect. It would have been fair to call it an ideal hunting ground.

First, Haruhiro eliminated his presence with Hide. Then, he moved with his presence eliminated with Swing. Finally, he utilized all his senses to detect others' presences with Sense.

Using the secret art of thieves, Stealth, to its fullest, Haruhiro moved like a shadow.

While he was using Stealth, Haruhiro's knees and elbows were never stiff. They were always bending smoothly. He lowered his hips, arched his back, and didn't let his neck stiffen. He was ready to respond to anything at any time. He maintained a posture that allowed him to breathe smooth and easily as his feet moved without hesitation.

Instead of focusing his attention on any one point, Haruhiro took in the whole picture. It was like his eyes had been pulled into the back of his skull. He used eye shifts and slight turns of his head to expand his field of vision. When done properly, he could even see behind him, where he wasn't supposed to be able to.

He didn't listen with just his ears. He felt sound with his entire body. His whole body was a sensor, and with it he picked up every stimulus, every kind of change.

He spotted a dead one poking its head out of the remains of a building in the Warehouse District, looking left and right.

Should we attack it together? Haruhiro wondered.

It was common for a dead one in the Northwest Quarter to run away as soon as it sensed a disadvantage. Especially a dead one like this, which was close to Ranta's size. It wore a helmet and light-looking armor and carried a short halberd-like weapon. There was something frightened and hesitant about it. It didn't look very strong.

That didn't guarantee it was weak, but it almost guaranteed it would flee. Haruhiro decided to circle around behind it. If he could finish it off, good. If he couldn't, then he could chase it to his comrades.

Ranta was the only one who had been against this plan, which meant they were going through with it.

Haruhiro closed in on the dead one's back.

It was less than ten meters away. Eight meters. Even as he catalogued the distance, Haruhiro still moved. It was seven meters away. Six meters.

If he said he didn't feel tense, it would have been a lie. But with his target's back in sight, he felt a strange calmness. It might have been part of his nature as a thief, or just part of his own nature. He often read the backs of living creatures. They provided Haruhiro with a lot of information.

The easiest thing to learn was whether they were a liar. Were they guileless or a schemer? Trustworthy or not?

This dead one was a liar, the dishonest, untrustworthy sort that tried to lure opponents into traps. Haruhiro sensed that from the way it leaned and the warped way it held itself. But this dead one was also shallow. It told obvious lies and relied on its nose to sniff out prey that would fall for simple ruses. If it didn't think it could win, it wouldn't hesitate before fleeing.

Sorry, Haruhiro thought, *but I'm not going to let you do that.*

He drew his short sword. Its sheath was well-oiled and maintained, so the move was utterly silent.

It was just a few steps away. He couldn't think any of those steps were special. If he placed importance on them, his target would notice him.

Here's the trick, Barbara-sensei had once told him. *When it comes to hiding, stealing, or killing, you do them all the same way. In this world, in any world, nothing is special. You can't think things are interesting or boring. You do them all the same way, without any attachments.*

I can't do that, Barbara-sensei, he had complained. The mysterious thing was, though, when it went well, he was able to do those things because they were *all the same.*

Haruhiro approached the dead one from behind, shifting until he seemed to hang over it. Then he wrapped his left arm around its head. With a backhanded grip, he stabbed his short sword into its neck, then gouged it, twisting its whole body to break its neck.

If he let out a sigh of relief, Barbara-sensei would have scolded him. No, she'd scold him, trip him, put his joints in a lock, and then make him faint. *"Do them all the same way! How many times do I have to tell you before you get it, Old Cat?!"*

The path was precarious. It was the sort of steep hill where, if he let his guard down, he would roll right down it. He didn't know if he would ever see Barbara-sensei again, but his master's teachings were still alive inside him. He was still persevering along this steep and narrow road.

The way of the thief!

"Heyyyy. I'm doooone," Haruhiro called.

While he called his comrades over, Haruhiro thought he was acting a little off. *Am I getting carried away? Like, things are going really well with the dead ones in the Northwest Quarter. This hunting ground is way too lucrative. I can work hard as the party leader, while still pushing forward along the way of the thief, even though I'm doing it all the same way. But, somehow... It scares me. It's all going too smoothly. This isn't what life is like, right?*

"Hey, Parupirorinnosuke!" Ranta jumped in and went to

work on the dead one. "Taking one down on your own is too much for a flea like you!"

"Kehe..." Zodiac-kun put in. "Talking like a human is too much for you, Ranta... Kehe..."

"No, Zodiac-kun, I'm an honest-to-goodness human, okay?! I mean, I'm a respectable human, all right?!"

Following quickly on their heels, Yume, Shihoru, Merry, and Kuzaku arrived. They came to a halt, then backed away.

"Huh?" Ranta looked to Yume and the others. "What? What's wrong? Does my way-too-respectable, special, and mature aura intimidate you?"

"Mature?" Shihoru scoffed. "Mature how?"

"Respectable?" Yume furrowed her brow, stuck out her bottom lip, and made a show of shrugging her shoulders. "How?"

Merry shook her head. "If you called him childish, I'd feel bad for actual children."

"You're all in sync, huh?! What a trio! What kind of threesome are you, huh?!" Ranta shouted as he rummaged through the dead one's possessions. "Well, fine! Say whatever you like! I've got my soul mate, Zodiac-kun, after all! What?"

"Just now." Kuzaku said and pointed above Ranta's head. "It vanished, man."

Haruhiro was surprised by that. "Wow, Zodiac-kun. You learned a trick just so you could harass Ranta."

"N-no!" Ranta jumped to his feet and rounded on Haruhiro. "N-none of you get it, okay?! Zodiac-kun's not doing it to harass me or anything like that! He does that as a way of showing his love!"

"What do you mean, 'he'?" Haruhiro asked. "Honestly, you two seem kind of distant."

"W-w-we do not! There's no distance between us. Me and Zodiac-kun are tight. We'll always be in loooove. You dummy, dummy, dummy!"

"I get it, I get it. Just keep looting, okay? You like that, don't you?"

"I do not! I hate, hate, hate it! You do it, you stupid moron!"

"Fine, I'll do it."

"Moron! I'm obviously gonna do it! Like I'd ever let you handle it, Parupiro! I'll do it all! Me! Don't you forget it, Paruparu!"

"What's a Paruparu?"

"Paaaruparuparuparuparuuuu," Ranta cackled. "Ehehehehe!"

There were times Haruhiro wanted to murder the piece of crap. He wouldn't do it, though.

Ranta got to work, finding two medium-sized coins and three small ones. There was a ring on the dead one's left hand, too. They might be able to sell it, so they decided to take it. Eventually another dead one would come along and clean up the body for them—in its own way. They could just leave it here.

"On to the next one," Haruhiro said. When their job was done, it was best to move on.

His comrades knew that, too, so even Ranta obeyed without any fuss. They departed, hurrying to find their next target. They had to return to Well Village before the flame set, so they couldn't afford to waste time.

We're hardly wasting any time, thought Haruhiro. *When things are going our way, everything seems to go well. Although good times can't last forever.*

Don't get carried away, Haruhiro reminded himself multiple times each day. *Stay on guard. There are pitfalls waiting for us everywhere. This is just a coincidence. It won't last. We don't know what tomorrow will be like. We don't know what today will be like. Misfortune could be coming our way. Someone could make a horrible mistake.*

His eyes met Merry's. For some reason, Merry smiled at him.

Everything's going well, huh? Haruhiro thought. *No, no, no, What am I thinking? No, I'm not thinking at all. I'm not thinking this, or that, or anything about Merry. I'm not thinking anything.*

But I can't help being conscious of her. It's Kuzaku's fault. Kuzaku didn't do anything wrong, it's just him opening up to me. That's what triggered this.

Haruhiro was the party leader. It was wrong for him to have unique or special feelings for a single party member. It wasn't a good thing.

Or at least, that's how it feels. That's gotta be right, right?

But Akira-san and Miho were married, he reminded himself. *That was an inter-party romance. There were Gogh and Kayo, too. Those two even had an adopted son.*

When he thought about it, Haruhiro started to feel it was perfectly natural for those sorts of feelings to sprout between them. They would form a strong bond because of all the danger. Besides, when he thought about a relationship with someone outside the party, it didn't feel right or real. Sure, he had relationships with people like Mimorin, but that wasn't a *relationship*. He didn't have romantic feelings for her. Besides, they might never meet again.

No, no, no, what am I thinking? Nothing! Maybe I'm getting a little too giddy? I need to seriously, diligently, earnestly focus on being the leader.

Honestly, I'm not good at this. Doing this and doing that at the same time—it's beyond me. If I don't focus on one thing, my head gets all jumbled up.

Haruhiro came to a stop on a narrow road in the Warehouse District.

He took point, with Kuzaku was ready to step in if needed. Behind them was Yume. Merry was somewhere where she could protect Shihoru. Ranta brought up the rear. This had become their standard formation for exploring the City of the Dead Ones.

"Haruhiro?" Kuzaku asked. He already had his longsword and his shield at the ready.

"Meow?" Yume let out a weird noise, looking around the area.

"Huhhhh? Whaaaat?" Ranta turned to look behind him.

Shihoru inhaled sharply, shrinking into herself.

Merry immediately got into a position, lowering her posture. She was gallant at times like this. It was a hard to deny, but Haruhiro didn't have time to admire her.

The blood instantly drained from Haruhiro's face. He wasn't sure how he managed to react, but somehow, he threw himself forward. Before he could do a roll, he heard something massive hit the ground right behind him. He felt the shock wave.

"Run for it!" Haruhiro shouted without checking to see what it was. Where had it come down from? The sky? The buildings here were relatively intact. The dead one must have been lurking on some roof, waiting for them.

Them, or just Haruhiro?

It was coming. Charging at him.

Haruhiro ran. He dashed at top speed, turning a corner. The only thing he knew about his enemy was that it was a dead one, and a big one. He figured with its large size, it couldn't make tight turns.

His hope played out. Just as he thought, the dead one couldn't turn suddenly or tightly. That put distance between them and gave Haruhiro the time to get a look at his pursuer, even if it wasn't a good look.

Aw, man, he thought. *It looks like a lion. I had a feeling it would. A lion standing on its hind legs. That's what it looks like.*

But it's a little—no, a lot—smaller than the one we saw before. Maybe it only looks that way because I want to it to? No, for real, it's smaller. Right?

If it had been that powerful dead one they had seen, Haruhiro would already be dead. It was still scary, though. He thought his stomach would jump out of his throat, but he wouldn't get off that lightly if the dead one behind him was that one. If it had been, Haruhiro would freeze, unable to move until it gobbled him up. This one wasn't that bad.

Haruhiro dashed into an alley and then jumped inside a building through a collapsing wall. What were his comrades doing? Had they gotten away? Haruhiro didn't think they were heartless enough to abandon him.

They wouldn't run away. They probably wouldn't run away. They wouldn't run away on me, I'm sure of it.

It—the not-so-powerful dead one—diligently chased after Haruhiro.

Haruhiro left the building through the entrance. The dead one bounded after him. He couldn't outrun it. That thing was faster than him.

"Haruhiroooo!" He heard Ranta's voice.

I'm amazed I managed to dodge it the first time it jumped at me, Haruhiro thought as he rolled inside another building.

This one had two floors. Haruhiro raced up some nearby stairs. They were wooden and weak. They gave in, and his foot almost got trapped. He didn't care. He took the stairs two at a time and kept going up.

The dead one destroyed the stairs as it tried to go up, then let out a roar.

Haruhiro made it to the second floor. There was a window. He could see outside through it. Ranta was there. So was Kuzaku. And Yume, Shihoru, and Merry. They were running this way. None of them had noticed Haruhiro on the second floor yet.

Haruhiro leaned out the window. "Run away! Come on, run away!"

"Whaa?!" Ranta looked up at Haruhiro, then immediately waved to him. "Man, get down here already! It's inside, right?!"

Haruhiro couldn't argue back. The dead one was still trying

to get to the second floor. Even with the stairs completely collapsed, it would get up here eventually. Ranta was right. For once.

Haruhiro did not jump out the window. He didn't have the guts. He straddled the window frame, got a firm grip on it, and then hung down. From that position, he let go. He didn't feel much of an impact when he hit the ground; his legs just felt a little numb.

"Come on, let's get outta here, you bunch of bozos!" Ranta had already taken off.

"Who're you callin' a booboo?!" Yume shouted after him.

"I didn't say that, you tiny-tittied monster! Hey, girls, if you stay next to that monster, your tits'll shrivel up and turn into miserable tiny tits like hers!"

"You're the worst, you vile monster man," Shihoru muttered as she caught up to Yume.

"If I'm the worst, that makes me number one, huh?! Hurrah! Hurrah! Gahahaha!"

"I respect that," Kuzaku ran, his armor clanking.

"No, go all the way and worship me! I'm offering a boon! You can become a thousand times more erotic! Gwahehehehehe!"

"That's not a boon. That's a curse you'll never recover from." Haruhiro muttered. He forced his slightly numb legs to keep going. He eventually caught up.

"Haru!" Merry shouted at him.

"Yes?!"

"For that, just now!"

"J-Just now?"

Merry was silent for a moment. It was slightly dramatic, and he was concerned when she didn't say the next part for a while.

While they bantered, or in Haruhiro's case waited, the dead one stuck its head out the second-floor window and roared.

Haruhiro sped up, catching up to Merry. They turned the corner. At that moment, she slapped him hard on the shoulder.

"You get one demerit!" She snapped.

"Whaa?!"

What did that mean? He thought maybe he understood, but also that he really didn't.

Merry wouldn't look him in the eye. Was she mad? Or embarrassed?

It might have been both.

Grimgar of *Fantasy* and *Ash*

11 | A Work in Progress

They could find themselves faced with a life-or-death crisis anywhere. If they made one misstep, it could be disastrous. There were countless times the worst almost happened. It would be fair to say it was almost a daily occurrence.

Haruhiro gazed into the campfire. Wrapped in a blanket made of some mysterious material he had bought from the flattened egg that owned the clothing-and-bag shop, he used his bag as a pillow. It was pretty comfortable.

He was tired, just starting to nod off but not fully asleep yet. This sort of state wasn't so bad. It was one luxury he could enjoy, although one he couldn't savor without first securing his safety.

His comrades were already asleep. While he listened to them sleep, he thought idly, *We managed to make it through another day. That's nice. It's amazing to have a tomorrow.*

Yume and Merry slept entwined in each other's arms. When Yume went to sleep, she tended to snuggle up to whoever happened to be nearby. Like she longed for another's warmth. Merry didn't seem to mind. Tonight, though, Shihoru stayed a little apart from them.

Suddenly, Shihoru sat up. "Haruhiro-kun? Are you awake?"

"Whuh?" Haruhiro pushed himself up a bit, supporting himself with his elbows. "Uh, yeah."

"There was something I wanted to...talk to you about. Is that okay?"

"You want to talk? Sure."

It would be awkward to talk where they were, so they stood and walked a bit along the moat. After a few minutes, they crouched down side by side.

"So, what's up?" Haruhiro asked. "You know, it's kind of weird, crouching like this."

"Yeah. Maybe. Uh, there're two things. The first is about what happened..." Shihoru stopped, as if it was hard to talk about. "It might not be my place to say, but, you know, it's just... It's been bothering me."

"Okay," Haruhiro said. "I'll hear you out. Talk to me."

"Haruhiro, you...you don't value yourself enough, I think."

"I don't? Is that how it looks?"

"Yeah," Shihoru told him. "If it came down to it, you'd sacrifice yourself, wouldn't you?"

"Maybe. I don't know. I don't plan on it, though, you know?"

"I wish you'd stop that." Shihoru looked down, her shoulders trembling. "I'm sorry, I don't know if I should be saying this, but... but it reminds me of Manato. I don't want you to die on us."

Haruhiro rubbed his forehead. "Well, I don't want to die, either. I mean it."

"Then...take better care of yourself, please."

"It's not that I don't value myself." Haruhiro pinched the bridge of his nose. "I just value everyone else more. I mean, without you guys, I couldn't do anything. Like, I don't think I could find the motivation to go on without any of you. So, if I had to choose between you or me, I'd choose to help you survive. It's not that I'd mean to do it. It'd be instinct, I think. A snap decision."

"If only one of us could survive, Haruhiro-kun, I'd rather it be you."

"It's a real dilemma, huh?" Haruhiro said.

"What if it were between you and Ranta-kun? Who would you choose?"

"Ranta," Haruhiro answered without hesitating, then was taken aback by his own answer. "Whoa. Seriously? This is Ranta we're talking about. I don't know that I like this."

"I'm glad."

"Huh? F-for what?"

"That you're our leader," Shihoru said. "Our comrade. And friend."

"You're making me want to dive into the moat right now."

Shihoru laughed, so Haruhiro could laugh, too. He was glad Shihoru was his comrade, and his friend. He felt that from the bottom of his heart.

"So, what was the other thing?" Haruhiro asked.

"The second thing." Shihoru closed her eyes, placed her

hand over her chest, and took a deep breath. What was she doing? Shihoru was trying to do *something*, he could tell that much, at least.

The air was tense. Haruhiro held his breath and waited.

Shihoru opened her eyes. "Elementals, come..."

"Whoa!" Haruhiro fell back on his rump in surprise.

In front of Shihoru's face was a whirling vortex. It was small, just about thumb-sized. It didn't have any concrete shape or form. But there was a whirling vortex, so he knew something had to be there.

Shihoru reached out with her right hand. She let the vortex sit in her palm.

"Float," Shihoru ordered, and it floated. "Fall," she said, and it descended back into her palm.

Shihoru repeated the rising and falling process a number of times with a degree of focus that was noticeably bizarre. It wouldn't have been an exaggeration to call her possessed. Shihoru ground her teeth, eyes unblinking and hair swaying restlessly. As he watched her, Haruhiro got goosebumps.

"Release," Shihoru said, forcing the word out.

The vortex let out strange noises and began to shift, like it was being pushed open from inside. Something came out. This dark purple thing, part way between a light and a haze, appeared.

No, it struggled to appear.

It looked like it was trying to be born. Depending on how you looked at it, it was star-shaped, or human-shaped even, and seemed to be kicking and struggling with its legs and arms. But then it ran out of strength and disappeared with a poof.

"No good." Shihoru sighed, shoulders slumping in disappointment. "I've tried it a number of times, but I just can't get it to work."

"To work? What?" Haruhiro rubbed his throat. He'd tried to swallow, but his mouth was dry. "What did you do? Shihoru, was that magic? But there was no chant. You didn't draw elemental sigils, either..."

"What Gogh-san said, do you remember it? He said, 'We set loose an elemental, then activated an alternate power. They won't teach you this stuff at the guild.'"

"Vaguely, but yeah," Haruhiro said.

"I've been thinking about it ever since," Shihoru said. "In the guild, we learn there are elementals in the world, magical creatures you can't normally see with your eyes. What I learned to do was to tame those elementals and use magic by bending them to my will."

"Honestly, I don't really understand, but go on."

"For a while now, there's something I've had my doubts about."

"Err, what's that?"

"Even in sweltering weather, you can call ice elementals and use Kanon ice magic," said Shihoru. "In the middle of the day, there's nothing obstructing your ability to use Darsh shadow magic."

"So, elementals are just elementals, and the material world—the heat, and light, and shadows, and stuff—they don't interact directly with those, is that it? Sort of?"

"But the thing is, with magic you can freeze things. Make them explode, do so much more," said Shihoru. "I wondered if it's not that they don't interact at all, maybe. I was thinking that was strange."

"I'm sorry, I'm not sure I'm keeping up. So, what you just did, it wasn't magic? Is that it?"

"I tried working under the theory that elementals are just elementals," said Shihoru. "Arve, Kanon, Falz, Darsh. I thought maybe they were just something humans came up with on their own, and not the elementals' true form. That seemed closer to the sense I had of them."

"Magic they won't teach you at the guild, huh?"

"I want to get better at magic," Shihoru said. "Everyone's always protecting me. I want to be able to lend you all my strength."

"You're already strong, you know that."

"Not strong enough, I think. But there's no guild in this place."

"Probably not," Haruhiro said. "Not a chance."

"If I can't gain new spells, new powers without being taught... I won't change. So, I wanted to do something about it by myself."

You're amazing. It was the one thing Haruhiro could think to say. Shihoru was truly amazing.

If Barbara-sensei's not here, I'll have to come up with something on my own. Had there ever been a time when he had thought that? It had never crossed his mind.

"But," Shihoru hung her head, frowning. "There's something that worries me. In a way, this feels like I'm... I'm rejecting how I've used magic until now. I think it might affect the magic I've learned from the guild, too."

"So, you haven't decided whether to keep pushing ahead with it or not?"

"Yeah."

"It'll be fine," he assured her.

I mean, not that I'd know, but still.

Haruhiro was no mage. Even if he were, he wouldn't be able to tell her anything definite. It was almost irresponsible to comfort her so easily. But he wanted to nudge her forward, to encourage her. He wanted to support Shihoru, who worked so hard. He thought he ought to, and it wasn't as if he couldn't help.

"Listen, if anything goes wrong, I'll be there to back you up," said Haruhiro. "We all will. It's gonna be fine. I mean, having a goal can motivate you. I'm sure that probably plays into it, too. I mean, this would be your own original magic, right? I wanna see it. I'm sure it would be good for the party, too."

"Thanks."

"I should thank you. I've got my energy back now. I don't know about magic, but if anything comes up, let's talk about it, okay? If you're okay with talking to me, I'll be all ears."

"Yeah," Shihoru said. "I'll do that."

"Magic they won't teach you at the guild, huh? I bet it's not limited to magic. I'll do some thinking myself, too."

"You're a good leader," Shihoru said.

"Huh?"

"You are, Haruhiro-kun." Shihoru gave him an uncharacteristic grin. "You're the best leader we could ask for, you know that?"

"Heh heh." Haruhiro couldn't help grinning, so he covered the bottom half of his face with one hand. "C-cut that out, would you? You're gonna give me the wrong impression."

"That wouldn't happen. Not with you, Haruhiro-kun."

"You think? I dunno... I'm trying to keep it from happening. I'm careful about that. Like, there are times I get carried away. Because it's scary."

"That's why we trust you."

"Are you trying to compliment me to death?" Haruhiro asked. "It feels like it, you know? You're making me feel giddy."

"Sorry." Shihoru looked at the moat, taking a short breath. "I just wanted to tell you what I was thinking. I talk about things as much as I can. I don't want to be left with regrets again."

Haruhiro found himself unable to speak. He nodded instead.

They crouched in silence, side by side, at the edge of the moat for a while.

It's kind of strange, he thought. *This silence isn't awkward at all. It's because it's Shihoru. If I were with Merry, it might not go like this.*

That was when it happened.

"Haruhiro-kun, do you like Merry?"

"Huhh?!" He pitched forward, nearly falling into the moat.

Haruhiro desperately denied her suspicions. It turned out Shihoru didn't have much reason to believe he did, and she seemed to accept when he told her he didn't. But Haruhiro was going to have to be careful not to cause any more misunderstandings in the future.

A misunderstanding? he thought. *Was it really?*

Grimgar of Fantasy and Ash

12 | Kinuko-sama

"I'M DYING! IT HURTS!" Ranta shouted as he used Leap Out to get in front of the enemy. "Clearly, our 49th day is cursed!"

The enemy tried to turn toward Ranta. However, with excellent timing, Kuzaku pushed in with his recently-acquired shield, preventing it from doing so.

"Grahhh!" Kuzaku shouted.

"Ngh!" Ranta swung the black blade he had bought into the enemy's flank. "Of course, I meant it's cursed for you, pal!"

While the lionlike dead one coughed blood from its terrifying maw, it wrapped its left arm around Ranta. Kuzaku was in the way of its right arm, so it couldn't move the way it wanted to. Kuzaku wasn't just interfering with its movements; he was shouting and stabbing his sword into its guts, too.

Yume released her drawn bowstring. Her arrow flew and struck the dead one in the forehead.

Nice one, Haruhiro wanted to congratulate her, but Yume cried out, "Mrrrow!" in consternation. She must have been aiming for the eyes. Still, she hadn't been far off.

Haruhiro kept a level head as he clung to the dead one's back, stabbing his short sword into its neck. Its thick, stiff mane got in the way. He pulled his sword back and stabbed again. Then he sensed it; its body was filled with an abnormal strength.

Haruhiro let go and jumped away. "Get away from it for now!"

"'Kay!" Kuzaku shouted.

"Dammit!" Ranta yelled.

Kuzaku and Ranta immediately followed Haruhiro's command and pulled back. In that instant, the lionlike dead one let out a truly heart-chilling roar. It was a noise that grabbed everyone who heard it by the guts, messing them up inside. Even if they had been prepared, it would have been harsh. It made them want to cover their ears and scream *Please, stop!* Haruhiro, Kuzaku, Ranta, and Yume all cringed. Even Zodiac-kun, who idly floated around nearby, flinched. So did Merry, but Shihoru, who stood beside her with her mind keenly focused, did not.

"Dark!" Shihoru cried.

When Shihoru called that name, the thing appeared as if coming out of a door from an unseen world. Long, dark strings twisted into a spiral and took on an almost humanlike form. It was just about the right size to fit in a person's palm. Palm-sized darkness. It was an elemental.

After much trial and error, Shihoru had settled on this form. If you asked about it, Shihoru would say it was a work in progress and that he must have a true form. One more appropriate for him.

Dark had grown attached to Shihoru, or at least that's how it looked to Haruhiro. Dark appeared next to Shihoru's face and then sat on her shoulder.

"Go!"

When Shihoru gave that order, Dark obeyed. He flew off Shihoru's shoulder with a mysterious whooshing cry. He hurtled toward the lion dead one.

Dark struck the dead one in the chest. There was no impact. Instead, he sank into its body. What Dark did, or caused, wasn't clear, but the lionlike dead one groaned and doubled over like it had taken a solid punch to the solar plexus. It dropped to a knee.

Before Haruhiro could shout "Now!" Ranta was charging in with Leap Out. He drew a figure-eight with his black blade and—no.

Ranta drew an infinity, not an eight.

"Infinite Black Purgatory Dance!"

First an infinity, then an eight. The eight was followed by another infinity. After the infinity, an eight. He chained, and chained, and chained them.

The dead one wasn't wearing actual armor, but its body was protected with hard, dense fur, impact-absorbing fat, and thick muscles. Thanks to that, slashing attacks were ineffective against it. Still, Ranta slashed it. Never learning his lesson, he slashed and slashed like crazy. In the end, he stumbled backward, short of breath.

"What about that?" Kuzaku panted. He stabbed the lionlike dead one in the belly again, right where he had stabbed it before, and twisted. "Was that supposed to be infinite?!"

"Nguhhhhhhh!" The dead one writhed, spewing blood.

"That's Ranta for you!" Yume fired off one arrow after another. She was using Rapid Fire. The first shot missed, but the second one landed a perfect hit in the dead one's right eye. The third shot pinged off Kuzaku's helmet.

"Whoa!" Kuzaku yelped.

"Meow?! S-sorry 'bout that!"

"Bwahah!" Ranta quickly shot back at her. "That's just Yume for you!"

"Shut up, stupid Ranta!"

"Ehe... It's true, you're too noisy... Shut up, Ranta. Forever... Ehehe..."

"Zodiac-kun! You're basically telling me to die there?!" Ranta screamed.

"Auugh!" The dead one tried to push Kuzaku away.

Kuzaku dug his heels in, standing his ground. He forced his longsword in deeper and twisted it. "Rahhh!"

Haruhiro jumped on the lionlike dead one from behind, stabbing his short sword into its back. He tore through fur, flesh, and fat, the blade passing between its ribs. But it was no good. He didn't reach any organs.

"Haru!" Merry called out. Haruhiro decided to put some distance between himself and the dead one. When facing an enemy of this level, a mere thief would hardly be able to land a fatal blow.

If he could see that line, things would be different, but it wasn't a thing he could see.

With a roar, the dead one tried to push Kuzaku away from it. Kuzaku resisted, but the odds were against him in a test of pure strength.

"Die already!" Ranta whacked the dead one hard on the head with his black blade. He still couldn't cut into it.

The lionlike dead one finally kicked Kuzaku, knocking him off balance.

"Guh!"

The dead one immediately turned and ran.

"You think you can get away?!" Ranta shouted, chasing after it. Or rather, pretended to. Ranta took two or three steps, then stopped and clicked his tongue. "We missed our chance to kill it! It's because you're all hopeless! If we'd had another me, we could've taken it out!"

"Yeah, just keep talking." Haruhiro looked around the area, checking for any other dead ones. He took a deep breath.

"Kehehe... If there were two of Ranta... this world would be a nightmare... Kehe... Kehehehe..." Zodiac-kun cackled.

"Whaddaya mean by that?!" Ranta hollered.

"Exactly what it sounded like," Shihoru muttered.

"Zodiac-kun's so kind," Merry said, smiling coldly. "If anything, that was a generous assessment."

"You peopleeeeee. What'd I ever do to youuuuuuuuu?!"

"You've been doin' all sorts of stuff." Yume puffed her cheeks and plucked the string on her bow. "Mrrrow. Was that a close one, you think?"

"Hard to say." Kuzaku lifted the visor on his helmet, bending his neck. "I thought I could push through, but I couldn't. It's like we were missing some decisive factor."

"But Shihoru's magic was effective." Haruhiro gave Shihoru a thumbs-up.

"You think so?" Shihoru's neck shrunk into her body with embarrassment. "I hope it was."

"You were great." Merry patted Shihoru on the back. "Creating magic in your own style. I could stand to learn from your example."

"Eh heh," Shihoru giggled self-consciously.

"Thanks to me!" Ranta puffed up his chest. "It's because I'm always showing off my freewheeling style! It was my influence! Clearly!"

"Kehe..."

"Wh-what, Zodiac-kun? If you've got something to say, then say it. We're buds. No need to hold back on me now. Wait, you're vanishing?! Because of that?! Hold on, Zodiac-kun, come back, okay?! If you leave like that, it's gonna be awkward when I summon you again, you know?!"

The lionlike dead one was a troublesome enemy that sometimes appeared in the Northwest Quarter. Until a little while ago, they had had no choice but to flee the moment it attacked. Now, though, they could fight it on even footing. They had engaged it several times, so they were getting used to it. And with the experience they gained each time, it was clear Haruhiro and the others were getting stronger.

Their equipment was getting better, too. Kuzaku had gotten himself a curved, trapezoidal shield—according to the black-smith, it was called "Gushtat." And Ranta, having gotten his hands on a pair of lightweight, sturdy gauntlets, had replaced his old armor with a lighter, more ominous looking set. He called it his "Death Armor," which was hardly original and fit the complete and utter moron.

As for Haruhiro, almost everything he owned—clothes and armor—had gotten so ratty and tattered they were beyond repair. He had bought some nice, dark-colored replacements from the clothing-and-bag seller and a matching set of snake leather pieces for armor. He was quite fond of them. He had to have a pair of seven-fingered gloves reworked for his five-fingered hands, but he'd gotten used to them, and now they felt strangely familiar and easy to use.

Yume had decided to increase her defense in a way that wouldn't impede her bow. She wore a number of different protectors. They were made of bone and coated with a sort of resin but were very light.

Shihoru's hat and robe had also been badly frayed, so the girls had gone together to buy suitable replacements from the clothing-and-bag shop. It looked a little tight in the chest area, or perhaps the robe she had been wearing had been a little too loose.

Ranta whispered to Haruhiro and Kuzaku, so quietly that Shihoru couldn't hear him, "She wasn't hiding big ones. Those are some serious torpedo tits she's rocking. I mean, she's more stacked than I thought."

Haruhiro agreed, but he still wanted to kill Ranta for saying it.

As a priest, Merry had been hesitant to do it, but she finally disposed of the priest robe that had been too badly damaged. She had looked for a white coat to replace it, but when she couldn't find one, she settled on a deep blue one. It was a good fit for her, and she looked good in it. She also acquired a staff with a painful looking head on it—not something Haruhiro ever wanted to get hit with, for sure—but they had looted that from a dead one.

They had all bought new masks or face coverings from the mask shop, which made the time they spent in Well Village a bit more comfortable. They also bought more daily necessities, since they could afford them. There were far fewer things missing from their lives now.

Other than that, the most notable thing was Shihoru's new magic. She had given form to the elemental she named Dark, which she could now control.

Dark resembled a shadow elemental because Shihoru specialized in Darsh shadow magic. Elementals fed on a mage's magic in order to take form and exert their power. Because of that, the mage and elemental directly influenced each other. Haruhiro didn't really understand it but thought it might be similar to a dread knight and its demon.

Shihoru's new magic, Dark, had only just been created. It was still a work in progress, and there was plenty of potential.

Shihoru had chosen the path of Darsh magic, which specialized in support and interference spells, but she had also picked up Falz magic which gave her some destructive power. She dabbled in Kanon magic, too. Her path had taken a number of twists and turns, but going from one to another was not what Shihoru really wanted to do. She was an earnest sort, the type who would pursue a single thing as far as she could.

Could Dark, perhaps, become that one thing? Haruhiro hoped so.

Their 49th day in this world ended, and the 50th began.

When they went into Well Village to wash their faces and get breakfast, they encountered him again.

"Oh ho!" Ranta jumped into the air. "It's Unjo-san!"

Wearing a braided hat, the walking arsenal—with axes, swords, crossbows, and more hanging from his hip and backpack—sipped at a bowl of bug soup. This was only the second time they had seen him, but he was unmistakable. It was Unjo.

When Unjo finished, he picked out the bugs and ate them. Then, when the bowl was empty, he said, "Ruo keh," returning it to the giant crab before finally turning to Haruhiro and the others.

"You people, huh. Volunteer soldiers. You still live, do you?"

"Thanks to you!" Ranta rushed over and did a fist pump. "I mean, that City of the Dead Ones! When you told us about that place, you really helped us out! Ever since, our quality of life has been on a serious upswing! You're the best, Unjo-san! Unjo-san for president! President? Maybe king would be better? Well, whatever. Ehehehehe. Would you like that, Your Excellency?! No, actually, how about Your Majesty?! You want that?!"

"Man, you are annoying," Haruhiro muttered. He fought off a pounding headache as he pushed Ranta aside, bowing his head in apology. "I'm sorry for our stupid, worthless piece of trash."

Unjo grabbed the brim of his braided hat and pulled it down. He didn't say a word.

Ranta gulped audibly and poked Haruhiro in the side. "Y-you moron. Th-this is your fault! Everything is!"

"Why?"

"You're the leader, damn it! That means everything's your responsibility, you worthless chunk of smegma!"

With a glance back at Haruhiro, who was so exasperated he lacked the will to get angry, Unjo started walking.

Where was Unjo going? To the general store that was beside the grocer's? It wasn't opened. It was rarely opened. Outside of the rare occasions when the lanky shopkeeper dressed all in dark grey was outside, the shop was permanently closed.

The owner wasn't outside now, so the door to the building was shut.

Once before, Ranta had said about a test of courage and knocked on the door. There had been no response.

The general store was the most mysterious shop in Well Village. Haruhiro and the others had just started calling it a general store on their own. It might not be a store at all.

Unjo didn't knock on the general store's door. He simply opened it; it was a sliding door. Unjo silently entered.

Wait, huh? Haruhiro thought, startled. *Is that okay?*

"Wh-what should we do?" Ranta had taken shelter behind Haruhiro at some point.

"What do you mean, 'what'? Just get away from me."

"Hey, man, I'm not clinging to you because I like it. Don't get the wrong idea, moron."

"Hmm." Kuzaku stretched his neck. "I'm interested, you know. Truth be told."

"Yeah," Yume said idly. "Let's try goin' in."

Well, we're inside Well Village. It's not like we'll get killed, reasoned Haruhiro. *Probably.*

The door was still open. Haruhiro peaked inside.

There wasn't a single window. The walls were dimly lit by a lamp and covered in stone or clay tablets. The sight of a great many rectangular tablets—large and small, with symbols and pictures carved into them—was overwhelming. Some of the pictures were even colored. Were those symbols some kind of letters?

Seated on a chair in the back, the lanky shopkeeper looked long and thin. Unjo laid his large backpack on the ground. He retrieved something from inside it. It was a stone tablet.

"Wowie." Yume crouched down at the door. "What's all that? It's amazin'."

Ranta raised the visor on his helmet and looked around. "Treasure, huh?"

"Is this all there is?" Shihoru sighed as she looked around the room. "Though, in a way, it might be a treasure."

"This might not be a general store," Merry said quietly. "It could be a museum, maybe?"

"Stuff looks old enough for it to be." Kuzaku wandered inside. He started reaching for one of the stone tablets, but then pulled his hand back. "Maybe touching them's a bad idea."

The lanky shopkeeper accepted the stone tablet from Unjo, placing it on the desk and holding both his hands over it.

Haruhiro shuddered a bit. The lanky shopkeeper's hands. They had five fingers, but the palms... There were eyes on its palms. The lanky shopkeeper used those eyes to scrutinize the stone tablet.

Unjo turned back to Haruhiro. "Here, there are no books. No paper books. There are records left, though. On stone, on clay. On tablets. The eyehand sage, Oubu, is a researcher. He collects tablets. If a tablet is of value, he will buy it from you."

The eyehand sage, Oubu, must be the lanky shopkeeper. When the sage's hands moved away from the tablet, it fished through the desk drawers and pulled out some black coins. Big black coins. Not small or medium-sized. Large coins. Two of them.

Two large coins meant two rou. Depending on the store, or rather its owner, the value of them could range anywhere from twenty to fifty ruma. It was a fortune.

Taking the two coins from Oubu, Unjo stuffed them unceremoniously into his backpack. "Ruo keh."

"Avaruu seha," the sage responded, his hands returning to the stone tablet on the desk. With those eyehands, he closely examined the newly-acquired tablet.

"Lumiaris and Skullhell," Unjo said, mentioning two very unexpected names as he pointed to a stone tablet. "The battle between gods."

"Ohh!" Ranta rushed over, pressing his face close to the tablet. "He's right! This guy, his face looks just like Skullhell's symbol!"

"Lumiaris is always just represented by the hexagram, never drawn, but—" Merry seemed intrigued. She squinted at the stone tablet. "The woman on the left, that's Lumiaris?"

The stone tablet was oblong. On the right was a man with a skull-like face, and on the left was a long-haired woman. The man held a large scythe in his right hand, a sword in his left, and had only one leg. The woman was naked, with a large sphere in her right hand and a tiny sphere in her left. There was a rainbow on her back.

The right half of the background was night, the left half was day. There were tiny creatures etched at the bottom, each aligned with the man or the woman. They were fighting one another, running each other through with swords, firing arrows back and forth. Many of the creatures had collapsed, but the bloody battle continued.

"It happened here," Unjo said in a low voice. "Lumiaris and Skullhell were here. Here in Darunggar."

"Darung...gar?" Haruhiro asked as he looked to the stone and clay tablets.

"That is what those here call this place."

"The God of Light, Lumiaris, and the Dark God, Skullhell, fought here in Darunggar," Shihoru said cautiously. "Long ago, the people of Darunggar sided with either Lumiaris or Skullhell, and they fought?"

"Who won, I wonder?" Kuzaku rubbed the hexagram carved into his own armor.

"Hey, man." Ranta snorted. "Look at how dark it is here. Obviously, my beloved Lord Skullhell won the day."

"But light magic works here, too?" Merry rebutted. "If Lumiaris lost, then why does her power still reach here?"

"You can say that, but my dark magic reaches here too, you know? Although, they're both not even half as effective as normal."

"Well, then." Yume was looking at another stone tablet. "It must've been a tie, don'tcha think?"

"So, now they've both gone to Grimgar?" Haruhiro tilted his head to the side. "What would you call a group of gods, anyway? A band? A crowd? A party? No. Maybe a pantheon?"

"The course of the battle remains unknown." Unjo shouldered his backpack. "The eyehand sage, Oubu, says he does not know. He is investigating that. Regardless, Lumiaris and Skullhell left Darunggar. Darunggar is a godless world."

"They left." Haruhiro tugged the hair on the back of his head a bit. "Wait, where'd they leave from?"

Shihoru gulped. "There's a path, somewhere? Without a path from Darunggar to Grimgar, they couldn't have left."

"That means one thing!" Ranta shouted. "We can get home, right?!"

Kuzaku glanced at Ranta. "If we could get back, wouldn't he have already done so?"

"Oh, yeah." Yume let out a deep breath. "With Konjo-san still bein' here, that's probably right."

"You mean Unjo-san, okay?" Haruhiro corrected her.

Really, he wasn't that shocked. He had been thinking, *I wanna go home. It'd be nice if we could,* but lately he had started to think, *Well, if we can't get back, that's fine.*

If they couldn't find any leads on getting back home after one hundred, two hundred, days of being here, they start working under the assumption they were going to live their lives out here. They would put down roots in Darunggar. Start families, maybe. That would be something they'd naturally consider and would be rather important. Haruhiro couldn't excuse himself from it, saying, *I'm the leader.* If anything, he would need to take the initiative.

There was no guarantee he wouldn't end up confessing.

No, that's not likely. I can't. Besides, what's a confession? What am I gonna confess? To whom? I don't even know what I mean.

While Haruhiro silently asked these meaningless questions, Unjo left Oubu's store, which was really not a store at all. He could have said something first, but this was Unjo. It seemed to be how he was, so they couldn't really blame him.

Haruhiro and the others left, too, and saw Unjo heading toward the largest building once again, the one made from piled stones and with glass windows. There was never a time the light didn't leak out from the glass windows. Someone lived there, but they had never seen them.

Unjo opened the door, glancing back at them. *Follow me,* he seemed to say. Haruhiro and the others followed him into the building.

As they did, Haruhiro got goosebumps. *Where is this place?* he wondered.

The world called Darunggar. They named the village Well Village. This place didn't feel like either of them. It felt different.

Unlike the other buildings in Well Village, this one had a proper floor, with carpet laid out. There were shelves, a single table, and five chairs. Another room lead off in the back. Curtains hung on either side of the glass window, and candlesticks sitting here and there provided light to see by, plus the constant stream of light they had always noticed.

Four of the chairs surrounded the table. The fifth one sat in the center of the room.

There, in the middle of it all, *she* sat.

She was human, wearing a red dress with white socks and black shoes. A red ribbon held back blonde hair from her blue eyes and pale skin. She looked very young, almost like a child.

That was what Haruhiro thought, but as he stared he realized she was not a child at all.

"A doll?" Haruhiro blinked and took another look.

She was well-made, but clearly old. Her skin was cracked in several places, and her eyes were wide, unnaturally open. But her hair was neatly combed, and while the colors of her outfit had faded somewhat, it wasn't torn or frayed.

"Hold on," Ranta murmured before falling silent.

There was more than the doll and the furniture. This room was overflowing with unique objects. On the shelves, across the table, even on the floor. What was more, many of the items seemed...familiar.

This, and that one, and that one over there. They're all familiar.

The picture frame-like thing leaning up against the wall. That round object sitting on the table. The thick, rectangular thing off to the side. The thing with two disc-like objects connected with a band. The thin, rectangular box that would fit in his hand. The board with lots of buttons on it. The box with glass on the front and rounded corners.

I've seen them. Probably. Somewhere.

He knew he must have, and yet the longer he looked, the more his confidence wavered. Had Haruhiro seen them before? How could he say for sure?

He didn't know. He couldn't recall their names, or when and where he'd seen them. How could he say he'd seen them before? What evidence did he have?

Still, there were things there he could firmly identify. There were pairs of glasses: black-rimmed, metal-framed, tortoise shelled. The lenses were broken—or lost completely—but they were clearly glasses.

The shelves had books. However, they didn't look like any of the books he'd seen in Grimgar. They were thin, and many were small. There were also cans and clear containers. But they didn't seem to be made of glass.

Unjo laid his backpack down and pulled something out. It was white. A small ball. When Unjo laid it on the table, it made a hard sound.

The ball didn't roll. Its surface was bumpy.

"Wh-what is that thing?" Kuzaku asked. "I know it, or I feel like I should. What is it?"

"Who knows?" Unjo slowly looked around the room. He might have been checking how far the candles had burned down. "I don't. Not me. But they're different, I can tell that much. The things in this room are different."

"Different." Shihoru shook her head. "I feel the same way. They're different."

Merry pressed a hand against her chest. "Did you gather all of them?"

"No," Unjo replied immediately. "When I first came, this room was here."

"Meow." Yume picked up a thin, rectangular object from the table. When she stroked it with her finger, the dust wiped away. It was awfully smooth. Yume tilted her head to the side and looked at it funny. "Nwuh?"

"Did the villagers start the collection, then?" Ranta looked at the doll, creeped out. "No one lives in this house? Other than that girl?"

Unjo gestured toward the doll with his chin. "Don't touch Kinuko."

"Kinuko? Wait, you mean the doll?"

"Everyone calls her that."

"Hmm," Ranta said. "Well, she doesn't look like a Kinuko to me. More like Nancy, if anything."

"She doesn't feel like a Nancy," Shihoru disagreed. "Not a chance."

"Well, what does she feel like, huh?! Speak up, Torpedo Tits!"

"Torp—" Shihoru covered her breasts with her arms. "M-maybe an Alice? Something like that."

"Alice, huh? Hmm." Ranta crossed his arms. "Either way, Kinuko's right out."

"The gods have left Darunggar." Unjo lifted his backpack. "She is their replacement. In this village, Kinuko is worshipped. She came from another world, they say."

"True enough." Haruhiro nodded. "She doesn't look like anything from this world. Yeah. Still, if you were to ask me, if she was from Grimgar—"

"Not a chance." Yume was still fiddling with the thin, rectangular object. "That's true, but Yume, she's got this mysterious feelin', y'know. It's all so nostalgic. Even though she ain't got no clue what this thing's supposed to be, she's feelin' like she knows. Weird."

"Foreign objects are worshiped, too," said Unjo. "If you find something out there that feels right, bring it here. Offer it to Kinuko."

"You mean, um, for free?" Ranta was always vulgar and tactless.

Unjo gave a low snort and didn't answer.

Haruhiro bowed his head a bit. "I'm sorry about him. Seriously."

"Huh? What're you apologizing for, Parupiroooo? You a moron, or something? Yeah, you're a moron, huh?" Ranta was unrepentant. "Well, y'know, I guess it works like that. Even if there's no money in it, he's saying Kinuko's a god. Maybe we can expect some sort of boon? That'd make it worth doing. Yep. If we find anything, let's bring it back here."

"But still." Kuzaku crouched down in front of the picture frame-like object. "Why is all this stuff here? Or is 'why' the question to ask? What is it? Isn't it weird?"

Haruhiro understood what Kuzaku wanted to say. He understood but couldn't put it into words. It was frustrating not being to say the feeling he had. But he did think it was just as weird.

"We're searching for a way back to our original world." Shima's words came back to him.

A way back to their original world.

Haruhiro's head hurt. At his temples—no, deeper—he felt a heavy, sharp pain. There was something there. Something he knew, something he remembered, but he couldn't reach it. Oh, if only he could!

"Unjo-san," Haruhiro said.

"What?"

"Unjo-san, you... Do you ever think about wanting to return to our original world?"

"'Original world.'" Unjo parroted the words, then fell silent.

"Wait..." Merry looked at Haruhiro from behind her mask. "By our original world, you don't mean Grimgar?"

"Huh?" Shihoru covered her mouth. "Not Grimgar, our original..."

Yume looked up to the ceiling. "Fwhuh?"

"Original..." Kuzaku was deep in thought. "Our original..."

"Hey, hey, hey. What do you mean, 'original'?" Ranta tried to laugh but stopped. "We came from some other world before Grimgar? Is that it?"

"Where did we come from?" Merry asked, as much to herself as anyone else. "I don't remember anything from before, but we had to be somewhere. There's no way we were just born looking like this."

"Where did we even come from?" Shihoru's voice trembled a little. "I mean, in my memories, I remember... I asked Haruhiro-kun, 'Where is this place?'"

Haruhiro remembered that too.

"...Um," the girl behind him timidly asked, "where is this, do you think?"

"Look, asking me isn't going to help."

"R-right, of course. Um, d-does anyone know? Where is this place?"

That's right, Haruhiro thought. That was Shihoru. But where were we?

"We were lookin' at Mr. Moon." Yume clapped her hands together. "He was all red. That sure was surprisin'."

That was right...

"Ahh," said Braids as she noticed it, too. She blinked repeatedly, then chuckled. "Mr. Moon is red. That's super pretty."

That had been Yume. He remembered. At that point, they noticed the moon. It had been ruby red, somewhere between a crescent and a half moon.

Why's it red? he'd thought. A red moon had seemed weird.

Where had they been?

"The hill?" Haruhiro murmured.

Yes, the hill. They'd been atop the hill next to Alterna. There were graves. Manato and Moguzo were buried there. And Choco, too.

Choco. Kuzaku's comrade. A thief. One of the junior volunteer soldiers. She'd fallen in the battle at Deadhead Watching Keep.

Was that all? Haruhiro didn't know. Something was bugging him. Like he'd forgotten something.

Big eyes. With bags under them. Pouty lips. A bob cut.

Choco.

Kuzaku's comrade. She'd died. He'd never see her again.

"We were there on the hill." Haruhiro said before looking at his comrades. "At the very least, Shihoru, Yume, Ranta—and Manato and Moguzo were there, too. Kikkawa. Renji. Ron. Sassa. Adachi. Chibi-chan, too. They were there. On that hill. We saw the red moon. Kuzaku, Merry, what about you?"

"The hill…" Merry mumbled to herself. "I remember it. Vaguely. I think my first memory is the hill next to Alterna."

"Me too." Kuzaku nodded. "It's sort of an… Yeah, I was there. With them. Dunno what we talked about, though."

"What a coincidence." Unjo smiled slightly. "I, too, remember seeing the red moon on that hill. 'The moon is red,' I thought. 'How creepy.'"

"Isn't that weird?" Haruhiro pulled out one of the chairs from the table and sat down. "That we were all on that hill with that moon, I mean. That's strange. No matter where we were before we came to Grimgar… There was a tunnel-like place, before Grimgar. Something like a tunnel. We must have gone through it, right? Then we appeared on the hill."

"There was a tower." Unjo took off his braided hat. His close-cropped hair had gone half-white. Though the lower half of his face was hidden by his scarf, his eyes were exposed. He had a pronounced forehead, like a man in his forties or fifties. Placing his braided hat on the table, Unjo took a seat, too. "If my memory is correct, it was the 'Forbidden Tower.'"

"The tower with no entrance or exit." Shihoru's entire body was shivering. "I never knew what it was for. I thought it was weird."

"Could it be..." Ranta sat down on the ground. "Maybe we came out of that tower?"

"Even though there's no entrance or exit?" Merry asked, doubtfully.

"Hmm." Ranta knocked on his own head. "There it is. That's the problem. But, you know, it's weird if no one can go in or out. There's gotta be a hidden door somewhere, right?"

"Hiyomu'd probably know, don'tcha think?" Yume said. "Hiyomu, she led us from the hill to Bri-chan's place in Alterna, y'know."

"It was like that for me, too." Merry nodded.

"Yeah." Kuzaku raised his hand slightly. "Me, too."

"For me..." Unjo pressed his brow. "It was a man, I think. 'Call me Saa,' he told us. Who is this Bri-chan?"

"Let's see," Haruhiro answered. "He's the office chief for Red Moon, the Alterna Frontier Army's Volunteer Soldier Corps. His name's Britney."

"Britney." Unjo's eyes went wide. "Was this a man who acted like a woman? With light blue eyes?"

"You know him?"

"His real name is Shibutori."

"Shibutori?!" Ranta exclaimed. "Bri-chan's name is Shibutori?!"

"Shibutori was from a younger generation," Unjo said. "Compared to me. He's the chief of the Volunteer Soldier Corps Office now?"

"Unjo-san," Haruhiro hesitantly asked. "How long has it been since you came to Darunggar?"

"Five thousand, six hundred and seventy-six times," Unjo said with a far-off look. "Since I started counting, that is. That is the number of times the dark night has broken, and the pale morning has come."

"Five thousand, six hundred—"

Was one day in Darunggar equal to a day in Grimgar? Was it different? It wasn't clear, but if they were the same, then Unjo had spent fifteen years and two hundred and one days in Darunggar.

"Before now, have you seen any other humans like us?" Haruhiro ventured.

"None. This is the first time. You people are the first."

"Seriously?" Even Ranta sounded pained by that. "That's... That's... Seriously, uh, that's gotta have been pretty tough, huh?"

"I've gotten used to it." Unjo lowered his eyes to the table. "I *was* used to it. I couldn't return. I had long since given up. Life here is not so bad. A man's home is his castle. Things that seem strange become normal. You learn the language. I have acquaintances here. Your language, it is nearly foreign to me. I've forgotten half of it. As we speak, I remember. But, either way, I cannot return. You people prepare yourselves for that, too. That hill. The forbidden tower. None of it matters. The hidden door. Even if it exists, you cannot find it. You cannot prove it exists. Live here.

That is the only option. Until you die, live. No matter where you are, it's the same. That is all there is for us."

"It's not just us." Shihoru choked the words out. "Lala and Nono. A pair who were far more experienced and skilled than us came to Darunggar, too. Besides, it's not like we came here directly from Grimgar."

"Where?" Unjo jabbed his right finger into the table. "Where did you people enter Darunggar from?"

It was hard for Haruhiro to remember clearly. The distance and direction they'd traveled was a blur. Even so, Haruhiro explained in as much detail as he could the events that led them to travel from the Dusk Realm to Darunggar, and then how they reached Well Village.

"Upstream," Unjo laughed, as if in amazement. "You people have good luck. It's a miracle you were all right."

From what he told them, the forest north of Well Village was home to the yegyorns—which, according to Unjo, meant "mist moths"—a species of venomous moth. Their poison was powerful, and in an instant of exposure, most living creatures fainted in agony. However, a weasel-like creature called a getaguna was the exception. Those creatures were immune to yegyorn poison; the yegyorns wouldn't even attack them in the first place.

Yegyorns swarmed their prey, knocking them unconscious—at which point, the getagunas rushed in and devoured the innards. The yegyorns drank the blood and then laid their eggs in the remaining flesh. In time, the eggs hatched, and the rotten flesh provided them sustenance as they grew. Eventually they emerged from the corpse as moths.

Yegyorns were small, only the size of the tip of a human pinky finger. They were impossible to avoid in the dark forests of Darunggar, and by the time you noticed them, you were already bitten.

In fact, Unjo said a dose of poison from one of them wasn't that big of a deal, but where there was one, there were hundreds more nearby. You could bet on being bitten many times in quick succession.

There were yegyorns in the river to the north, too. Furthermore, along the river there were tobachi—which meant "nasty," or "hard to deal with"—a group of creatures that specialized in sneak attacks. They lurked all over the place, so caution was necessary. Tobachi came in many types, so it was more of a collective name for the fierce, carnivorous creatures living along the river.

Tobachi often fell prey to yegyorns and getagunas.

There were also the ape-faced creatures called gaugai—what the party before called inuzarus—which spread out over a wide area. They were omnivorous, but their favorite food was getaguna.

The northern moth forest, Adunyeg, was therefore incredibly dangerous. People with good sense wouldn't go in there.

If they planned to cross the Adunyeg to return to the Dusk Realm, they had to be prepared to die trying. Unjo couldn't imagine traveling through the Adunyeg without encountering yegyorns. And if they encountered them, that would be the end. There were times when one or two yegyorns would wander into

Well Village, and when that happened there was always a panic, Unjo told them.

"W-well, aren't you glad we didn't go and find out?" Ranta gulped. "Not that returning to the Dusk Realm'd do us any good. That place was crazy dangerous in its own way. Still, I'll bet you Lala and Nono aren't doing so hot. I mean, I can't imagine they're as lucky as I am. They've gotta be dead. They used us as much as they could and then threw us away, so I've gotta say they had it coming."

"They haven't come to this village, right?" Kuzaku asked.

"Probably not." Unjo was starting to sound fluent. "Still, there are other villages. Or towns rather than villages."

That made sense. It would be strange and totally unnatural for this to be the only village left after the clash between Lumiaris and Skullhell.

But Haruhiro was still shocked.

"What?" Haruhiro was at a loss for words. He traded glances with the others.

"Mrr." Yume pressed her hands against both cheeks. "So, there're towns."

"Wh-where're they at?!" Ranta corrected himself. "Wh-Where, pray tell, might we locate them, good sir?!"

"'Pray tell'?" Shihoru's voice dripped with loathing.

"I wouldn't mind telling you people." Unjo put on his braided hat. "The reason we can't return to Grimgar. While I do, I can take you to the town of Herbesit. That is only if you wish me to."

Grimgar of Fantasy and Ash

13 | Revelation

BEFORE SETTING OUT, Haruhiro and the others heeded Unjo's advice and made thorough preparations.

The town of Herbesit was west of Well Village: a three-day trip on foot. Along the way, they would have to camp in the woods. There were a few yegyorns in the forest to the west, but there was also a colony of gaugais in the area. There were other vicious carnivores and omnivores, as well as durzoi—which meant "old ones"—a humanlike race that had four arms.

According to Unjo, the durzoi were proud hunters, who roamed in solitude or small bands to hunt large beasts called vaguls. If a party stole their prey, they became vengeful and dangerous enemies, but as long as their interests weren't undermined, they stayed to themselves. Still, they would need to watch out for vaguls, as well as beasts like siddas, wepongs, and gaugais. Each beast used different tactics and were clever about exploiting advantages.

There was one method that would let them avoid most beasts, and that was a bell like the one on the charcoal burner's wagon.

They bought a beast-repelling bell at the blacksmith's. It didn't come cheaply. It cost a full twenty ruma, but it was a necessity for getting through the forest. It was worth it.

In the western forest, they needed to ring the beast-repelling bell at all times. Unjo had a bell of his own, but he told them that it was hard to make it through the forest alone. Having comrades would make the journey easier. When he rested, the others could take turns ringing the bell.

The forest was also home to venomous insects and snakes. They weren't as dangerous as the yegyorns, but it was best not to leave skin exposed while sleeping.

The party bought thick fabric from the clothing-and-bag shop to make tents. They also made new undergarments. They procured preserved food and candles at the grocery store, as well as oil made from some plant.

Haruhiro and the others had been treating Oubu lab as a general store, but the real general store was the grocer's.

With their preparations done, the party followed Unjo from Well Village.

They traveled the road to the charcoal burner's place. Haruhiro and the others knew the path didn't end there. If they continued on, where would they arrive? According to Unjo, the road came to a three-fork intersection.

Unjo led the way, his beast-repelling bell hanging from his backpack. As long as they had Unjo's bell, they might not need to have a bell themselves. The thought crossed their minds, but that would be relying too heavily on a stranger.

The charcoal burner was working at his kiln when they arrived. Unjo was acquainted with him, too, because they had a pleasant conversation before he ordered Haruhiro and the others to rest here.

"There is no safer place in these woods," Unjo told them. "There is no man friendlier past this point. Once you understand that, rest to your heart's content."

From the way Unjo spoke, the people of Herbesit might not be friendly.

Haruhiro was filled with unease, but a small piece of hope kept him from backing down. They had to know. They had to know firsthand. Seeing was believing. There were things they wouldn't be able to understand until they saw and felt them for themselves. It would be wrong to act on information they had only heard. And since the information could affect their lives, it was all the more important.

Once they had rested, Unjo pushed them to depart. Everything beyond the charcoal burner's shack was new to Haruhiro and the others. They were tense, but Unjo walked quickly and without concern. Nothing happened as they traveled. The beast-repelling bell was doing its work.

In the forest, they couldn't see the distant ridge. The sky still brightened, though, so they could tell night from day.

The party arrived at the three-fork intersection that same day. Unjo chose the path leading southwest. He said if they went northwest, they would reach steep mountains. They could see the outline of the range off in the distance.

The road with the wagon tracks hadn't been left by the charcoal burner; it was something that had existed for a very long time. It was the same for the kiln. There had been a charcoal burner before the current one.

According to the clay and stone tablets, even after Lumiaris and Skullhell had left, the war between the forces of the Light Goddess and the forces of the Dark God had raged on for a long time. With Darunggar firmly divided into two camps, the world had been unable to come together after their leaders had left.

That tragic conflict dragged on to this day. The dead ones were descendants of Skullhell's worshipers. They killed and devoured one another, praying for the eventual destruction of everything. The people gathered in Well Village were descendants of the followers of Lumiaris. They handed down tales of the day Lumiaris would return, bringing light to the dark Darunggar. They also thought, though, that those tales were mere legend, much like the prediction that the world would end in darkness. The village's worship of the Kinuko doll and otherworldly objects were a response to those warped feelings.

Unjo had learned, through the tablets, that certain races had built kingdoms, and that elements of the warring factions had reconciled to create shared communities in the past. However, any group larger than a village or a small city was guaranteed to collapse under internal or external pressures. Whenever a king who had managed to build a country in Darunggar died—of natural causes or murder—the land he had unified quickly de-volved into civil war. Everything went to ruin.

Darunggar meant "the Land of Despair." It hadn't always been known by that name, though. Originally, it had been Fanangar: "Paradise" ruled by the one god, Enos. When Enos split into the conflicting Lumiaris and Skullhell, it had become Jidgar, the Field of Battle. When the world had been aban-doned by the gods, despair had enveloped the heavens and the earth.

They followed the wagon tracks through the deep for-est. There was still no sign of beasts, and they were grateful to the bells for that. At nightfall, Haruhiro sensed someone watching him. When he informed Unjo, he was told it was the durzoi.

"In these woods, it happens all the time," Unjo told them. "Don't try to search for them. You will never find them. If they become hostile, you will be targeted. No good will come of it."

Haruhiro should have done as Unjo said and not let it bother him. But he wondered.

It was late into the evening, so they pitched tents. They slept in shifts to keep the beast-repelling bells ringing. He didn't feel it when he was inside the tent, but when it was his shift, Haruhiro felt strangely restless.

The durzoi made noises sometimes. It must have been deliber-ate. They were trying to see what he'd do. If Haruhiro acted in a hostile manner, an arrow might come his way immediately. The durzoi might be closer than he thought. He could turn to find them right behind him, only to have his life snuffed out in the very next second.

Or perhaps they were having fun intimidating the party and putting them on guard.

Haruhiro didn't get much sleep. When morning came, he no longer sensed the durzoi's presence.

They're gone, he thought. *No, there's no way to be sure of that. I can't let my guard down. Or maybe I'm overthinking this.*

"You keep worrying like that, and it'll make you go bald one of these days, man." Ranta laughed scornfully.

It pissed Haruhiro off, but giving Ranta the time of day would only make things worse. Haruhiro sighed, "Yeah, yeah," and let it go. But then Ranta leaned in close to Haruhiro's ear and whispered, "B-A-L-D, okay?"

If only Ranta could have disappeared instead of the durzoi... I wish I could trade Ranta for a durzoi.

While he thought it, his fear and unease toward the durzoi lightened. Even trash could be useful, once in a while.

There was an incident later that day, when the sky began to darken. Something blocked the path ahead of them. Worse yet, whatever it was, it moved. No, it writhed.

They were thin creatures. An incredible number of long, thin creatures.

At first glance, they looked like intestines. Or perhaps worms. They were as thick as Haruhiro's wrist. There was a great mass of them blocking the wagon track road.

"What're those?" Kuzaku asked in a hoarse voice.

Unjo shook his head. "Who knows."

"Eek!" Shihoru let out a little shriek and backed away. Haruhiro didn't blame her.

"I-It's gonna be fine, okay?" Yume looked to Haruhiro. "Y'think it'll be fine, right?"

Don't ask me. "W-well, I dunno."

"Parupiro!" Ranta slapped Haruhiro on the back. "Go! Jump over them! You do that, and we'll know if it's safe or not. Do it! You're the leader, man! Come on!"

"No way," Merry snapped, stepping up to Ranta. She was scary at times like this. "Why don't *you* jump instead? We'd be in trouble if anything happened to Haru."

"What, and you don't care what happens to me?! It'll be too late for regrets once I'm gone! Did you ever think about that?! Do you properly understand my greatness, how special I am, my contributions, and my future potential?!"

"Oh, yeah, you're special all right, Ranta-kun," Kuzaku said.

"Kuzacky! Good, good, good! I thought you'd understand! You're not just a beanpole after all! You've gotta be, like, a level 2 beanpole or something! No, maybe even level 3?!"

"Not much of a compliment."

"I'm singing your praises here. Can't you tell that, you moron? Honestly, are you all height and no brains? That's why you're a beanpole, huh? Ahaha! Makes sense!"

"Hey." Unjo grabbed Ranta by the collar and started dragging him.

"Whuh?! Wh-what?! What's going on?! Whoa, Unjo-san?!

I mean, Unjo-sama?! What, what?! S-stop it?! Whoa! That's, wahh!"

Unjo was strong. He easily dragged Ranta along with one arm, then threw him into the middle of the mass of giant worms.

"Noooooooooooooooo!" Ranta landed flat on his backside in the middle of the swarm. "Gwahhhhhhhhhhhhhh!"

It happened in an instant. The giant worms engulfed Ranta. The group completely lost sight of him. If Zodiac-kun were here, Haruhiro was sure he would be making the worst sort of commentary. Although now might not have been a good time to think about that.

"R-Ranta?" Haruhiro called out hesitantly.

"Bwahhhhhhhhhhhh?!" Ranta leapt out from the center of the giant worms. There were still worms wrapped around his neck, arms, legs, and torso, trying to pull him back in. Ranta struggled. "I'm dying! I'm dying here, save me! I'm gonna die! S-save meeeeeeeeee!"

"If we have to..." Kuzaku muttered, reaching out with his long sword to rescue Ranta.

It was a brave thing to do. Haruhiro was impressed. But wasn't it also dangerous? Just as Haruhiro had worried, the giant worms attacked Kuzaku.

"Wah! Oh, crap!" Kuzaku shouted.

"Dark!" Shihoru summoned the elemental Dark and had him plunge into the giant worms. That drove off a few dozen of them, but it was hardly enough.

If it had just been Ranta, Haruhiro would have abandoned

him, but Kuzaku was caught now. He had no choice but to save them. In the end, everyone but Unjo had to pull the giant worms off Ranta and Kuzaku one by one. They moved away from that spot for a little while, waiting for the giant worms to fully cross the road. By the time morning came, the strange wriggling creatures were gone.

What were those things, anyway?

Thinking about it wasn't going to tell them. Reminding himself that things like that could, and certainly would, happen, they walked for a quarter of a day, until the forest suddenly ended.

The wagon track road continued down a gradual slope. A town spread out on the other side of it. While it was half-crumbled, there was still a defensive wall around it. The wall was about a kilometer and a half on each side.

The town was bright with light. Without a doubt, there were hundreds, possibly thousands, of people living in this town. They could clearly see figures walking up and down main streets. There were a lot of stone buildings, some with single floors but others with two, three, or even more floors. Towers rose into the sky.

The wind suddenly blew, and the trees in the forest rustled. Shortly after, they heard a bell. It was different from the beast-repelling bells Unjo and Haruhiro's party carried. It was a larger, heavier, and somehow sadder sound. There must be a belfry somewhere, and its bell was swaying in the wind. One of those towers might be a bell tower.

"This is the town of Herbesit." Unjo, at the head of the group, removed his braided hat. "Don't hide your face in Herbesit, but don't make eye contact with anyone. It will be taken as a challenge. If you are provoked, ignore it. The people in this town love to fight. If you don't want conflict, keep your heads down and keep quiet. If you want to fight to the death, then that's different. Do as you please."

Haruhiro and the others shuddered.

Just how dangerous is this place?

As it turned out, it was very dangerous. No sooner had they come to the end of the wagon track road and entered the town when a pair of humanoid creatures—hunched over as far as possible, but still taller than Kuzaku—picked a fight with them.

They couldn't understand the pair, but it was clear they were making some false accusation. One jumped back and forth in front of Unjo, making taunting sounds and clapping his hands. The other kept sticking his face up close to Shihoru's, making high-pitched, *hee-haw, hee-haw* sounds.

Shihoru was practically crying. Haruhiro wanted to help, but if he glared at those creatures and said, *Hey, cut that out,* a fight would break out right then and there. Shihoru needed to endure. They would all have to endure.

Eventually, when the two had left, Yume let out a strange cry. "Yow!" When Haruhiro looked, she was rubbing the back of her head. Someone had thrown a stone at her.

"Yume?! You okay?!" Ranta looked around the area. "Damn it! Who did that?!"

"Stop!" Merry quickly hit Ranta on the shoulder with her head staff. "It's an obvious provocation. Don't fall for it so easily."

"Merry, you sure you're not trying to provoke me?" Ranta returned. "That hurt pretty bad, just now."

"Oh, did it?" Merry brushed him off lightly. "Yume, I know it must hurt, but bear with it. I'll heal you later."

"Meowwww. Thanks. This li'l thing came flyin', and then, bam! It was just a surprise. There's only a little bleedin'. Yume's gonna be okay."

"You're bleeding?!" Ranta continued looking downward, clicking his tongue. "Those punks think they can mess with us. I'll tear 'em limb from limb. Seriously."

"He never learns..." Kuzaku wore a small, wry smile.

Shihoru laughed coldly. "Of course not. It's Ranta."

"So what if it's me, huh?! Well, Torpedo Tits?! I'll grope you! No, let me grope you!"

"Man..." Haruhiro started, but then closed his mouth. It was pointless to engage with Ranta.

There were frequent provocations by the residents after that. They stalked and insulted the group, throwing things and blocking the road. That was just the least of it. There were residents who suddenly tripped them and others who went so far as to tackle them. No matter how much they ignored, dodged, and evaded, the assailants still appeared, one after another. It was exhausting, physically and emotionally.

Had Unjo not been there, they would have fled the town within minutes or gotten into a fight.

Were Haruhiro and the others being targeted because they were outsiders? It didn't seem like it. Violence broke out all over town, and they even heard bloodcurdling death screams occasionally. It was hard to believe—they certainly didn't want to believe—but people weren't just getting injured. They were getting killed. What was wrong with this town?

It was such a state of acceptable chaos that when melees broke out on the streets, onlookers gambled on the results.

Unjo moved away from the main streets, leading Haruhiro and the others down back streets. These were a little better. On either side of the somewhat narrow street, there were people of various races squatting. They spoke in pathetic voices, holding out their hands. If Haruhiro let his guard down, they pulled at his coat. Many of them were injured and were likely beggars. They were depressing, and he was soon fed up with them. Still, the back streets were better than the main streets, where everyone was ready for a fight and death was constant.

Could they live like this? There were beggars on the verge of death, and some not moving at all. The rotten smell of the dead hung in the air. Many of these beggars hadn't been able to survive and were now no longer among the living.

"Don't touch anything that you don't need to. Don't let anyone touch you, either." Unjo avoided the beggars as he said that. "You wouldn't want to catch something. I can't say deadly diseases are uncommon here."

"Yikes," Ranta muttered. Even Ranta, a plague unto himself, was scared of getting sick.

Haruhiro was afraid of disease, too. Merry had learned Purify, a spell for removing poison, and it worked on some diseases.

Some being the operative word. Ordinary colds, for instance, could not be healed with magic. If they got sick, they had to rely on medicine they could procure and their own stamina to get them through it. Haruhiro wasn't especially robust, and he wasn't particularly strong-willed, either. When it came to disease, prevention was his best medicine.

While they weaved between beggars, they ran straight into a tower. It was not particularly tall, only about five meters high. Unjo used the metal knocker on the door. Not long after, the door swung open.

A woman in a brown robe and almost translucent white skin came out. Her combed hair was gray. She almost looked human, but her eyes had no white. It looked like someone had pressed glass balls into her sockets. She also had three slits on each cheek, which opened and closed slightly, almost like gills.

"Unjo," the woman said before looking at Haruhiro and the others with her glassy eyes. "Akuaba?"

"Moa worute." Unjo gestured with his chin, as if to say, *Let us in.* The woman let them all into the tower.

The ceiling was high. Did it open all the way to the roof? They couldn't tell. The walls were lined almost entirely with bookshelves, which were covered with clay and stone tablets, arms and armor, equipment, and various unusual items, like potted plants. There were lamps here and there, as well as ladders and stools.

"This is Rubicia," Unjo introduced her.

The woman pressed her hands together in front of her chest

and bowed to them. That must be how residents greeted one another in this town.

"H-hello," Haruhiro said as he tried imitating Rubicia. "I'm Haruhiro."

"I'm Ranta." Ranta crossed his arms arrogantly. "They call me Ranta-sama!"

"Kuzaku." Kuzaku bowed his head slightly.

"Yoo-may!" Yume said in a loud voice, clearly enunciating, and then smiled. "Ehehe."

"I'm Shihoru." Shihoru imitated Rubicia like Haruhiro had.

"I'm Merry." Merry gave a proper bow. "Nice to meet you, Rubicia-san."

Rubicia nodded slowly. She exchanged a few words with Unjo before descending the stairs by the wall. There must be a basement room.

"It's safe here," Unjo said as he set his pack down on the floor. "If you want to rest, rest. Rubicia will bring water. It is not infected or contaminated. Don't worry."

"Righto!" Ranta sat down immediately. "Come on, if you've got yourself a nice safe house like this, say so sooner, Unjo-saaaan, sheesh. By the way, what's up with Rubicia-san? Is she your *y'know*? Nah, no way."

"Yes," Unjo responded. "Rubicia is my wife."

Haruhiro couldn't help but whisper, "Wow..."

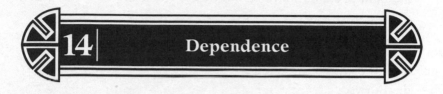

14 | Dependence

L OVE WAS DEEP.

Maybe.

Well, not that Haruhiro really understood.

Birth, upbringing, race, none of that had anything to do with love, although it wasn't entirely clear whether or not Unjo and Rubicia were a loving husband and wife. Unjo may have gotten lonely, being a stranger in a strange land, and sought comfort with a woman he once met. She might be indulging him out of pity. Haruhiro didn't know, but that sort of thing could happen. Was that a type of love? Could he call that love? He wondered.

The fact that Unjo and Rubicia didn't act particularly close made something feel off. It could be because Haruhiro and the others were there. Perhaps they were embarrassed to be affectionate or flirtatious with people around. Or maybe affection was uncommon in Darunggar. It was hard to imagine a Herbesit couple enjoying what Haruhiro thought of as married life. Maybe the simple fact that they hadn't killed each other meant they were in a good relationship. But Rubicia seemed to be a quiet and intelligent person, so she didn't quite fit in with the residents of Herbesit at all. Or maybe there were other peaceful pacifists living quietly in town.

With Rubicia's tower as their base of operations, they learned quite a bit as Unjo showed them around the town over the next day or two.

In most of Herbesit, provocations, violence, and robbery went on without end. Seemingly empty streets were often the territory of robber-gangs, so it was important to remain cautious. The bell tower in the center of town was controlled by a faction called Garafan, which meant "sharp claw." That area was especially dangerous; Unjo said he never approached the bell tower.

There were two other gangs in the town: the Jagma, (great storm), and the Skullhellgs (the children of Skullhell). There was a violent struggle for territory between them. In the broadest terms, Central Herbesit belonged to Garafan, Western Herbesit to Jagma, and Eastern Herbesit to the Skullhellgs. If they picked a fight with any members of these three groups, they were in trouble.

In the oldest part of Herbesit, Old Town, there were underground aqueducts as well as graveyards. The Zeran, or Scholars, ruled here and were an exceptional group in that they *didn't* favor violence. Of course, they weren't against using force to keep the fighting under control. If anyone started a quarrel underground, punishment would be waiting for them. And the Zeran knew everything about the complicated underground and had a sizable number of fighters. Neither Garafan, Jagma, nor the Skullhellgs tried to encroach on the underground.

That being the case, Herbesit's underground wasn't a paradise for the weak. The Zeran didn't refuse guests, but they were elitists and never allowed outsiders to settle in the underground. Furthermore, there were sealed districts only the Zcran could enter. And to become one of the Zeran, you had to understand their doctrines and undergo training.

Rubicia was a former Zeran. She had lived underground before but moved to the surface for unknown reasons. She still had connections in the underground, but she was treated just about the same as any other outsider.

Haruhiro and the others tried visiting the underground. There was a market there, where they could shop with black coins. With blacksmiths, grocers, clothing stores, and more, there was greater variety and selection than what was available in Well Village. However, the prices were easily double to triple those of Well Village, making even basic things pretty expensive. Everyone worked with base ten.

The party learned early how the Zeran looked down on outsiders. According to Unjo, when outsiders shopped in the underground market, they were usually charged double what the Zeran would pay. Outsiders could complain, *That's not fair,* but they'd be told, *If you don't like it, get out, and never come back.* And that was the end of it. There were marketplaces on the surface, too, but the three major gangs were involved in all of them, which didn't create a leisurely shopping environment. They wanted to avoid trouble, so they had no choice but to use the underground market.

In the basement of Rubicia's tower, there was a furnace with a smokestack, a cooking area, an incredibly deep well, and a drainage pipe leading to a sewer—all things they needed to live. In addition, there were two small mezzanine floors. Unjo's and Rubicia's bedrooms were on them.

They were married, but they slept in separate rooms. Even if Haruhiro wanted to ask about that, he couldn't and wouldn't. They were already imposing on the two. It would be rude to pry needlessly on top of that.

On the third day, when they had learned more about Herbesit and were feeling more at ease, Unjo said they would be leaving town.

"I'll show you people the exit. The entrance to the exit, to be precise. I came to Darunggar through there. My comrades all died, I was the only survivor. I no longer have any intention of returning home. There is a path back. There is a way, but I value my life too much to take it. To live, I've learned that is the one thing I desire."

Before they set out, Rubicia held Unjo's right hand in both of hers, pressing it against her cheek for a short while. It was a silent moment of contact, as if it were some sort of ritual.

Unjo said he had no intention of returning home. Was Rubicia the reason? Perhaps in meeting her, Unjo found the reason to go on living here.

When they exited Rubicia's tower and left Herbesit, they headed west, opposite the ridge where the flame rose each day.

It was hilly to the west of Herbesit, and there were farms—large and small—surrounded by fences. On the farms were creatures with tiny, childlike bodies, who turned over dirt or pulled up dark gray stalks that looked like weeds. There were times when collared gaugais barked at them from the other side of farm fences.

"Never go inside the fences," Unjo strictly ordered them. "It will cause trouble."

They had no intention of going inside them. There weren't just tiny laborers who looked like slaves and gaugais. The farms had lions that stood upright and muscular humanoids with bull-like heads. They were armed and kept a close eye on the laborers' work. They also ensured no intruders entered their farms. If they trespassed, the guards would spot the party directly. If they didn't, the gaugais would. They'd bark and alert the guards.

Once they were past the farms, white things covered the gently rolling hills. They didn't need to pick them up to know what they were: bones.

The Field of Bones, Zetesidona. According to Unjo, it was a battlefield where the forces of Lumiaris and Skullhell once waged an intense battle. Some great power had caused the death of tens of thousands. The dead rotted, their possessions were stolen, and now only their bones remained. He said those bones were gathered up, ground, and spread across the farmers' fields. It made an effective fertilizer, apparently, and Zetesidona had so many bones that it would never run out.

When they arrived at a place where the bones ran deep, they risked falling and getting buried. If they looked closely, they could find spots where dirt peeked through the bones. Those spots offered safe footing.

They had to watch their step as they crossed the Field of Bones. But they couldn't keep their eyes down. That was dangerous, too.

There were birds called skards here. These carrion birds looked like large crows, but they couldn't fly well. Their bodies were much too heavy. Their leg strength more than made up for it, though. It was terrifying to watch a skard take aim and then charge in a straight line to tackle its target.

If any of them were flying by one of those, and landed deep in the bones, that would be the worst. But that was how skards hunted. They dropped their prey into the deep bone piles and then pecked them from above. They were ferocious birds.

By the time they reached the reddish-brown river, the Dendoro, it was already night. The Dendoro was not large, with the opposite bank only ten meters away, but it was deep, and its current was swift. They couldn't walk or swim across it. There was a bridge further upstream, but they decided to make camp by the riverside.

When the fire on the ridge set, the skards cawed ominously. They could hear them even down at the riverside. It made it hard to sleep.

When the ridge in the distance began to burn, the skards stopped cawing. Haruhiro hadn't slept at all, but that wasn't new. He was used to it.

They walked along the river, and after a quarter of a day the bridge came into view. Haruhiro had a bad feeling about it. As they got closer, they saw the state of it. The piers were still there, as were the girders, but the planks were gone. Haruhiro, as a thief, might have been fine, but they couldn't expect the heavily-armored Kuzaku or Shihoru the mage to make the crossing like that. It would be cruel.

However, Unjo said, "This is the only bridge."

It's either go on or go back, thought Haruhiro.

It took Shihoru and Kuzaku a long time. Several times it looked like Kuzaku would fall, but they made it across somehow. Unjo and the rest of them made it without trouble.

There were ruins on the other side of the bridge. Or Haruhiro called them ruins. They weren't as intact as the City of the Dead Ones. They covered a vast stretch of land.

"There was a city called Alluja here," Unjo explained. "If you search, you'll occasionally find tablets."

"Huh?!" Ranta jumped, then pointed off into the distance. "H-h-h-h-h-hey, there, there's something over there?!"

"Probably just a pillar or something." Haruhiro put his hand on the hilt of his short sword and squinted. Whatever Ranta pointed at didn't move. It looked person-shaped, but he would give good odds that it was building wreckage.

Wait... No.

Haruhiro lowered his hips and drew his short sword. "It just moved? That thing, just now."

"See!" Ranta held his black blade at the ready, hiding behind Unjo. "T-take it out, Unjo-san! I'll back you up! Totally!"

"Yeah, I'm sure you totally will," Kuzaku muttered. He readied his longsword and shield then moved forward. "There's something, right? Something here."

"Logoks," Unjo said. "Tree people, they're called." He drew the ax hanging from his hip.

The thing that looked like building wreckage walked toward them with swaying steps. Gradually it picked up speed, until it was running. It was coming. The logok, a tree person. It certainly looked like a tree, with a stump-like torso and branch-like arms and legs. Its movements were awkward but fast.

Kuzaku was ready to meet it head-on, but Unjo threw his ax. The ax spun through the air, then chopped off one of the logok's legs. The logok lost its balance and fell.

"Logoks don't die," Unjo calmly explained. "Smash it, keep it from moving."

"Roger Wilco!" Ranta sprang at the logok and chopped it up with his black blade. "Ohohohoho! Easy peasy! Gahahahaha-haha!"

"Listen, man." Haruhiro was so disgusted with Ranta.

"Meow!" Yume let out a strange cry. "There're still more!"

Haruhiro had figured as much. *Well, no, but it isn't strange that there are more. Looking around, I see others have popped up. They're probably logoks. Five, six of them?*

"They're not strong," Unjo said as he drew another weapon from his pack. "However, they're numerous and troublesome."

"I'll watch Shihoru!" Merry held her head staff and stood in front of Shihoru.

Shihoru nodded, as if to say, *I have Merry, so don't worry about me.*

Numerous and troublesome, Haruhiro thought. It was true. There were *a lot* of them. By the time they were able to take a break, they had dismantled forty of the things. Fifty, possibly.

Ranta wheezed and dropped down on all fours. "A-are are we gonna h-have to fight these things f-forever?"

"No. I'll use this." Unjo picked up a dried branch that might have once been a logok's arm or leg. When he lit it, white smoke rose up from it and let off a bittersweet smell. It wasn't intolerable, but it was unpleasant.

"Um, does the stench drive off logoks?" Haruhiro asked, trying not to breathe through his nose.

"Yes." Unjo looked around. "Just to be safe, take as much as we can."

"Yuck," Ranta complained, kicking around pieces of logok. "This stuff stinks. It smells nasty. Bwuh?!" Unjo had kicked him in the butt. "I-I'm sorry! I-I-It smells lovely, right?! It's a sweet smell, yeah?! Okay, time to pick up as much as I can!"

Haruhiro didn't think Unjo would kick anyone other than Ranta, but he didn't want logoks swarming them everywhere they went, either. They all gathered up pieces of logok before continuing on.

Then it happened.

Haruhiro turned back with a strange feeling. Had he imagined it? He turned back and walked.

No, there was something strange. He knew it.

Haruhiro raised his hand, forcing a stop. "Um, Unjo-san?"

"What?"

"We're not being followed, right?"

"It's possible," Unjo said like it was nothing. "The smell of logok repels logoks. However, in exchange, it draws nivles."

"Nipples?" Yume tilted her head to the side. "What're those?"

Unjo pulled his braided hat down. "It's '*nivles*.'"

"You moron." Ranta pointed at his own chest. "If it were nipples, you've got a pair. Why would nipples come up here? Are you nipple-obsessed or something, Yume?"

"So, what is a nivle?" Shihoru asked, ignoring Ranta.

"Lizards," Unjo responded immediately. "About four meters long."

"Four!" Kuzaku let out a short, strange laugh. "K-kinda big, huh?"

"It's certainly," Merry looked around, "not small, no."

Unjo drew the ax at his hip. "They're less like lizards, more like small dragons."

"Oh, man." Haruhiro slouched forward. His stomach hurt. "Personally, I don't want to meet any dragons. Not here, not anywhere."

"Y-y-yeah, w-w-well, I say I w-w-wanna meet 'em!" Ranta declared.

"You say that, but your voice is shakin.'"

"Y-Y-Y-Yume! Why're you perfectly calm?! It's a dragon, dammit! You know, a dragon?!"

"Y'think they're cute, these drangos?"

"Not drangos, dragons, you dolt!"

"Yume's not a dolt!"

"H-h-h-h-h-here it comes!" Haruhiro exhaled strongly.

The creature was five meters, from head to tail. It peeked out from around the corner of a ruined wall. It stood less than a meter tall, but it was big. Really big. It was a deep green creature—more like a dragon than a lizard as Unjo had said—and it had a fleshy crest on top of its head.

"Do we run?" Haruhiro hesitantly asked Unjo for advice.

"They're persistent," he said. "It'll chase us for days. We have to take it out. It's venomous. If you're bitten, it will be serious. Be careful."

"Yes, sir," Haruhiro responded like a kid without meaning to.

I need to keep it together. I've been loosening up because Unjo is with us. I'm the leader here, Haruhiro told himself. *When there's a reliable person beside me, I depend on them. I'm weak. It happens every time, but I still don't like it. I'm weak. I really am hopelessly weak, but I need to try to keep it together.*

The nivle steadily walked toward them. Its footsteps were so silent, it was a wonder Haruhiro had noticed it. If he hadn't, it would have ambushed them. It would be difficult to lose, too. Even if they ran their fastest and managed to shake it, it could easily sneak up behind them.

Unjo was right. They had to finish it here.

"Kuzaku, I'm counting on you," Haruhiro said. "Take the head. Yume and Ranta, the sides. Merry, stay with Shihoru. Shihoru, support us with Dark. Use whatever timing works best for you. Unjo-san, if it comes down to it, please help."

"Very well," Unjo responded, his voice sounding just a bit kind.

Haruhiro probably looked and sounded exhausted.

"Okay," he said. "Let's do it."

15 | Because He Has a Reason

A LLUJA HAD ONCE BEEN a massive city. There were theories that it had been prosperous before the conflict between Lumiaris and Skullhell.

It took a whole day to cross the ruins of the great city Alluja. They took plenty of breaks, and those who could nap did so. But they were few because even if they could set aside their fear of logoks, there were still the nivles.

Nivles mainly fed on logoks, but humans were far more appetizing to them. If they saw, heard, or otherwise detected a human, they chased them to the ends of the world. They didn't just blindly attack, either; they were extremely good at finding good openings to do so with advantage.

Unjo said they were four meters long, but that varied. Nivles ranged from three to five meters. Males were crested, females weren't. The larger and showier the crest, the more violent the male was, but those nivles attacked them head-on. The confidence ended up making them easier for the party to handle. Surprisingly, it was the females, more subdued in their appearance, that were more dangerous. They were calculating, and fast, which made them fearsome opponents.

Haruhiro and the others took down seven nivles as they crossed the ruined city. Four males, three females. Every fight had been to the death. They were fortunate nivles didn't hunt in groups. If they'd had to face more than one at the same time, they wouldn't stand a chance.

Nivle hides sold for a fair price, but they were bulky, so the party didn't bother with lugging them along. They cooked and ate the meat, which wasn't terrible.

When they came to the end of the ruins, there was a downhill slope. The incline wasn't particularly steep, but it went down a long way. It felt like they descended into the depths of the earth. It went so far that, even during the day, it was too dark to see what was right in front of them.

If they hadn't had Unjo to guide them, they would never have gone down. It was scary, after all.

"Um, what's past here?" Haruhiro worked up the courage to ask.

"Orcs," Unjo answered, indifferent as always.

"Walk?" Yume repeated.

No, Yume, thought Haruhiro. *Well, we are walking, though.*

"Wait." Merry checked with him. "By orcs, do you mean...?"

"They're similar, at least," Unjo said as he descended one step at a time. "They're called orcs here in Darunggar, too."

"Whoa!" Ranta shuddered. "Well, damn. Now I've got goose-bumps. It's like, you know. In our world, orcs are the enemy, but here, I almost feel an affinity with them. Well, no, not quite, but still."

Unjo snorted. "They're the enemy here, too."

"These orcs," Shihoru said in a voice as quiet as a mosquito, "could they have come from Grimgar?"

"The entrance to the exit," Kuzaku whispered to himself.

Unjo said, "Who knows?" Then, after a long silence, as if he were just remembering it, he said, "This might be their homeland."

The hill was rocky, covered in fine pebbles as slick as sand. They had to be careful or they would slip.

The slope was nivle-free. That was probably because the logoks lived primarily in Alluja.

Here and there were holes about a meter in diameter. Unjo avoided them. When asked, he said, "Because there are gujis."

A guji was a creature between a monkey and a bear, and they fought to the death to defend their dens. If you poked at their den, sometimes more than ten gujis would come out to defend, and that quickly turned into a huge problem. If you could catch them, gujis were edible, but they were muscular, making their meat tough even when cooked. You could stew it until it softened, which made a fairly good broth. But they didn't plan on catching one and trying it.

Eventually, they saw occasional red lights. The temperature rose. Steam puffed up everywhere. The word "crater" flashed through Haruhiro's mind. Could the light be lava?

They passed by a light soon enough. It bubbled and steamed

and looked very much like lava. If they slipped and fell in, burns would be the least of their worries.

They came across a river as well. It was barely knee-deep and kind of hot. Not too hot, though.

"A hot spring?" Merry questioned.

"Mixed bathing!" Ranta exclaimed.

"Not a chance!" Yume whacked Ranta on the back of the head.

"It's potable, too," Unjo said, gesturing to the hot spring river with his chin. "The taste is strange, but it won't cause indigestion. We'll rest here."

The party didn't go for mixed bathing, but they dug a bathing hole in the side of the river. The guys and girls took turns washing themselves. Unjo volunteered to be the lookout, thankfully.

"I dunno what to say," Kuzaku said once he had sunk in up to his shoulders. "Doesn't it make you feel glad to be alive? Is it just me? Like, I could die satisfied right now. Nah, I don't want to die, though. Feels so good."

"I know how you feel." Haruhiro scooped water in his hands and gently washed his face. "This is nice. I mean, damn, this is the best."

"Whaddaya mean?" Ranta crossed his arms. "I'm disappointed in the two of you! We totally coulda gotten them to get in with us. If you two had just agreed, they'd have been like, 'Well, this time, I guess we'll have to.' Are you morons? Just how crappy do you guys have to be?"

"I'm curious how you thought there was any chance they'd go along with it?" Haruhiro asked.

"Huh? It's all about feelings, man. Feelings. They say when you're traveling, you leave your sense of shame behind, right? If everyone did that, they'd be down for some mixed bathing, don't you think? I mean, the girls aren't stupid."

"Well, Yume, Shihoru, and Merry aren't stupid like you, so they wouldn't think that."

"Oh, shut up! I wanted to do some mixed bathing! I wanna bathe with some girls! I wannaaaaa!"

"You're some kind of mixed bathing fiend, huh?" Kuzaku sighed deeply. "Man, this feels good."

Maybe it was the bath, or the lack of sleep finally caught up to him, but Haruhiro slept well. Yume had to shake him awake in the morning. He felt a little bad about that.

Unjo told them he had survived using the Hot Spring River as his watering hole. That was when he had eaten guji meat, too.

Once they crossed the Hot Spring River, the ground leveled out. The moment they noticed that, though, a steep cliff rose up in their way. It wasn't a dead end. There were fissures all up the face of it.

The fissures snaked inwards, narrowing and broadening. They couldn't see even a few meters ahead, which made them incredibly uneasy. Had Unjo found this path and come through on his own?

If Haruhiro had been in Unjo's position, he wouldn't have done it. He didn't even need to think about it. It would've been impossible for him. He didn't have the ability, or the attachment to life.

When he was doing something for the others, Haruhiro tried hard. When it came to himself, though, he was useless. He couldn't bear pain, suffering, or even lack of hope. For better or worse, that was who Haruhiro was.

The others? Kuzaku, Yume, Shihoru, and Merry were probably similar to Haruhiro in that regard. The only one who would hold on for his own sake would probably be Ranta.

This was the strength of the party, and also its weakness. They could get along, with one glaring exception. They cooperated, but they were all highly codependent. Individually fragile. If one of them died, they'd probably lose the will to fight. It wasn't a situation he wanted to think about, but as the leader, he had to think about it.

"Whoaaaaaa..." Ranta breathed as they reached the end of the twisted fissure path.

He sounded like an idiot, but it was an incredible view.

They could see hundreds, maybe thousands, of lava streams rising and falling. There were hills, mountains, and boulders. There were buildings, big and small.

Yes, buildings.

Most were carved out of boulders, reinforced and decorated with iron struts. There was a building that looked like a shrine or temple, and numerous towers. There were medium-sized buildings here, too. What they were, none of them could guess.

Sandwiched between two narrow flows of lava, a road—a real road—stretched from one end to the other, streets branching off from it. There were large buildings lining the bigger streets and rows of tiny buildings along the smaller ones.

The sky was already dark, but thanks to the lava, this town saw no real night.

A town.

It *was* a town. Or perhaps a city.

"No way." Kuzaku's voice cracked as he spoke.

"Is—" Haruhiro couldn't find the words.

"Is that..." Shihoru asked in a vanishingly small voice, "the orcs' town? All of it?"

"Whew," said Yume. "Sure is a big city, huh?"

Yume took it in easily. Too easily, if anything.

"Is this it?" Merry asked the question Haruhiro wanted to. "The entrance to the exit?"

"Yes." For some reason, there was slight laughter in Unjo's voice. "The entrance to the exit. I came through this city, Waluandin."

"They're our enemies, yeah?" Kuzaku rubbed his lower back. "The orcs."

"Clearly," Unjo declared. "The orcs won't let anyone but their own go. Livestock, however, are a separate matter."

"Y-y'think we should let them raise us? Might be easier—" Ranta looked to the others, then cleared his throat. "I-I'm kidding, obviously. There's no way I'd be serious, y-you morons."

"Might not be a bad move." Unjo stroked his beard. "More realistic than running through, at least."

"I-I-I-I know, right? Right? Heheheheheheheh.…"

"He's being sarcastic," Haruhiro sighed. "Figure that much out on your own."

"Shut up! I knew that! I was just playing stupid, you moron!"

"So." Yume puffed up her cheeks and pointed toward

Waluandin. "What now? We're already here, y'know. It'd be nice to try gettin' closer."

"Yume-san's got guts." Kuzaku looked seriously put off by the suggestion.

"Well, only if it's not dangerous, y'know?" Yume said. "If it'd be dangerous, Yume thinks we'd be better off leavin', too."

"Obviously it'd be dangerous!" Ranta stomped his feet. "You should know that much!"

"If it's just a li'l bit dangerous, it might be fine!"

"It might not be." Shihoru looked ready to collapse at any moment.

"Wh-where..." Haruhiro pressed on his throat. He had to pull it together. He might be in shock, but he'd been prepared, to a degree. "Where did you come through? Unjo-san. I mean, like, what area?"

"I don't remember. I was desperate." Unjo slowly laid down his backpack, crouching next to it. "The one thing I know for certain is that two of my comrades died in Waluandin. Iehata and Akina. They were killed by orcs. I escaped. Alone."

From what Unjo told them, his party had encountered difficulties on the border of the former kingdoms of Nananka and Ishmal.

The territory of Nananka was overrun with orcs, and Ishmal was full of undead. Unjo and his comrades, back when he was young and full of vigor, had daringly stormed the enemy's main base and fought powerful undead. However, one day, they'd been caught by a surprise attack. One of their comrades, the thief Katsumi, died.

While running through enemy territory, they'd wandered into a foggy area and gotten lost. They passed through a cave and came out into a dark mountainous area bright with rivers of lava. They had thought they were safe. Although, when they saw the lizards leisurely swimming in those rivers, they had sensed something was off.

Fortunately, those lizards—which they called salamanders—hadn't attacked them, but a terrifying dragon then attacked and ate the salamanders. Unjo's party had been chased by that dark-red fire dragon.

Two more of Unjo's comrades, the paladin Ukita and the mage Matsuro, had been eaten by that fire dragon. While as they were devoured, Unjo, the warrior Iehata, and the priest Akina had fled.

And then they'd reached Waluandin. What had awaited them there was tens of thousands of orcs.

Haruhiro tried sorting out his thoughts.

There were currently two ways out of Darunggar.

The first was taking the path they'd come through. They would return to Well Village, then travel through the good old nest of gremlins back to the Dusk Realm. The northern forest, however, was infested with yegyorns. Well, they had been fine on the way here, maybe they could make it back. Haruhiro didn't really think so, though. It was a miracle they had made it to Well Village without encountering any yegyorns. He couldn't expect that to happen twice.

Counting on a miracle to get them to the Dusk Realm was a

huge gamble. Even if it worked out, was there any hope for them in the Dusk Realm? They would have to hunt for that seed of hope while being chased by cultists, white giants, and hydras. Which sounded incredibly difficult.

The second way was to get through the Fire Dragon Mountain, which was on the other side of Waluandin, and then somehow reach the foggy place. That was in dangerous territory but getting there might be impossible. Waluandin was going to be a problem. Was there a way to reach Fire Dragon Mountain without passing through Waluandin? If there was, they would still have to deal with the fire dragon.

Yeah, no.

He couldn't see any potential there. Zero. So, what then?

It might be time to accept things as they were. They could forget Grimgar and live here. In Darunggar. If nothing came up, they could live out the rest of their lives here.

What did they have to do to manage that? Share their knowledge, work together, build a stable foundation for their lifestyles. Step by step. They could move forward at their own pace. No need to rush.

Could they live here, in such a different world, without issues? Unjo was a living testament to the fact it was possible. Unjo was awfully pale, probably due to the lack of sun, but he seemed healthy. They could live for a decade or two.

With the reality shoved in Haruhiro's face, it finally set in.

It could work, right? This place is fine in its own way. I mean, Grimgar wasn't our homeland to begin with, I'm pretty sure.

When we came to, we were in Grimgar. We were forced to live there. That's all.

This world was dark. Too dark, and, honestly, gloomy. He didn't know the language well. There were practically no other humans. It was full of danger. So many concerns, but they could be overcome. They could get used to it, eventually.

Besides, unlike Unjo, they still had each other. They weren't alone. Haruhiro wasn't alone. His circumstances weren't as bad as Unjo's had been.

Even as he realized it wasn't like him, he dared to be cheerful and optimistic about the future.

Grimgar had been the first chapter in their story. The second chapter began in Darunggar. There would probably be a third and fourth chapter, and no idea where they would be. But they would continue on. He could hope for that, at least.

The next chapter might be here in Darunggar, or it might be elsewhere. He'd never predict where it was going to be. It was all unknown. Things might not always be good, but they weren't always bad, either. If there were troubles, there would be joys, too. Even in gloomy Darunggar, it wasn't all darkness. There was light.

"Well." Unjo stood up and shouldered his pack. "I think you get it now. That there's no returning to Grimgar. You see the reasons why. I'm going back to Herbesit. You do as you please."

Haruhiro closed his eyes and nodded. He couldn't stand to be left behind here. They would turn back. It wouldn't be right to impose upon Unjo's kindness much more, but he wanted to maintain a good relationship with the man. After all, they were fellow humans and volunteer soldiers. No, *former* volunteer soldiers. Unjo was their senior. Haruhiro wanted to count on his advice and tutelage in the future.

For now, thought Haruhiro, *we'll follow Unjo, doing our best not to burden and annoy him. Let's do that.*

"We're—" Haruhiro began to say, but then his eyes went wide. "Seriously?"

He stuck his hand down his shirt and pulled the necklace out.

At a time like this? Seriously?

It was a black, flat, stonelike object, but it was no rock. It vibrated. The lower end glowed green.

"The receiver," Shihoru whispered.

"What's that?" Unjo pushed up the brim of his braided hat, eyes shining. "Is it an otherworldly item?"

"Haruhiro," came the voice from the receiver.

"Soma-san." Haruhiro's hands, and his voice, trembled. His comrades gathered around, desperate to hear what he'd say.

"Are you listening?" Soma asked. "Haruhiro. How many times have I called you now? We're in Grimgar. Akira and Tokimune and their groups are all right."

"Oh, man..." Ranta half teared up. "Yeah, of course... Of course they would be. Damn straight they're all right. Man, I just... I'm so glad. Yeah. We're in a bad spot, but I'm glad."

"Haruhiro. Ranta. Yume. Shihoru. Merry. Kuzaku," Soma said. "I know you're out there somewhere, listening to this. I believe in you."

"Damn." Kuzaku held his head. "Soma-san called me by name."

"How many times..." Merry hung her head.

How many times has he called? was what she meant to ask.

"We're looking forward to seeing you all again," Soma said. "Not just me. Everyone."

"Whew..." Yume fell flat on her butt.

"Kemuri," Soma added.

"Hmm," said Kemuri. "How's it going?"

"Shima."

"Yeah," said Shima. "Haruhiro. Do you remember what I said? Let's talk about it next time."

"Hm? What's this about?" asked Soma.

"What? Does it interest you, Soma?"

"Yeah. It does. Well, I guess it's fine. Here, Lilia."

"I have nothing to say to a bunch of immature kids," said Lilia. "Fine. Just... try to be careful. Believe in yourself and your comrades. You must always look and listen to what's important and turn your heart to the light. If you never stop walking, eventually you'll find a path. Now, listen here. If you give up, I will never forgive you. Th-that's all!"

"For having nothing to say, she sure talked a lot, huh?!" Ranta sniffled. "Ohhh, Lilia-san's so cuuuute! I wanna see her again."

"Pingo?" said Soma.

"Drop dead. Uheheheh... I kid. Hey, Soma. You can try to make Zenmai talk, but it won't work. You moron... Uheheheh..."

"Oh, I see," said Soma. "Well, it's not just us. Akira-san, Miho-san, Gogh-san, Kayo-san, Branken, and Taro, too, they're all worried about you. And Rock, Kajita, Moyugi, Kuro, Sakanami, Tsuga, Io, Katazu, Tasukete, Jam, Tonbe, and Gomi. You haven't met them yet, but I told them all about you guys. Everyone's interested in you."

"Rock's and Io-sama's squad!" Ranta squirmed a little. "And wait, what kind of names are Tasukete and Gomi? That's like being called 'Help Me' and 'Trash'! Well, whatever, I hear Io-sama is a total hottie. Damn, I wanna see her."

"He never stops," Shihoru said coldly. "But—"

"Haruhiro." Soma called each of their names once more, as if committing them to memory. "Ranta. Yume. Shihoru. Merry. Kuzaku. We'll be waiting. See you."

The receiver stopped vibrating. The light on the lower end vanished.

Haruhiro held it, unable to breathe.

"Akira, he said?" Unjo suddenly let out a low laugh. "And Gogh? Preposterous. Impossible. No way."

"You know them?" Kuzaku hesitantly asked.

"I know *of* them—" Unjo stopped and let out a sigh. "They're not necessarily the same people. They're different people with the same names, most likely."

Akira and Gogh were the same age and had been volunteer soldiers for twenty years. Haruhiro figured they were probably in their forties. Unjo had to be around there, too. It wouldn't be strange if he knew them.

Haruhiro took a deep breath, mind still numbed. "I think they must be Akira-san and Gogh-san."

"Soman was sayin' he called a buncha times," Yume said in a fluffy, half-dreaming voice. "So, why'd we never hear it before?"

"Hold on, Soma—" Haruhiro started to correct her but decided against it. *The nickname's fine, I guess,* he thought. *Maybe it isn't? I don't really know anymore.*

"Maybe..." Merry looked beyond Waluandin. "It's because we're close?"

"That's it!" Ranta pointed at Merry. "Merry, girl, you're smart! Well, I'd figured that out, too, and was just about to say it!"

"Girl?" asked Merry. "I take it you never want to get healed again?"

"Ah! Sorry, I-I got a little too chummy there. I need to be more polite, m'lady. My bad. No, seriously, seriously. It won't happen again. So, forgive me! Pwease!"

"That pwease was infuriating," Shihoru muttered. Haruhiro agreed.

But setting that aside.

"We're close, huh?" Haruhiro looked down at the receiver. "We're close. We're close to Grimgar."

Yume held her hand tightly against the center of her chest. "Yume, she wants to go home. Yume wants to see Master. If she couldn't ever see him again, well, Yume wouldn't like that."

"Yeah." Kuzaku looked up to the dark sky. "I've gotta agree."

Stop it, Haruhiro thought. *Please, just stop. Don't tell me the truth like that.*

Because even if that's how you feel, it's just not possible. If you'd ask me, I'd say, "I wanna go home." I mean, I wouldn't even joke about wanting to stay here. But what choice do we have? If we try to go back, we're risking our lives. If we do risk them, there's no guarantee it'll pay off. I can't imagine it would.

I can't be adventurous like that. I can't let you be, either. I don't want to lose anyone. I can't let you die. We're gonna live. All of us. That's the best option.

"*If you give up, I will never forgive you,*" Lilia had said. What was that supposed to mean? That they should not give up? That they should struggle and survive here?

Or...

"*We'll be waiting,*" Soma had said. "*See you.*"

"We can't take risks," Haruhiro said. "Not big risks. No way. But we can ensure our safety while looking for a way."

"Huh?" Ranta crossed his arms and cocked his head to the side. "What's that mean?"

"Huh?" Kuzaku asked. "Are you stupid?"

"Kuzacky! You're mocking your super senior! I'll throw crap at you, you jerk!"

"That's filthy! Geez!" Yume scowled. "Basically, it means just that. It means that, right? So, it's that, right? Right?"

"You don't get it either!" Ranta shouted.

"We'll do our best not to put ourselves in danger. We'll be careful," Shihoru said. "We move forward with our investigation, and if someday, we reach our goal—"

"—we can go back," Merry finished for her. She bit her lip. "To Grimgar."

"That's what it means," Ranta said, puffing up his chest arrogantly. "I knew that, you moron."

With his pack on his back again, Unjo turned to go. "Do as you please."

Even if he could return, Unjo wouldn't. It might not be for a simple reason, but he would stay in Darunggar. That was clear.

Well, different strokes for different folks.

Haruhiro bowed his head deeply. "Umm, thank you so much, Unjo-san. For everything. Really!"

Unjo stopped. He didn't turn back. "Don't die, my juniors."

Grimgar of *Fantasy* and *Ash*

16 | A Good Day to Wait for a Better Day

THERE WAS A MOUNTAIN OF THINGS to be considered, and a mountain of things to be done.

For a start, Haruhiro decided to test how close he could get to Waluandin. He didn't need his comrades for that. In fact, not going solo would have been bad.

Haruhiro used Stealth and headed toward Waluandin alone.

Waluandin was built at the foot of Fire Dragon Mountain, near a mountain basin. Haruhiro tried to cut across the basin to reach Waluandin, but it wasn't exactly an empty field. Villages dotted the basin rim.

The villages contained anywhere from ten to a few dozen igloo-like buildings, and hot springs welled up in them and between them. From a distance, he managed to spot the village residents.

They were humanoid but green-skinned. They had smushed noses and large tusks protruding from their mouths. Tall, with broad thick frames, they looked just like orcs. They could only be orcs. Male orcs wore short pants and nothing else. Which made sense. It was hot here, so they didn't need shirts. Their bodies were utterly smooth. Did they shave, or just not grow body hair?

Female orcs dressed similarly, although they included a wrap around their chest and head.

The village orcs dug in the dirt, doing some sort of work at a basin shelf. He observed them raising large caterpillar-like creatures in pens. They were a bit like the pigworms he had seen at the Cyrene Mines. Were they for eating?

There were holes in the ground, and he saw the orcs were doing something or other inside of them. Perhaps they were producing food for Waluandin.

The farmer orcs had such impressive physiques. Haruhiro worried. No. These were farmers, he insisted to himself. They had grown strong by working. He wanted to think about it that way.

But all of them, male or female, are bigger than the ones we fought at Deadhead Watching Keep, he thought. *Or am I imagining that? I hope so.*

The orc villagers were so busy that they never noticed Haruhiro. But if he hadn't been alone? If his comrades had come with him? It was hard to say, they might have made it past them unawares. Besides, the orcs probably didn't work day in and day out. It was hard to tell how bright the sky was because of the lava, but they had to sleep at some point.

Haruhiro slipped past the orc villages without difficulty. Of course, it took time. Almost three hours. If they kept to the path he took in his head, they could cut that in half. The problem would be everything that came after.

Beyond the villages was a river of lava. Once they crossed it, they'd be in the city of Waluandin. This river was less than a meter across. There were many bridges, but they could probably just jump over it. It was a simple border, not a barrier.

The city streets just beyond the river were lined with square-ish buildings. They were all two-story, but an awfully short two-story. The first floor must be half-underground. Their doors all faced away from the river.

Haruhiro saw orcs sitting in the windows with their legs dangling down. They were thin and tiny for orcs. They must have been children.

Could he cross the river without being spotted? Haruhiro was cowardly, so he didn't risk it. He was sure it would be suicide to enter Waluandin from the front.

Haruhiro followed the lava river to the left. Eventually, he started to hear a familiar sound: hammering. In a large work-shop—little more than a bunch of poles with a roof over them—there were way-too-muscular orcs swinging hammers.

Waluandin's smithy made effective use of the lava. They didn't light fire, instead drawing high-temperature lava directly into their furnace. It probably wasn't just the smithy; nowhere in Waluandin had need for fuel. It was incredibly dangerous, but also incredibly convenient.

The workshop district went on for a while. The orcs of Waluandin worked metal, manufacturing a variety of products in large quantities. That meant they needed raw materials and got them from somewhere.

When Haruhiro reached the end of the workshop district, the lava river came to a stop at a rock wall. He didn't think there was any way he could climb that, but he noticed there were holes bored into it. Large holes.

Orcs went in and out of them. They pushed wagons filled with what had to be ore. There was an ore pile, too. This must be a mine.

He saw an orc who seemed to be the foreman. It wore shoulder and hip guards that gave off a dim light, carried a long stick, and acted with extreme importance. He was also noticeably larger than the rest.

The orcs in the farming villages were about two meters and thirty centimeters tall. The orcs working the smithy hadn't been much taller, but their shoulders were broader, their frames thicker. The miner orcs were roughly the same size and shape as the farming orcs. But the foreman orc. He was nearly three meters.

And he wasn't the only big one.

Haruhiro realized as he saw several big orcs that the first one wasn't a foreman. He was just...bigger. There were more of the smaller variety than the bigger variety—nearly ten to one—and he wondered if perhaps the big orcs belonged to a different social class rather than a different position. They all seemed to do similar work.

Either way, the bigger orcs, well-built and armed as they were, had to be tough. The mine was dangerous.

When he finished his investigation of Waluandin, Haruhiro headed back to his comrades.

Ranta made a pain of himself, asking, "Well? How was it? Huh? Huh? Huh?" Haruhiro ate some of the less-than-delicious preserved food they'd brought as he relayed what he had seen. He was incredibly tired, though, and passed out soon after giving the report.

When he woke, his comrades, who had been observing the villages in shifts, had their own reports for him.

Yume went first. "In the night, the orcies, they go beddy-bye, like you were thinkin'."

Only Yume would nickname orcs "orcies." As cute as it was, it didn't do anything to change the orcs' nature.

"But in Waluandin, there wasn't much change, I think." Shihoru didn't seem confident. "I know the villagers were asleep until a little while ago, though."

"I was out like a light and didn't see anything," Ranta announced.

"Why do you sound so proud?" Merry sounded mystified. "Because you're off in the head, or because you're rotten to the core? Could you just tell me?"

"Excuuuuse meeee," Ranta sneered. "Haven't you been a bit harsh with me lately? It wouldn't kill you to be a bit nicer, okay?"

"I dunno about that," Kuzaku muttered.

"Hey, Kuzacky! You're my underling! Don't get smart with me!"

The party decided to try slipping past the villages as a group. Haruhiro wished he could leave Ranta behind, but he couldn't.

Though Haruhiro had gotten the hang of the journey during his scouting trip yesterday, he had foreseen the difficulties involved. When they tried it, the six of them walking together made them stand out. There had been places where he laid low yesterday, but they were too tight for six. He tried to have them follow the same route, but they were almost discovered by farming orcs on multiple occasions. It took time and effort to move forward, and Haruhiro occasionally wanted to give in and turn back.

Minus Ranta, his comrades followed Haruhiro's orders obediently. But that was all they did. If Haruhiro didn't make a decision or give them an order, none of them did anything. There was nothing they *could* do. They didn't know the route, and they didn't have his training. He understood that, but it still pissed him off.

There were times when he wanted to snap. But he didn't. He'd take a deep breath and continue on. He could get emotional, but he couldn't let them control him. If he let his emotions swing him around, he'd become exhausted, and that would lead to mistakes.

It took four, maybe five hours, to reach Waluandin. There was no way they could cut the time shorter. When Haruhiro was alone, it had taken an hour and a half. It took three times longer with six people. It had to. They would burn a third of a day going and coming back.

Hiding near the lava river in front of Waluandin was hard for six people, too. Haruhiro was a thief, so he didn't need things to hide behind. He could lie down or crouch down and use Stealth, but that was out of the question for his comrades. If they stayed in one place, they'd be found. They had to keep moving.

The blacksmiths were to the left. The mine was past that. Haruhiro and the others went right. Occasionally there were orc children sitting in the windows of the buildings across the river. They looked around often, so the party stayed vigilant.

"Orcies're cute when they're little," Yume whispered quietly.

"How?" Ranta spat distastefully. "You call them little, but they're probably bigger than you or me."

"Size's got nothin' to do with it."

"Yeah, it does. They've got some pretty vicious looking mugs, too."

"They're just lookin' out' cause they're bored," Yume said. "Ranta, you're just seein' 'em that way 'cause you're scared."

"I'm not scared," Ranta retorted. "In a fight, I could take them easy. If you think I'm lying, I don't mind proving it. I mean, I'm not scared. I'm seriously not scared."

Thanks to the idiotic piece of trash, Haruhiro broke into a cold sweat. The orc children could easily detect them, but fortunately they didn't. Eventually, the party came to a dead end.

When they reached the end of the small street, it opened up. They hadn't come to an empty lot. There was an incredible number of orcs talking at once. It almost sounded like they were shouting at one another. Items were strewn across the ground. Was there an orc selling things? Was it a shop? Haruhiro noticed carts, and orcs standing or sitting as they ate and drank. They must have come to a market place, or some area for entertainment. Maybe both. It was chaotic. Haruhiro watched a group of orcs jump from one side of the river to the other. He didn't know what was so fun about jumping lava, but the orcs were having a great time, laughing with their throaty voices.

Approaching was dangerous. They'd be found. They could take the long way around to avoid them, but they'd have to go back to the farming villages for that.

After considering everything, Haruhiro decided to turn back. For now, at least, they'd return to Herbesit.

They needed to investigate Waluandin slowly and carefully. It wasn't something they could do in a few days. They had to gather information and prepare themselves. They'd need food and supplies. They couldn't acquire those things on the spot. Their only option was returning to town.

Even though they were going back the way they came, Haruhiro knew they would be helpless without Unjo to guide them. Once they rested by the Hot Spring River, there were no more chances to let his guard down. Every time they encountered nivles in the ruins of Alluja, he felt his heart being ground down.

There were injuries.

They crossed the bridge over Dendoro River. They were repeatedly tackled by skards in the Field of Bones, Zetesidona.

When the farms west of Herbesit came into sight, Haruhiro's tension broke despite his best efforts. He teared up. Would he ever want to go back to Waluandin? He might not. He never wanted to go through Zetesidona or Alluja. Or see orcs. Couldn't they just live in Darunggar now?

No.

Herbesit was still a dangerous city itself, so he pulled himself back into his cautious mindset. They made it to the underground of the Zeran somehow. Once they finished shopping there, though, he was at a loss for what to do.

They weren't with Unjo, so it felt wrong to visit Rubicia's tower. They weren't Zeran, so they couldn't stay in the underground, either. The people above ground were noisy and frightening.

What now? What should they do?

"Hey, even up top, there're good people, like Unjo's wife," Ranta said. "Maybe there's something like an inn, where they'll let us stay if we pay them? If we look, there's probably one somewhere, don't you think? I mean, there's gotta be. Kuzacky. You go nip up top and find one for us real quick. We'll be waiting down here. I'll even be nice and wait for you, okay?"

"Why'd you make it sound like you're doing me a favor? And why me?" Kuzaku complained.

"Because you're the lowest ranked here, duh! I mean, you're my gofer, right? You're my gofer, so you've gotta do what I tell you, y'know?"

"I don't get what you're saying."

"Oh? Acting rebellious now? I don't mind. I'll take you on anytime you want. I'll beat your ass, though. You want that? Huh?"

"This is the first time I've wanted to set that curly hair of yours on fire, Ranta-kun."

"What? Did you just call my hair curly? You did, didn't you?! Curly!"

"It *is* curly, though," Merry said coldly.

"Curly," Shihoru agreed.

"It sure is curly, huh," Yume decided.

"You jerks! Curly, curly, curly, curly, you keep saying it! People who call me curly are the ones who are really curly! Don't you know that?!"

"Hey, curly hair hasn't done you wrong, so don't be besmirching its good name," Haruhiro said.

He sighed as he looked around. Herbesit's underground had once been aqueducts and graves, so there was water flowing in some places. Most of it, though, was just underground tunnels. It was dank, but there was something almost refreshing about the smell. The people must be mixing something with the fuel for the lamps. Mint, perhaps. Thanks in part to that smell, the customers in the underground marketplace were calm and quiet. When the party made a ruckus, the Zeran who had shops open on either side of the tunnel looked bothered by it. It would be best to shut Ranta up and then beat a hasty retreat before they got thrown out.

After thinking it over, Haruhiro and the others decided to return home. To Well Village.

They considered using Herbesit as their base of operations while searching Alluja for tablets they could sell. But Herbesit was too hard to live in.

They prepared a bell, crossed through the forest, and headed for the charcoal burner's place. The charcoal burner didn't give them a warm welcome, but he didn't drive them away, either. They rested in the corner of his place for a night. When they woke, the charcoal burner was preparing his wagon for travel.

When they signaled they were willing to help him out, he didn't refuse. So they helped load the wagon and then accompanied the charcoal burner back to Well Village. They didn't have a house or anything, but it was amazing how much they felt like they were coming home when they saw the familiar gate and bridge.

The Well Village residents were taciturn, but the giant grocer crab smiled, happy to see Haruhiro and his group again. Admittedly, it was hard to read the giant crab's expression, but he looked like he was smiling to Haruhiro and his voice sounded pleased.

They talked about what to do next while eating familiar stew, but not one of them mentioned Waluandin. Should Haruhiro bring it up himself? He debated it for a while, but ultimately decided not to.

Now is the time for patience. Let's wait for the time to be ripe. He could think of reasons, but, ultimately, he just wanted to wait for a better day.

Grimgar of Fantasy and Ash

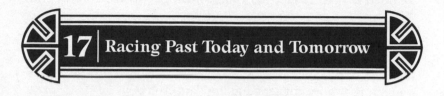

17 | Racing Past Today and Tomorrow

AFTER SPENDING TEN DAYS working in the City of the Dead Ones, though, Haruhiro wondered if everything was all right like this. They all did.

When hunting in the City of the Dead Ones, there were times when they didn't focus on the task at hand. Obviously, when they were fighting a dead one, everyone stayed focused, but they clearly had a hard time maintaining it. Haruhiro struggled with it too, so he understood.

It took courage, but finally he suggested it might be time to go back. No one objected.

This time, they planned for a fifteen-day trip. It might be a few days longer or shorter, depending on the circumstances, so they prepared for that possibility. Once they decided it wouldn't be too long of a stay, he felt more motivated.

That's right, he thought. *No use dragging it out. Staying focused for a short time is best.*

Their second trip to Waluandin went smoothly, considering Unjo wasn't with them.

We've gotten used to Darunggar, was something Haruhiro avoided thinking. Getting used to things was dangerous, and scary. It was best to jump at every little thing, to feel the pain in his stomach.

Haruhiro scouted Waluandin on his own. That was overwhelmingly more efficient and less dangerous.

Past the entertainment quarter, he found a space packed with igloo-like houses similar to those in the farming villages. These were the slums, where lower-class orcs lived. Even on the steep hills, igloos were built so that they seemed stuck to them. It was kind of impressive.

Fire Dragon Mountain was on the other side of Waluandin. There was a path there, somewhere, which led to Grimgar.

There were two ways to reach Fire Dragon Mountain. One was through Waluandin. The other was traveling around Waluandin and crossing the mountains.

If they were going to cross the mountains, they would have to pass the mine or the slums. Both areas were dangerous, so they wanted specialized equipment for the task.

If someone asked Haruhiro what that specialized equipment might be, he'd have no answer. He was no specialist. Even Yume, their hunter and outdoor specialist, had no experience with mountain climbing. Crossing the mountains was going to take thorough preparation. It wouldn't be the next thing they did, but the thing after next, no doubt.

If they were going to go through Waluandin, they'd have to try when the orcs were less active, choosing a route where orcs weren't likely to find them.

They knew the village orcs slept at night, so it stood to reason city orcs did the same. Using Stealth to investigate on his own, Haruhiro had seen the Waluandin orcs—waluos for short—distinguishing night and day in their lives.

The entertainment quarter bustled with waluos at all times. However, there were more waluos in the afternoon and at night, and fewer in the early morning and before noon. At both the workshops and the mine, no one worked at night. The slums were always kind of noisy.

Then again, Haruhiro only knew what he could see from his side of the lava river. Even if they successfully snuck through the mine or workshops at night, there could be obstacles afterwards that would prevent them from going farther.

He wanted to infiltrate Waluandin and learn more, but he couldn't bring his comrades for that. If he were to come out and say it bluntly, anyone he brought would just get in the way. This was something Haruhiro had to do alone.

When the predetermined fifteen-day period was up, Haruhiro and the others returned to Well Village. They spent the next day heading out to the City of the Dead Ones and earning money.

For the next day, and the day after that, and the day after *that*, and the day *after that*, and they worked in the City of the Dead Ones.

Hunting was a volunteer soldier's job, but they couldn't let it become routine. They had once earned the nickname the Goblin Slayers, so they were used to spending ridiculous amounts of time on the same hunting grounds. But they knew to be wary of getting used to things.

"Urgh!" Kuzaku earnestly tried to hold off a lionlike dead one.

Not just with his shield. He used his longsword for defense, too. Kuzaku lowered his center of gravity while being careful to stay balanced, then held in there.

He kept a fixed distance from the lionlike dead one, making adjustments to his position and stance based on his opponent's movements. He did a splendid job staying at range, and the lionlike dead one had a hard time with him. One-on-one, Kuzaku kept the dead one easily occupied. He had gotten good at it.

Everyone knew Kuzaku was improving as a tank. They trusted him, and that was why Merry could move up and trip the dead one with her staff.

Kuzaku would never let the dead one get away. If she didn't fully believe that, Merry wouldn't leave Shihoru's side.

Merry wasn't unusually strong, but the priest's self-defense techniques had been created to defend the weak. She had developed from there. Making use of centrifugal force, she amplified her weak power into blows against her enemies. When she got a clean hit in, her strikes could be more powerful than Ranta's.

The lionlike dead one tripped. Kuzaku was quick to jump on it. But this time, he didn't have the chance.

"Gwahaha!" Ranta, who had been watching and waiting for his opportunity, used Leap Out to jump in and assault the lionlike dead one. His willingness to go all in was his one praise-worthy quality. His black blade plunged through the dead one's right eye. "Take that!"

"Get back!" shouted Haruhiro.

Ranta jumped back, possibly even before he heard the command. His black blade remained in the dead one's eye. Even as it writhed in pain, the dead one tried to hug Ranta with all its strength. Ranta had gotten away just before it had managed to break his back.

"Eheh... Let there be curses..." Zodiac-kun, who floated nearby, often said things that could be either auspicious or ominous; it was hard to tell which.

The dead one rose up. Yume loosed an arrow, but it twisted to avoid it. Right after her, Shihoru cried, "Dark!" and sent out her elemental.

The star-shaped elemental Dark sank into the lionlike dead one's chest. It immediately began convulsing and fell to one knee.

"Hah!" Kuzaku swung wide with his longsword, striking the dead one on the side of its head. He followed up by whacking it in the chin with his shield.

"Yeah!" Merry slammed its neck with her staff.

"There!" Ranta leapt at the dead one. He tore his black blade free of its eye, and then slashed it. He slashed it like crazy. Whenever Ranta rested, Kuzaku and Merry delivered one or two hits, and then Ranta jumped back in and resumed his flurry of blows.

Haruhiro watched over his comrades as they fought, taking

in their surroundings for any new threats. Yume, next to Shihoru, was also on guard with an arrow nocked.

The party had shifted their hunting grounds in the City of the Dead Ones from the Northwest Quarter to just inside the Southwest Quarter. The Southeast Quarter should have been their next location, a level up after the Northwest Quarter, but the east side was mostly covered in mist.

The dead ones of the Southwest Quarter were clever and vicious, but Haruhiro and the others had found the dead ones in the area closest to the Northwest Quarter were comparatively easy to take down.

They were mostly like the lionlike dead one they were fighting now. They were still powerful enemies, but if they focused their efforts properly, they could practically guarantee they'd take them down.

Enemies at this level were good. Even if they wanted to relax, they couldn't. They couldn't just defeat these dead ones in a routine manner. The tensions always stayed just a little high, forcing them to improve themselves. They had to adjust things day by day, or they would never survive. As long as they did things right, and didn't relax, they managed.

"Haru-kun." Yume gestured toward a building to the south with her chin.

"Hm?" Haruhiro squinted.

Something poked its head out from the collapsed section of the second floor. No, it just looked like it. Nothing to worry about.

Haruhiro shook his head. "No. It's fine."

"Yume got it wrong, huh? Sorry 'bout that."

"Hey, it's fine."

"Take that! Let Skullhell embrace you!" Ranta landed a finishing blow on the lionlike dead one. "Bwahahahaha! I'll drink well again tonight!"

"What are you, a mountain bandit?" Haruhiro muttered. He was a thief himself, but he didn't want to think he was in the same class as Ranta. Ever.

They hunted in the City of the Dead Ones for ten days, then left on another fifteen-day expedition. When they spaced it out like this, they spent their days actually looking forward to the next one.

It wasn't good to think too much about the future, but if they only thought about what was directly in front of them, they would suffocate. Striking a balance was important. If all they did was charge blindly toward hope, they would forget to watch their feet and fall into danger. If they kept looking down under the weight of despair, they would become exhausted and unable to walk.

They couldn't live on hard times, and good times wouldn't last forever. It was best to cry when they needed to and smile even when they didn't feel like smiling.

In the middle of their third expedition, when Haruhiro was out investigating alone, Ranta and the others were attacked by orcs. There were only two. While they managed to kill them, Kuzaku and Yume were both wounded. Things looked bad for a while after that.

Both orcs had looked thin and young. They had worn no armor, but carried bows, arrows, swords, and knives. They had been outfitted like hunters, and perhaps chanced across Ranta and the others while leaving for a hunt.

After the attack, they changed where the other five who stayed would wait during their fourth expedition. They set up their base camp moved near the Hot Spring River. Haruhiro had Ranta and the others hunt gujis, which were like badgers, while he investigated Waluandin. He'd gotten to the point where he could slip into the city at night, if he was alone.

During their fifth expedition, they found a small stone tablet in the ruins of Alluja. When they returned to Well Village and showed it to Oubu the Eyehand Sage, he bought it off them for one large black coin, a rou.

When they camped outside the village later, Ranta said, with uncharacteristic sincerity, "You know, I can sort of understand how the people here felt, clinging to Skullhell. When it's this dark, anyone would want to be embraced by Skullhell."

"I think it's easier to understand why they clung to Lumiaris," Merry countered. "When it's this dark, it's normal to seek the light."

"I'm sure that's normal for you," Ranta retorted. "But listen, what's normal is different for everyone, you know that?"

"'You'?" she repeated.

"I am really sorry," Ranta said without emotion. "Merry-san, please, forgive me."

"He's not putting his heart into it at all," Shihoru said.

Ranta got down and performed a kowtow. "I'm so sowwy! I was wong! Fogibe me!"

"There's nothing more worthless than a kowtow from you," Haruhiro said with a wry smile. He poked the fire with a stick. "Gods, huh? It doesn't feel real to me. I mean, there're actual gods? They exist? I always thought they were, like, fictional? Or something."

"If they weren't real, I couldn't use light magic." Merry showed him the palm of her hand. "But I'll admit, until I came here, I... might not have fully believed in them myself."

"Oh, yeah." Kuzaku nodded. "I could see that. Gods are an example for us, y'know. Or the source for obe? The reason? The basis? Something like that. Like, there's Lumiaris, and if we assume she's always watching, we behave righteously, maybe."

"Elhit-chan the White God's real," Yume said. She rested her head in Shihoru's lap, while Merry held to her leg. "Elhit-chan shows up in Yume's dreams and everything. Yume wishes she could meet Elhit-chan."

"So, let's talk seriously here." Ranta disabled his kowtow mode, sitting with legs crossed and arms folded cheekily. "Really, everyone's afraid of dying and stuff, right? Since we're alive, we don't want to die. But still. We're gonna die. Someday, for sure, we're gonna bite it. There's no getting out of it. It's the conclusion of our lives, you could say. When you think about that, I dunno... It feels overwhelming, right? It's hard to deal with."

"Even for you?" Haruhiro asked, struck by an unexpected feeling.

Ranta snorted and laughed. It was forced.

"I'm talking generally, man, generally. I'm above and beyond all this stuff. Besides, dying is just a part of my life, right? Even if other people's deaths feel, well... y'know. You've got to accept your own death, or you can't live. You're born, and then you die, and that's life. It's a cycle, man, a cycle." Ranta spun his index finger around in circles. "I'm sure you people don't get it, but Skullhell's teachings include views on life and death like that."

"We have those in Lumiaris's teachings, too," Merry said quietly as she rubbed Yume's thigh. "In the beginning, there was light. All life is born from that light and will return to it. That's why we see the light when we die."

"When we die, we fall into the darkness, obviously," Ranta snorted.

"No, we do not. Darkness is a side effect produced by the light not shining somewhere. If you avert your eyes from the light, you'll be mired in darkness. That's all."

"You're wrong. Darkness is the original, and the light came after it. I'm telling you, the root of all things is darkness."

"This is why I can never get along with a dread knight who blindly follows Skullhell," Merry muttered.

"I don't need to get along with you! I don't want anything to do with the cowardly believers of Lumiaris!"

"Don't fight over this nonsense." Haruhiro tried to step in as leader, but Merry and Ranta both glared at him.

"Nonsense?!"

"Whaddaya mean, nonsense?!" Ranta yelled.

"I-I'm sorry."

"Both…" Shihoru said, trying to help him out. "Can't it be both? In the beginning, there was light and darkness. I think they're conflicting but complimentary elements."

"Like everyone here, huh." Yume rubbed her cheek against Shihoru's lap. "It's 'cause everyone's there for her that Yume's able to keep on livin', y'know."

That got everyone to settle down.

Conversations like this were bound to happen since they were almost always together. And when they weren't? Well, the guys always talked about pretty stupid stuff, but the girls? Haruhiro wasn't actually sure. Did they talk about love and romance amongst themselves? Haruhiro was curious, but he couldn't ask them. So that mystery would remain just that, a mystery.

Ranta used the ten rou he had saved to buy a two-handed sword from the blacksmith. The hilt was long, but the blade itself wasn't overly large, which made it surprisingly light.

Most swords had an unsharpened section just above the base of the blade called the ricasso. The ricasso of Ranta's new sword was long and had a protuberance at the top of it. Apparently, gripping the ricasso made performing a finishing blow easier for Ranta, and he insisted there were other uses for it, too. Knowing Ranta, he would come up with all sorts of things for the ricasso through trial and error.

He named his sword RIPer and bought armored gloves so he could hold the ricasso good and tight. He'd borrowed money for those gauntlets from his comrades.

His black blade was still usable, so he handed it down to Kuzaku. Kuzaku purified the sword by carving a hexagram into the blade and marking it with blood as proof. By doing this, he could use the light magic spell Saber to bestow Lumiaris's blessing upon it.

The party acquired a helm reminiscent of a hawk's head in the City of the Dead Ones. Kuzaku's helmet had been badly damaged by the time they found it, so he swapped it out for the new helm. Ranta named it the Hawk Helm, but Kuzaku really didn't like that.

Yume had made the curved sword she'd picked up in the City of the Dead Ones weeks ago one of her favorite weapons. Haruhiro kept calling it a wantou—which was the word for a curved blade—so Yume decided to nickname it Wan-chan, which was a cute word associated with puppies. Honestly, Haruhiro thought it was kind of wrong.

Merry's head staff broke, so she bought a staff with a hammer on the end from the blacksmith. She had chosen her weapon with an eye toward its destructive power, since she had been participating more actively in battles now.

Though Shihoru didn't change her equipment, her elemental Dark was gradually getting stronger. The more attached Dark got, the bigger he grew. And the cuter he became. On top of that, he could now produce effects similar to Sleepy Shadow, Shadow Complex, and Shadow Bond. He wasn't all-powerful, and Shihoru had to will one of the impact, confusion, sleeping, or stopping effects into him, but he was still amazing.

According to Shihoru, she would eventually be able to mix and match different effects. When she could, she would deal damage while stopping the enemy, weaken them on top of dealing damage, and other possibilities. That was even more amazing.

Haruhiro ended up with a stiletto he would use exclusively for skewering attacks, and a knife with a hilt guard for sweeping, slashing, and stabbing. The former he had found in Herbesit's underground, the latter he had looted off a dead one.

They hadn't seen Unjo. He visited Well Village occasionally, but Haruhiro and the others spent a lot of time away on expeditions, so they were probably just missing each other.

Every time they visited Herbesit, Rubicia's tower crossed Haruhiro's mind. He thought about going there but never did.

One day, Ranta invited them to the grocer's in Well Village, where they got absolutely hammered. All of them. Everyone drank as much as they could, and they had a great banquet with the blacksmith, the flattened egg with arms from the bag shop, the off-duty guards, and the giant crab grocer. Ranta, Haruhiro, and Kuzaku took turns arm wrestling with the blacksmith. They all lost badly. Then the three of them took him on as a team and still lost. He had only vague memories of this.

As they had gotten drunker and drunker, he recalled sitting next to Merry. They talked, but he couldn't remember about what. What *did* they talk about? He felt like he'd had a good time, but he didn't remember a word they had said.

Well, as long as he hadn't said anything weird. The next day, Merry acted the same as ever, so it was probably fine.

It's fine, right? he tried to convince himself.

After that one time, the receiver hadn't vibrated again. No one commented on it. It was probably just a matter of bad timing. That was all. That was what Haruhiro decided to think.

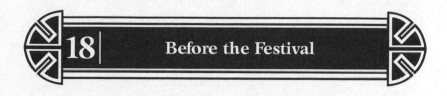

18 | Before the Festival

"OH. TWO HUNDRED, HUH," Haruhiro said.

While infiltrating Waluandin, he realized this had been their 200th night in Darunggar. Not that it mattered. Whether it was their 200th, their 300th, or even their 666th night, it made no difference to the denizens of this world.

Still, there was something strange about Waluandin tonight. Strange even in the outlying villages.

The village orcs tended to go to bed and wake up early. Earlier than the waluos, for sure. Haruhiro usually crept through their villages as they slept, then entered Waluandin through the workshop district once the blacksmith orcs left. There were many places to hide in the workshop district, so even if there were waluos, he could get past them easily enough.

Tonight, however, the village orcs were up late. Light leaked out from inside their igloo-like houses, and he heard talking. He even spotted a handful of orcs outside, doing...something.

He didn't feel they were a threat to his ability to sneak past them, but it bothered him.

In the workshop district, work had ended for the day, and all was quiet. However, everything past there was different.

Beyond the workshop district was a mixed residential district. Usually, there weren't many waluos walking the streets at night. This time, though, there were boisterous waluos everywhere. Every house was lit up.

Some waluos were inside their houses, busily moving around, while others were outside talking. It wasn't just this residential area. All of Waluandin bustled with activity. It wasn't *quite* festive, but it felt like they were preparing for a festival or holiday.

There were waluos loitering around, so it was dangerous to linger. Based on past experience, though, Haruhiro knew they weren't even remotely on guard. There was a coliseum-like place in the entertainment quarter, and waluos often bet on fights there. Haruhiro had watched some showy fights; the waluos loved displays of martial ability.

But oddly enough, this city had no real defenses.

They probably never considered the possibility of external enemy attack. They never imagined humans like the party would make it into their city. As long as Haruhiro was careful and didn't draw attention, he was certain he wouldn't be spotted.

Being a coward, Haruhiro was afraid, but he stayed calm and looked around the area. On their 200th night in Darunggar, Waluandin was definitely different. Why? Were they preparing for a festival? He wanted the details. Haruhiro went from alley to alley, occasionally climbing to and jumping across rooftops as he observed them. Gradually, he figured things out.

Because of the lava flowing nearby, night never came to Waluandin. Even so, the city was brighter than usual. The waluos were building something. Many things, in fact.

The windows of their houses generally had no shutters, so you could see inside them when the lights were on. Haruhiro saw waluo women working at looms. What work needed to be done so late at night? Couldn't they just do it during the day? Haruhiro didn't know, but he did know that he had never seen these women weaving at night before.

Waluo men decorated the front of their houses with sticks, too. Like the weaving, he had never seen waluos do this before. They chatted with their neighbors and ate as they worked, but they didn't seem to be getting much pleasure from it. They weren't doing it for fun.

Haruhiro had no clue what the sticks were, but there had to be a reason for them.

Waluo children messed with something that looked like a cage. Older waluos gave directions to the boys, and they had them help with the stick work.

Preparations. It was clear the waluos were preparing for something. They produced costumes and decorations, and then they put them on, used them, and did *something*. It had to be a city-wide event. A ritual? A festival? Whatever it was, Waluandin was enveloped in an atmosphere entirely separate from their usual routines.

The center of Waluandin was dominated by a particularly large building that resembled a crouching dragon. It wasn't clear if the waluos had a king or not, but Haruhiro called it the palace, for convenience's sake.

The palace was surrounded by wide streets and thin rivers of lava. One main road stretched out toward Fire Dragon Mountain. Impressive buildings surrounding the palace, and waluos were always going in and out, day and night. Armed waluos also patrolled this area late into the night. With so much activity, and so many waluos, it was a hard area to approach, but tonight Haruhiro decided to work up the courage to slip inside.

It was a calculated risk. Being no exception to the new atmosphere, the palace district waluos were hard at work. Usually, waluos here enjoyed leisurely nighttime strolls, but not tonight. Most were absorbed in their work. If Haruhiro used Stealth well, he wouldn't be found easily.

But... he couldn't help but think.

They led cultured lives here in Waluandin. Well Village was the sticks, and Herbesit a lawless, barbaric outback compared to here. There was order in this city. The waluos didn't rob one another for the most part. They worked together as they earned their keep and lived their lives. They didn't just eat, work, and sleep. They had leisure, too. It was a highly stratified society, but it afforded half—no, most—of the waluos with a safer and more prosperous life than Haruhiro and the party had.

As he mused, Haruhiro saw it. He tilted his head.

"An altar...?" he murmured to himself.

Up on the roof of one building facing into the plaza, Haruhiro tried to let the tension out of his body. It was the first time he had come this far. However, he had seen the plaza before, from a distance. That thing hadn't been there then.

It was a stage about two meters square and three meters high. There was another platform on top of it, and on that platform— there was a cage. Gilded, decorated, and gaudy. Normally, cages were used for holding criminals or prisoners, but it didn't look like that was what this one was for.

The plump waluo woman in the cage didn't look like a prisoner. The cloth wound around her head and breasts, and the skirt she wore around her hips, were standard waluo women's fashion, but of clearly high quality. They sparkled with what looked like gemstones and were embroidered with vibrant patterns. Her green skin was glossy, as if she were shining. And she almost looked like she was wearing makeup.

She didn't act like a prisoner, either. She was calm, even dignified.

Besides, even though she was in the cage, she wasn't alone. Waluos came up onto the stage, one after another, to greet her. They spoke through the bars of the cage, sometimes holding her hand. Perhaps they were acquaintances of hers. But the woman was better dressed than any of them.

Haruhiro took a closer look at the gilded cage. The decorations on the four corners were... dragons? All the decorations were dragons. Dragons were scattered around the rest of the altar and covered the woman's clothing. The pattern on her skirt was a dragon, and on top of her cloth-wrapped head, she wore a dragon-like crown, too.

Now that he thought of it, Haruhiro realized all the decorations the waluo men had put up were dragons. The palace, he noticed, resembled a dragon, too. How had he missed it before? Waluandin was overflowing with dragon-based designs. There were dragons everywhere.

Haruhiro turned his eyes toward Fire Dragon Mountain, which looked ready to erupt at any moment. Like its name suggested, there was at least one dragon there: the fire dragon.

The waluos had built their city and now willingly lived at the foot of that mountain. The fire dragon ate salamanders, and Unjo said it had eaten his comrades. Could it be orcs didn't taste good to it? That was hard to imagine. The fire dragon had to be dangerous. Haruhiro didn't know why, but the waluos were living right next to that creature. They were *prospering* right next to it.

Perhaps the waluos worshipped the dreadful fire dragon. The fire dragon might be a god to them.

Right now, they filled the city with dragons in preparation for something. It might be a festival, with some ritual involved. Then what was the woman in the cage?

"No, she couldn't be a sacrifice, could she?" Haruhiro murmured.

The waluos kept visiting the woman in the cage. It looked like maybe they were saying their goodbyes. There was no air of tragedy to it, so perhaps it was an honor to be a sacrifice. Well, no, he wasn't *sure* she was a sacrifice yet, and there wasn't definitive proof they worshiped the fire dragon, either. Maybe Haruhiro's imagination was getting the better of him.

He couldn't help but think there was room for different possibilities, but if he speculated too much while scouting, he would make a careless mistake. He was going to have to leave when the night ended anyhow. Now was a good time to pull out, so he did.

For his return, he went back through the workshop district, like he had decided in advance. On the way back, he repeated, *Going in is easy, but getting out is scary.* It was easy to become hasty on the return trip and to let his guard down. It was better to stay overly cautious.

When he crossed into the workshop district, he felt the hairs on his neck stand on end. Haruhiro hurriedly ducked inside a nearby workshop. He sensed something, though he didn't know what. Should he hide, wait and see?

No. He decided to move.

Haruhiro kept his posture low and walked under Stealth. He couldn't hear his own footsteps, the rustling of his clothes, or even his breath. It was as if Haruhiro wasn't there. Was anyone else moving? He didn't see them. Had he imagined it? Not necessarily.

He focused. There was no issue with how he was walking.

He sensed something.

Is there someone, something, out there? Am I being watched?

Well, who cares, he decided.

If they were watching, let them watch. If they were going to come, let them come. If they got closer, he would know. He would be able to react. He had trained a lot during his solitary expeditions. It wasn't just for show.

Don't get conceited, he immediately warned himself. *Don't get carried away. Don't think you're doing well. Think you've got to try harder. Always give it your all.*

Haruhiro was already convinced. There was something out there, and it was watching him. Following from a distance. He could only call it a presence at this point, but he felt it. It was there constantly.

Not only that, but there was more than one of them. Usually behind him, sometimes to the right or the left, but always there. The presence right behind him was unchanging. It watched Haruhiro from a fixed distance. The other presence would close in, then move away. It vanished sometimes, too, but always came back.

It wasn't that he wasn't disturbed; Haruhiro was, and scared, too. However, they hadn't attacked yet. Nothing good would come from giving in to fear. He understood that, so he kept himself under control.

He leapt over the lava river from inside the Warehouse District, leaving Waluandin behind. He stopped after a bit, turning back.

The presences had vanished. Were they gone? He couldn't be sure yet. Haruhiro had stopped, so they could have stopped, too. If they had, it would be harder for Haruhiro to detect them. That might be all. It was too early to be relieved.

The villages had gone to sleep by this point, so he risked dashing through them.

Who were his pursuers? Waluos? That was likely. Humans had thieves like Haruhiro, so it wouldn't be strange for some orcs to specialize in thievery and stealth, too. Had a pair of waluos detected Haruhiro and decided to tail him, to discern his identity and motives? Well, it was probably something like that.

This was embarrassing. He had been worried after they'd killed the waluo hunters, but fortunately that had never been traced back to them. But if the waluos became aware of Haruhiro, they might become more cautious. If they put proper security in place, he wouldn't be able to get in and out of Waluandin, at least not the way he had been.

It was best to assume the waluos could prepare themselves to deal with enemies from outside. This was true of the orcs back in Grimgar, but the orcs of Waluandin were roughly as intelligent as humans. Though they were different, and there were a lot of things one couldn't accept about the other, neither side was superior or inferior. In Grimgar, humans had been defeated by the Alliance of Kings, which included orcs, and had been forced to withdraw to south of the Tenryu Mountains. For humans, orcs were an enemy more than equal to them.

He did his best not to enter the villages' fields. It was hard to call the footing there good. It would lower his speed, making it hard to respond quickly. He moved quickly down the thin paths that ran between the fields.

On the way, he felt the presences again, as expected. They had no intention of letting Haruhiro go.

He hadn't come up with all the details yet, but he had decided on a general plan. First, he'd probe the presences while getting out of the villages as quickly as possible. If they attacked, he'd have to flee immediately. Could he get away? There were too many unknown elements, and he couldn't be sure until he tried, but if it came down to it, he'd have to.

Ohh, this is scary.

He caught sight of moving shadows twice. He stopped sensing the pursuing presences once he entered the twisting path through the rift, but it was best not to assume they'd given up. It was incredibly difficult to keep a level head in this situation. It just wasn't going to happen.

Still, somehow, he managed to keep himself from panicking. That was pretty good. He wanted to praise himself for it. Well, no, not really. He wasn't safe yet. He should wait for safety before singing his own praises.

He came out of the rift and into the flat lands. He was almost back to the meeting point at the Hot Spring River.

Night wasn't over. His comrades were probably asleep, with one rotating guard. If it had been daytime, they would be hunting gujis, or perhaps heading to Alluja. Either work would make regrouping difficult, so it was best to think of this as good luck within bad luck.

Was it?

My stomach hurts, Haruhiro thought. *Nothing new there. Maybe I'm developing an ulcer? If I am, I guess we could treat it with light magic. Does it work on internal diseases like that? I dunno. I'll have to ask Merry.*

He was thinking things that didn't matter—proof that his concentration was breaking.

Haruhiro reapplied himself to the task at hand. He could see where the others were waiting.

Who stood guard? Shihoru, it seemed. Everyone else was lying down. Shihoru was the only one sitting.

Not good.

Haruhiro broke into a cold sweat. He felt an unpleasant feeling rising in his chest. Had he screwed up?

He'd practically led his pursuers back to his comrades. That might have been their aim all along. They'd discovered a suspicious individual, but they'd been sure he wasn't alone. They'd known others were out there somewhere. So, to catch them—or slaughter them—in one fell swoop, they'd tailed Haruhiro. That was why they had deliberately chosen not to attack him.

They had been letting him swim, so to speak. Now the enemy might leave Haruhiro for later and ambush his comrades as they slept.

What should he do? What was he going to do? There was no time for indecision. Haruhiro dashed forward.

"Shihoru! Wake everyone! Run away!"

"Huh... Haruhiro-kun?! Ah!" In great haste, Shihoru whacked Ranta in the head with her staff. "G-get up!"

"Ngahh?!" Ranta jumped up. "Wh-wh-what?! What're you doing?!"

"Whuh?" Yume rubbed her eyes as she sat up.

"Gah?!" Kuzaku shouted as he quickly got up.

"I'm gett—" Merry tried to run as soon as she woke up but tripped. "—Wah!"

Oh, man, Haruhiro thought frantically. *That made my heart race. No, now's not the time to be smitten with her. I've got bigger concerns. I mean, I might have bigger concerns.*

Haruhiro looked in every direction, running as he shouted, "We've got enemies! Run! Don't split up!"

"Yoink!" Yume pulled Merry to her feet, then shouldered her pack.

Merry said, "Thanks," and picked up her own things. Shihoru was already running.

Kuzaku took the lead, while Ranta drew RIPer.

"Enemies?! Where? I'll take them—" Ranta began.

Before Haruhiro could shout anything—

"Hold it!" he heard a familiar voice say.

"No." Haruhiro came to such a sudden stop, he nearly pitched over. He turned toward the voice.

Wait, what's a no? What's no? She's not a no, she's, uh, what was she again?

It came from behind him, to the right. The woman wearing a dark cloak and a wide-brimmed hat stepped out of the darkness. She immediately threw off her coat and hat, revealing herself to be—no matter how you looked at her—a dominatrix.

Why did she have to accentuate herself so expertly, exposing everything but the pieces she really shouldn't let them see? When she stuck her chest out, it was hard to look away.

She isn't a No, she's a La.

"Lala-san?" Haruhiro said slowly.

"Long time no see," Lala said with an amorous smile, licking her lips. "I'm surprised to see you alive."

"The ones who tailed me here from Waluandin...that was you and Nono-san?"

"Well, yes," said Lala. "Though I hadn't expected you to notice. Nono!"

The man appeared from the direction of the rifts. He was white-haired, with a black mask covering the lower half of his face.

Nono came up next to Lala and got down on all fours. Lala sat down on Nono's back, crossing her legs.

"So? What were you up to in the orc city, right before the Fire Dragon Festival?"

"Festyfull?" Yume cocked her head to the side in confusion.

"H-hold on!" Ranta had nearly returned his sword to its sheath, but he readied it again. "Haruhiro, they're the enemies you meant, right?! Just because they're human, and we know them, doesn't mean they're on our side! These guys abandoned us once before!"

"Abandoned you?" Lala snorted. "Did we do that?"

"Y-y-yeah! You left us behind and took off on your own, didn't you?! I haven't forgotten!"

"That wasn't our intention, but even if it were, why bring that up now? You're such a tight-ass. I can't even work up the motivation to train you and expand it."

"E-expand it..." Shihoru stuttered.

Um, Shihoru, Haruhiro thought. Why was she, of all people, the one to react to that?

"Shut up!" Ranta was whining. "Listen, we've had a real hard time since then! We've been through a lot! We didn't know left from right, and it was really tough!"

"It was the same for us," said Lala.

"S-still! I understand what you're saying, but still!"

"Ranta-kun," Kuzaku whispered to him. "Politely. You're talking to her politely."

"You're imagining it, moron! Dumbass! You're too big for your own good, damn it!"

Merry looked at Haruhiro. *What do we do now?* her expression asked.

Haruhiro rubbed his lower back, subtly placing a finger on the hilt of his stiletto. "I don't really think you abandoned us. No... none of us do. Except for the idiot. It's probably some kind of sign that we met up again like this. I'd like to trade information."

Of course, if Lala and Nono tried to harm Haruhiro and the party, or intended to use them, he wouldn't stop there.

"We feel the same way, of course." Lala narrowed her eyes, touching her own lips playfully. "You're a strange one. Haruhiro, was it? You've got a good face."

"I get told I have sleepy eyes." Haruhiro had to work to keep his expression straight. *She sees right through me.* "So, what's this about a Fire Dragon Festival?"

"You saw them preparing for it, didn't you?" Lala asked. "We don't know how often yet, but they hold it relatively frequently.

It's a big ritual where they offer a sacrifice of an orc to the fire dragon. The whole city celebrates. The Fire Dragon Festival is just our name for it. We're not sure what they call it. It's too bad, really. Looks like we can't make friends with the orcs."

"Sacrifices and rituals, you say...?" Ranta sheathed his sword and knelt. It looked like he was getting ready in case he had to kowtow. What was with that guy?

"So, uh...basically they're....you know," Haruhiro said. "They're offering a sacrifice to the fire dragon? Seriously?"

"That's what she said," Shihoru said in a low voice filled with revulsion.

You can say that again, thought Haruhiro.

So was that it? The Fire Dragon Festival. The sacrifice. The streets packed with revelers.

Maybe, just maybe, could this be it? Could it be what, exactly?

Could it be their chance, maybe? Their chance at what?

That was obvious. If they took this opportunity, they might actually make it. The thought occurred to him. He'd gone and done it now.

Everyone could charge through Waluandin and reach Fire Dragon Mountain. They could search for the cave, then maybe they could return through it.

"Looks like you've got some useful information." Lala put on a sensuous smile and motioned for Haruhiro to come closer with one finger. "Tell Lala-sama everything. You might just get a lovely reward for it, you know?"

Grimgar

of

Fantasy *and* Ash

19 | Over the Rainbow

ALL THE ORCs had decorative cloth tied over one shoulder and wore red and black body paint. Men and women, young and old.

Orcs beat on drums and played stringed instruments. Orcs blew on flutes. They clapped their hands, stamped their feet, and sang in unison.

The orcs carrying sticks with dragon designs weren't singing; they chanted instead, saying something in loud voices. The way they spoke in rhythm, making gestures with hands and body, gave the impression of a speech or directions to the musicians and singers.

They were wonderfully lively, and though it felt like it could fall apart at any moment, for the moment they were unified. They may have been wild, but they were by no means crude. The event was highly refined. Beautiful, even. Overwhelming to watch and listen to.

No, Haruhiro thought, *shaking his head in the shadow of a giant caterpillar enclosure's fence. Don't listen. Sure, it's incredible. I know it's worth hearing. It feels like something I have to listen to, but I can't. This isn't the time to be falling in love with a song.*

Haruhiro poked his head out from behind the fence to get another look at the orcs celebrating in the central plaza. It was noon, but alcohol was already flowing. The children were worked up, too. Thankfully, he was more than twenty meters from the plaza. Even during the day, they wouldn't be able to see him. There was no way they would spot him.

Haruhiro waved his hand, motioning to the others in the rear. Then he gave the signal for Lala and Nono. There was a momentary incident where Yume whacked Ranta, who had been staring off into the distance, over the head. When he tried to complain, Merry clubbed him with her hammer staff. But nothing came of it. Everyone kept low and came this way.

In Kuzaku's case, his armor clanged loudly as he moved. But the noise of the festival covered it, which made this a good arrangement.

Haruhiro nodded, then moved to the next point. He confirmed it was safe, then called over his comrades plus Lala and Nono. It was boring and repetitive work, so he was a little surprised when not just his comrades but also Lala and Nono did as instructed without a word. There was no telling when those two would turn on him, though.

Lala had a pocket watch, so they could mark the time with relative precision. The raucous festival had begun three hours after the flameset. Haruhiro and the others had entered the village area one hour later, then spent an hour and a half making their way to Waluandin.

Incidentally, the time from flamerise to flameset was roughly ten to fifteen hours, and the time from flameset to flamerise was also ten to fifteen hours. There was variation in the length of the day and night, but if you added them together, they were around twenty-five hours. So, a day in Darunggar was one hour longer than a day in Grimgar.

Regardless, in another hour and a half, they would be out of the village area, or so he thought when the next incident occurred.

Oh, crap, thought Haruhiro, *It's a dragon.*

The dragon was coming from Waluandin!

To be more precise, it was a dragon model.

It was over three meters high and ten meters long, painted red and black like the orcs' bodies. Its two eye sockets were filled with sparkling yellow gems. Its neck, jaw, body, tail, and four limbs were movable, and more than thirty orcs in black costumes were carrying and manipulating it with sticks.

When the portable dragon came, the village orcs got super excited. This was probably another part of the Fire Dragon Festival. The singing and playing of instruments increased. The voices of the ones holding the dragon sticks grew louder. The orc children ran away in fear. The portable dragon chased them, and some of the children cried and wailed. The women who were presumably their mothers laughed as they soothed their children.

Ranta was clearly itching to join the festivities, but that was out of the question. Haruhiro moved on toward Waluandin. If things were this lively in the villages, there was no way they'd be discovered in the city. That was their aim, and the reason they had waited for the Fire Dragon Festival to start.

The villages were noisy wherever they went, but the noise was concentrated in certain places. All the farmer orcs from throughout the villages were gathered in plaza areas with their families. They sang, played instruments, enjoyed the portable dragon when it was brought to them, and got totally smashed. Everywhere else was deserted, not a person or orc in sight. Even so, Haruhiro didn't relax. He made sure not to rush, always taking the proper steps before moving forward. He was so thorough that even he got exasperated with himself.

Waluandin was boiling over with festive spirit. It seemed to be a holiday, so there was no sign of waluos in the workshop district or the mine. The blacksmiths' workshops had warehouses. He found one that was not too big and not too small, used Picking on the lock, and decided to use it to lay low temporarily.

Ranta, Shihoru, Yume, Merry, Kuzaku, and Lala went on standby. When Haruhiro and Nono split up to do some scouting, they found the situation in Waluandin was roughly the same as in the villages. The waluos were concentrated on the main streets, singing, performing, dancing, and making a ruckus. Every waluo wore decorative cloth and body paint, and one in every twenty to thirty carried one of those dragon sticks in full festive attire.

There was food and drink everywhere, and the waluos seemed free to take any of it.

Haruhiro headed back to where his comrades were hiding, masking his footsteps and walking down the back alleyways. There were no orcs to be seen. Every house was empty. That said, there could still be waluos who were at home for some reason. He couldn't let his guard down. Haruhiro made sure he was on task as he entered the alley.

He gulped.

There was a waluo, clearly very young and still thin, crouching there. He held his head with both hands. He wore body paint, but he had taken off his cloth, which was a tangled mess at his feet.

What do I do? What do I do? What do I do? Haruhiro asked himself that more than ten times in the span of a second. He found his answer. Haruhiro decided to turn back quietly.

That was the exact moment the orc looked in his direction.

The young waluo inhaled sharply, the start of a scream. Haruhiro's body moved on its own. He jumped on the orc, pushed him to the ground and strangled him.

If he did it while standing, he might strike his head or some other part of his body on the wall or ground as the waluo struggled and thrashed around. If he pinned him first, well, he was more or less safe. Haruhiro's right arm tightly wrapped around the waluo's neck. He braced his right arm with his left so it wouldn't be easy to break free.

The waluo tried to scratch at Haruhiro's face with both hands, but he managed to defend himself.

I can do this, Haruhiro told himself. *It looks like this will work. Okay... He's out.*

The waluo passed out with fangs bared. The strength had fully drained from his body. There was no mistaking it. This wasn't an act; he was out cold.

Haruhiro rolled him over and then got up. He was about to leave, but then—

No, no, no. Haruhiro shook his head. *Isn't this bad? I mean, sure, he's unconscious. He'll probably be out for a while. But I can't just leave him like this, right? I have to do something. Make it so he can't move? Tie him up? Or...make it so he never wakes back up? Like, snuff him?*

"Damn it." Haruhiro pressed his palm to his forehead.

I don't know what to do. I'm torn. I'm hesitating. This waluo was all alone, even though it's the middle of the Fire Dragon Festival. Why was he all alone in a place like this? Was he bad with groups? A loner? Maybe he was being bullied? That could be why. None of it matters. He saw me. It'd be dangerous to let him live. I'll kill him. Just a quick stab. Time to do it.

With that deed done, Haruhiro left the alley. He hurried back toward their hiding place.

Don't let it shake me up. Stealth, Stealth. Concentrate. It happened once, it could happen again. I might encounter another waluo. It's fine. I handled that appropriately. It's fine. No problem. Good grief. Things like that can happen. Man, he surprised me. I've gotta be more careful. Of course. I'll be careful, okay? I'm gonna be real damn careful. Obviously. That goes without saying. Geez.

Haruhiro turned and looked back. Nono was there, standing like a corpse, if corpses stood. Haruhiro was often told he had sleepy eyes, but Nono had a dead man's eyes. Was he looking at Haruhiro? There was no way to tell.

Haruhiro bowed to him and raised one hand a little. "Hey there."

Nono's head twisted to the right, and then slowly back to the left. His expression didn't change. Or rather, because of the mask, Haruhiro couldn't read it at all.

Um, you're kinda scary.

"Erm... You wanna go back?" When Haruhiro hesitantly pointed to the hideout, Nono nodded. He knew the man didn't talk, but Haruhiro couldn't help but think, *Say something!* Maybe the harness-like mask prevented him from speaking.

It was strangely tense returning with Nono. When had Nono gotten behind him? Had Haruhiro turned because he'd noticed Nono's presence? Or was it because he'd been vague? He couldn't be sure.

They finally reached their warehouse hideout. Nothing seemed out of the ordinary. When they entered, Ranta, who was sitting in the corner, jumped up. "Hey!"

That was when it happened.

Nono suddenly grabbed him by the neck.

It was a surprise. He hadn't seen it coming, so he couldn't dodge. Even if he had been ready for it, Haruhiro wasn't sure he could have avoided it.

Nono pressed his masked mouth close to Haruhiro's ear. His

voice was muffled, almost like a groan. It was hard to make out what he was saying, but for some reason Haruhiro knew very clearly what he meant.

When Haruhiro responded, "Got it," Nono let him go.

Nono walked over to Lala and immediately got down on all fours. He'd just gotten back, but he was already a chair again. Lala gave him no words of gratitude. Instead she sat on Nono's back, as if that were perfectly normal, and crossed her legs. She seemed satisfied.

Haruhiro walked over to the others, dragging his feet like a corpse.

"Wh-what was that about?" Shihoru asked worriedly.

"Nothing." Haruhiro shook his head. "It's nothing, really."

"Did he say something to you?" Ranta indicated Nono with a glance. "Hold on, can that guy even talk? Well, I guess he must be able to."

"Don't call him 'that guy,'" Haruhiro corrected without much strength. "It's Nono-san, okay?"

"S-sure," Ranta said. "Hold on, pal, are you okay? You're acting weird, you know? Did something happen?"

"Ha ha, if you're worried about me, I'm probably done for."

"You're one rude guy, you know that?" Ranta snapped. "I may not look it, but I'm full of love, okay? I'm the Dread Knight of Love, got it?"

"You love Haruhiro?" Merry asked, sounding annoyed.

"Y-y-you moron, of course not! That's not what I'm saying!"

"It's not just any love, it's romantic love, huh?" Yume snickered.

"I don't love him, romantically or otherwise, damn it! That's obvious, you moron! Damn it!"

Kuzaku let out a short laugh. "When you're so desperate to deny it, that makes me more suspicious."

"I'll make mincemeat out of you, Kuzacky! Seriously, seriously! Don't make light of a dread knight!"

"Hey," Lala spoke up. "You, the monkey over there. You're annoying. Be quiet."

Ranta immediately stood ramrod straight and saluted her. His mouth moved but no voice came out. *Sir, yes, sir!* It looked like, at some point, he'd been fully trained by Lala.

Terrifying.

Honestly, she was terrifying. Haruhiro shuddered. It wasn't just Lala. Nono was, too. What he'd done a moment ago, that was terrifying.

What Nono had said to Haruhiro rang in his ears:

"If Lala-sama gets so much as a scratch because of you people, I'll kill every last one of you."

That was it.

It wasn't an idle threat. Nono had been serious. Besides, the guy didn't look normal. And he was hyper competent. If Nono decided to kill them all, he could do it without them managing to move so much as an eyebrow to defend themselves.

The question was, why had Nono chosen that moment to tell Haruhiro? It wasn't like no ideas came to mind, but he didn't want to think about it. It wasn't a thing Haruhiro could do anything about by thinking. He decided to forget the matter for now.

There were other things that needed thinking about. Lots and lots of other things.

The party left the warehouse. They went out of the workshop district and passed through the residential area beyond it. Haruhiro led the way, checking that everything was safe before calling everyone over, the same as before. They were avoiding the festival areas, so there were few waluos passing by. Still, he had to be careful of stray ones. Even if he thought there were none, nothing was absolute. That said, if he was too timid, they wouldn't move at all. If they were found, or if they found a waluo, they would just have to deal with it immediately. He had to accept it. Nothing was perfect.

Right?

His stomach hurt. He sweated like crazy. His throat was dry. The road coming up next was a big one. But when he'd scouted it earlier, it'd seemed they could cross it without incident.

He poked his head out a little. No waluos. He gave the signal, then crossed the road first. His comrades, along with Lala and Nono, followed.

They were still in the residential area, but the slope got steeper here. It was a pretty sharp climb. It was hard to see the top from the bottom, but there was a good view from above. He had to skillfully hide himself as he advanced.

His stomach really hurt. He was aging a year for every second that went by. He couldn't help feeling that way.

Instead of heading straight toward Fire Dragon Mountain, he chose side streets as much as possible. No matter what kind of road they took, he made sure to check it thoroughly before entering. He had to be sure that, no matter what happened, he didn't lose his head.

He was straining himself. Pushing his whole body.

Don't force it, he told himself. *Stay calm, stay calm.*

He couldn't do it. His heart felt ready to break into a thousand pieces. He was barely holding himself together, with guts, or pure stubbornness. Something like that. That was the condition he was in, but Haruhiro probably had sleepy eyes and looked disinterested as he did his job. He didn't know if that was a good or a bad thing. Either way, he wasn't at his limit yet.

I can manage.

Since that last time, he hadn't seen a waluo. Maybe they would make it through Waluandin just like this? Whenever he thought it would be easy, something bad happened. Well, his harsher predictions also tended to come true, so maybe it would be the same no matter which way he leaned.

"The sound of the drums. Isn't it kind of close?" Ranta asked.

Even before Ranta mentioned it, Haruhiro had noticed the noise. Lala and Nono had to have been aware of it well ahead of him. Yet they'd said nothing.

Once again, Haruhiro was reminded he couldn't trust them. He didn't know if they were evil, but Lala and Nono only ever thought about themselves. They accompanied Haruhiro and the others because, at the moment, they had decided they were worth using. If that changed, they would abandon the party without hesitation. Use them as sacrificial pawns, if need be. They wouldn't even feel guilty about it.

To be fair, Haruhiro and his comrades worked with them because it benefited them, too. So, in a sense, they were even. Well,
sort of. If he had to, he wasn't sure if he could abandon Lala and
Nono. He'd probably have a hard time bringing himself to do it.
Was he being naive? He might be.

Haruhiro had the others wait while he clambered up onto
the roof of a nearby building. When he got to the top, he saw
columns of lights that he assumed were torches moving around
Waluandin. One column was less than one hundred meters away.
That was close, all things considered.

What do we do?

Haruhiro came down from the roof. How should he explain
it? His head wasn't working right.

When he just stood there, Ranta rounded on him. "What're
you staring off into space for?! What's up, man?! What's going
on?! Haruhiro! I'm asking you a question, so say something, you
balding idiot!"

"We may be in trouble."

"In trouble how?!"

"They may be searching for us."

"Searching for us? Wait, whaaaaaaaaaaaaaaaa?!"

"Ranta's been talkin' real loud for a while now, after all," Yume
said.

"Shut it, Tiny Tits! Just shut up! We're having an important
conversation here!"

"Why would they be looking for us?" Shihoru asked.

It was a perfectly reasonable question. From his comrades'

perspective, it must have been a mystery. However, it wasn't a mystery to Haruhiro. In fact, he had it mostly figured out. He didn't want it to be true, but he assumed it was.

"We need to run," Merry said as if trying to convince herself. She looked at her comrades. "Whatever the cause or reason, it can wait."

"Sounds about right." Kuzaku nodded. "We should run before we're found."

"Where're we gonna run to?!" Ranta shouted. "We're pretty deep inside Waluandin, you know?! You think there's anywhere for us to run here?!"

"No need to run." Lala licked her red lips, then pointed to Fire Dragon Mountain. "For the orcs of Waluandin, Fire Dragon Mountain is probably sacred land. They wouldn't chase us there, would they?"

Nono fixed a contemptuous look on Haruhiro.

S-Scary, Haruhiro thought. *He's totally pissed. They're on to me, damn it.*

Or at the very least, Nono knew. He knew who it was who'd brought them to this.

Yes. That was right. It was Haruhiro's fault. Probably. Almost certainly. Haruhiro would have given eight to nine out of ten odds he was to blame.

He hadn't killed the young orc. He hadn't been able to do it. He'd bound him hand and foot, gagged him, and left him there.

Do I have to tell them? Haruhiro wondered. They were short on time, right? Maybe not now. Still, why didn't Nono condemn him for it? No matter how Haruhiro looked at it, this was a crisis he had caused. Lala was in danger, too. So why didn't he?

Because Nono didn't want to talk? Would he rather kill Haruhiro first and lay blame later? Was he looking for the opportunity?

It didn't matter. Whatever the reason, it didn't change the fact they needed to hurry.

Merry was right. Whatever cause or reason, that could wait.

"Let's go! To Fire Dragon Mountain!" Haruhiro directed.

The waluos beat their drums, swung their torches, and shouted as they searched for Haruhiro and the others. Even at a rough count, the number of torches reached triple digits. What was more, the walios weren't all necessarily carrying torches. It could be one every ten, or even less than that.

It was best to assume there was ten times as many searching as there were torches. That put their numbers over a thousand, possibly multiple thousands of waluos hunting for Haruhiro and the others.

Haruhiro did what he could to lead the group, but Nono went on ahead of him. He had to follow. He couldn't say, *Leave this to me.* Nono would probably kill him. Besides, he felt like he'd mess up again.

It was best to put what happened with the young waluo out of his mind for now. He knew that, but he couldn't forget it. Honestly, Haruhiro didn't have any confidence in his decision-making ability right now.

Right now? What about in future? Was he ever going to be

able to say, *Okay, I'm good now*? He couldn't see it happening.

Nono advanced smoothly, sometimes going straight without hesitation, sometimes turning, sometimes heading down alleyways. How could he keep going without hesitation like that? Every once in a while, Lala would call out to him from the rear, telling him to go right or left or straight. Was it thanks to Lala? If he was going the wrong way, would Lala correct him? If he messed up, would Lala cover for him? Did they trust each other like that?

What about Haruhiro? Did he believe in his comrades? It wasn't that he didn't believe in them, it was just, well, that—

"Stop!" Lala shouted. A band of waluos had appeared in front of them.

The waluos were over two meters tall and wearing body paint, so they were frightening to look at. Haruhiro's heart jumped, causing a sharp, intense pain to run through his chest.

Nono attacked the lead waluo. Kuzaku readied his shield and charged in. Ranta followed.

Nono used his right-hand knife to cut open the first waluo's neck in the blink of an eye, then sprang at the next. Kuzaku smashed into one with his shield, probably meaning to knock him down. The enemy, however, was bigger and managed to hold firm. Ranta slashed at the waluo carrying the torch, but though he'd managed to drive him back, he hadn't dealt a serious wound.

Haruhiro grabbed the hilt of his stiletto, adjusted his grip, and then held it tight.

Oh, crap. Oh, crap. This was not good. No. He was standing bolt upright, his legs like sticks.

What was he doing? Nothing. Haruhiro was doing nothing.

He looked around. Looked and thought. Well, he pretended to think. The truth was, he wasn't thinking a thing.

"This way!" Lala shouted.

The moment he heard Lala, Haruhiro was incredibly relieved. She pointed to an alley a little way back the way they had come.

He sent Yume, Shihoru, and Merry on ahead, then waited for Ranta, who had turned and run, and Kuzaku, who was slowly pulling back while using his shield to block a waluo's kicks. Nono used martial arts techniques of varying speed along with his knife to great effect. He was stalling the waluos. He wasn't big, and all he had was a short knife, but he ran circles around the waluos. How could he pull off a trick like that?

Now wasn't the time to stare in admiration.

Ranta went into the alley. Kuzaku hadn't managed it yet. There was a waluo harassing him.

I've got to do something, thought Haruhiro. *That's right. I've got to. I need to do that much at least. Do it.*

Haruhiro raced past Kuzaku and the waluo, then made a sudden turn and slammed a Backstab into him. He'd been aiming for the kidney by going through his back, but the stiletto didn't reach the organ.

The waluo turned.

Kuzaku hit it in the jaw with Bash, then followed up with a Thrust using his black blade. There was no need for them to say, *Let's go.* They headed for the alley together. Nono followed them, too.

To the alley.

It was narrow, maybe only about a meter across. Lala was there, elegantly pointing to the right. Why hadn't Lala abandoned them? What was Nono thinking?

It didn't matter. Not now. He'd shut up and do as Lala said. It was his only choice, the best thing to do. After all, Haruhiro couldn't handle it himself. He had no plan for getting them out of this. He could only run around blindly.

Lala was different. She showed no signs of panicking. Nono was the same way. They were calm. Like always.

I've gotta be like that, thought Haruhiro. He wanted to be like that, but could he? Well, probably not. There was no way. He could work at it his whole life, and he'd never be like Lala and Nono.

When they came out onto a large cobblestone road, they got a good view of Waluandin in its entirety. They were at a high elevation, already on the far edge of Waluandin. The waluos pressed in on them from the far end of the road.

"Aha!" Lala laughed. "Slowpokes! We've won!"

Had they really? Lala took the lead, racing up the big road on the hill.

Ranta shouted, "This is so damn cool!"

The waluos had caught Haruhiro and the others now. This road stretched from the palace district, meandering as it went all the way to Fire Dragon Mountain. How did he know? Torches lit up the path, and he could see how it wound and moved toward the mountain.

There was an incredible number of waluos.

If Kikkawa had been here, he might have called it "tally-to some-awe." Yeah, maybe not.

Haruhiro missed Kikkawa. He was supposedly all right. Would they meet again? There wasn't much hope of it. He couldn't help but feel that way.

A muddy stream. With their body paint and decorative cloths, the waluos swinging around their dragon sticks and torches formed a muddy stream that surged backward up the road in an attempt to swallow up Haruhiro and the others. It was hard to tell how many meters were between Nono at the rear of the group and the waluos, but it had to be less than ten.

Nono could shake them if he got serious. But Shihoru and Kuzaku would have had trouble, and Merry didn't seem like she'd have an easy time avoiding them, either. It was only a matter of time now; they all felt it in the air.

Were they out of moves? Was this the end?

It was all Haruhiro's fault. He had ended it.

I'm sorry. I'm sorry, guys. I'm really sorry. It was me. It was my fault. I'm the one to blame. All of it. Me. What can I do to get you to forgive me? Yeah, nothing, I'll bet. Of course not. I mean, it's my fault, after all! No one else is to blame. It's all on me!

Haruhiro ran as fast as he could, crying and screaming despite himself. He didn't turn back. He only looked ahead. He was scared. He didn't want to see anything or know anything.

Enough. It was over anyway. Because of Haruhiro, it was all over. They were all going to die. They'd be beaten to a bloody pulp. Brutally killed.

It was strange. No matter how much time passed, it didn't happen. It should have been any moment now, but Haruhiro was still alive.

He passed between two stone pillars with a dragon motif. He'd finally left the city. The steep cobblestone road continued, but there were no more buildings. The rocky mountain spread out on either side, and not so much as a single tree grew. Here and there, lava spurted up as if from a pulsing vein with a puff of smoke.

"They're not comin' after us!" Yume cried, her voice full of cheer.

I see that. Haruhiro wiped sweat, tears, snot, and saliva from his face as he turned back. The waluos were there. They hadn't turned back. But they had stopped at the stone pillars, as if some invisible dam held them back.

Sacred land. Fire Dragon Mountain was sacred land to the orcs of Waluandin, so they wouldn't chase them here. That had been Lala's read on the situation, and in the end, it had been spot on.

Lala had won them a calculated victory. Not just Nono, but Ranta, Yume, Shihoru, Merry, and Kuzaku might all have hope now.

Haruhiro was the only one who didn't.

He was alone in his despair.

He'd panicked so badly he'd lost the ability to think straight. He was incredibly embarrassed. He wanted to just disappear. He didn't want to live in shame any longer.

The road turned into stone steps. It was so steep that, had they not been on a staircase, they would have tumbled down. When they got past that incline, it leveled out to near flatness. The road came to an abrupt end.

"Oofwhah!" Ranta let out an odd exclamation. "There! There they are! Those're salamanders, right?! Hold on, how are they okay in that molten lava?!"

From there, there were real ups and downs in the mountain slope, and rivers and springs of lava bubbled up. The salamanders floated in the lava, swimming and jumping around in it.

Actually, if he had to describe them, the salamanders looked like clumps of molten lava shaped like lizards. When they weren't moving, they were indistinguishable from lava. That was why Haruhiro had no idea how many salamanders there were. It was possible that all the lava was salamanders. Well, that was probably not true, but he couldn't deny the possibility.

"Let's take it a little more carefully from here," Lala said quietly, as if they hadn't been careful up until this point.

What kind of nerves did she have? Or was she just putting up a strong front? No, that couldn't be it. She had nerves of steel.

Nono stood in the front, checking his footing as he moved. Lala went second, and behind her went Ranta, Kuzaku, Merry, Shihoru, Yume. Haruhiro brought up the rear. They hadn't discussed it beforehand; it had just ended up that way. Probably because Haruhiro hadn't done or said anything, everyone assumed he meant to bring up the rear.

Haruhiro hadn't been thinking anything, but he had no complaints. If anything, he was grateful. He was happy to be in the back; the back was great. He didn't feel anyone's eyes on him. He couldn't be a leader in this state anyway.

"The reason we had our eyes on this place," Lala explained, without anyone asking her to, "was because of the orcs. They're in Grimgar, too. As a general rule, when a race exists in two different worlds, you can assume those worlds are connected. Based on our experience, if a race has put down roots in a specific place, there's usually a path between them. Though, in many cases, there's a reason they can't go back and forth."

"There's a fire dragon here." Shihoru held her hat down as she fearfully jumped across a thin stream of lava.

Immediately after she did, a salamander hopped out, nearly touching Shihoru's leg.

"Ohhh!"

"Y'think there really is a fire dragon?" Yume easily jumped over. Of course, the salamander jumped again, too. Yume easily cleared both the lava and the salamander. "It's too quiet here, after all."

Haruhiro ran up and jumped as hard as he could, trying not to look at the stream or the salamander. He had to say something. It was strange for him to stay quiet. But what could he say? It wasn't like he didn't have things he should be saying. If he said it, though, what would happen? He didn't know. He didn't want to imagine it.

"Y'think that's the summit there?" Kuzaku pointed to the left in front of them.

There was a dark mountainous shape in that direction. How far was it? A few hundred meters ahead? More?

"Hold on." Ranta came to a sudden stop. "Haruhiro. You were saying something earlier, weren't you, pal? Back in Waluandin. Also, man, were you crying? Was I just imagining that?"

Haruhiro just shook his head. He didn't answer. When he tried to keep going, Ranta pushed aside their comrades to close in on Haruhiro.

"You were saying something, something about how it was because of you. What'd that mean? Like, you said it was all your fault. You're acting weird, too, you know? I mean, I know you're weird most of the time. You've got those sleepy eyes and all. But, even so, you're not acting normal. Man, what's gotten into you?"

"Later," Haruhiro whispered.

"Huhh?"

"I'll tell you later. I promise I will. For now, it...it doesn't matter."

"It does matter." Ranta grabbed Haruhiro by the collar. "There's no way it doesn't! Don't give me that crap! Listen, man, there's nothing I hate more than things being kept vague like this!"

"That's why I said I'd tell you later! Think about the situation!"

"What situation? You're not getting out of this! When I decide to do something, I do it! I'm gonna chase you down and get the truth out of you no matter what it takes!"

"Ranta, stop!" Yume tried to interpose herself between them.

That pushed Haruhiro backward. "Ah!" He lost his footing, and where he had stepped to catch his balance was a pool of lava. His foot didn't land right in it, but his heel brushed the lava. It sizzled and burned. "Urgh!"

"H-Haru-kun?!" Yume cried.

"No, I'm... I'm fine." Haruhiro crouched down and rubbed his heel. He had pulled his foot out immediately, so he didn't think it was anything major. That was what he hoped, anyway. He traced the outline of his boot with his fingers. The heel seemed kind of melted. Was it just the boot? What about the inside? It felt painful, and kind of hot.

"I-I'm not gonna apologize, okay!" Ranta said arrogantly. "Th-th-that was Yume's fault, and your own! I'm not in the wrong here, not one insignificant bit!"

"You're insignificant," Shihoru murmured.

"Huh?! What was that, you rotten saggy titty bomber?!"

"R-Rotten, s-saggy?!"

"Haru! Let me look!" Merry pushed past Shihoru, Yume, and Ranta and crouched next to Haruhiro.

Lala shrugged, looking at them in utter amazement. Nono brought his face close to Lala and whispered something in her ear. He might have been pressing her to make a choice. *Isn't it about time we abandoned them,* maybe?

That wasn't good. Not good at all. The party needed them, or they'd be in trouble.

"Whoa, wai—" Haruhiro pushed Merry aside as she tried to heal him and stood up. The pain shot through his right heel, and he let out a bizarre little shriek of pain.

"Huh?" Kuzaku said, which was incredibly strange. "The summit moved?"

"Mountains don't move," Lala said with a joyous purr in her

voice for some reason. "That's no mountain, is it?"

"I-If it isn't..." Ranta turned and looked up at the summit. No, the thing they had thought was the summit. "Wh-what is that thing...?"

It shook left and right and made a sound, almost like it was vibrating. Or rather, like the ground was shaking.

The ground *was* shaking. The thing was approaching.

"Run!" Haruhiro shouted reflexively.

"Wh-which way?!" Ranta shouted back.

"I don't know which—"

Which way? Where would they run? Back the way they came? How far? Could they go down the mountain? They couldn't flee into Waluandin. That was obvious. What should they do? How could he know? Haruhiro naturally tried to cling to Lala and Nono.

They were gone.

They had been there until just a moment ago. No. He could see their backs. They were moving on. He'd lost sight of them for a moment when the shadow of a boulder blocked his view. They were already more than fifteen meters away.

"A-after them! Follow those two! Hurry!"

"Damn it! That bitch!" Ranta shouted.

"Shihoru, go on ahead!" Yume cried. "Yume's gonna be right there behind you!"

"Y-yeah! Got it!"

"Merry-san, you go, too!"

"Okay! Haru, can you run?!"

"I-I can, yeah! Now hurry! Kuzaku, you too!"

"'Kay!"

The tremors grew larger and more violent. Haruhiro desperately chased after Kuzaku's back. When his heel touched down, pain shot all the way to the top of his head. All he could do was avoid putting his heel on the ground by running on the balls of his feet. It wasn't easy, by any means.

With the weight of their gear and possessions factored in, Haruhiro was usually the fastest, or the second fastest runner, in the party. Kuzaku was the slowest. Today, that wasn't the case. Not only was he not catching up to Kuzaku, he was being left behind.

Kuzaku would look back, slow down, and wait for Haruhiro. He was so happy he could cry, but it was no solution. Even when he closed the gap a little, it quickly opened back up. Sometimes, it got worse.

He suddenly lost sight of Kuzaku. Had he finally given up on him? No, that couldn't be it. Haruhiro passed through a narrow gap between two boulders and came out into a more open space.

Everyone was there. Even Lala and Nono, though they were off in the distance.

Kuzaku turned back, looking at Haruhiro, and then at something further up.

Kuzaku let out an ominous silent cry.

Haruhiro felt like he was being told about the end of the world.

He couldn't decide. Should he see it for himself, or was it best not to? Before he could decide, his eyes were drawn toward it. He didn't wish he hadn't seen it. He wasn't glad that he had seen it. He was just dumbfounded.

He had encountered his fair share of terrifying living creatures, like the giant god in the Dusk Realm. Well, there was room to debate on whether that had been living or not, but it had been huge.

This thing wasn't bigger than them like the giant god had been. But there was something in its eyes that made him feel a special, deep kind of emotion. They weren't beautiful. They weren't pretty.

In a word. There were terrifying. Absolutely terrifying.

That was the word, but that was certainly not all they were.

Its body was covered with reddish scales, or perhaps black scales with a red luster. It was almost similar to a reptile in that respect. In fact, it might have been fair to call it a giant lizard, but after the scales, it was very different. It walked on four legs, but its front legs also looked like they could grab things. It had surprisingly dexterous hands. Its neck was long, and its head rather small, but it was probably still large enough to swallow a person whole.

It wasn't fat and moved quickly for its overall large size. If it ran as fast as those powerful rear legs would take it, it would out pace them easily. It didn't look slow-witted either. It lifted its long tail, stretching it out.

That's a dragon.

Most likely, even if they hadn't known that dragons existed, anyone would know this creature was one. If someone had been told this was a dragon, they would accept it immediately. Even

though they didn't know what dragons were, they would no doubt think, *Oh, I see, so that's a dragon.* Dragons had to be engraved in everyone's instincts.

It was little wonder the orcs of Waluandin worshiped it. It was easy to understand why they wanted to offer it sacrifices.

Haruhiro trembled. This fear wasn't something he felt normally. However, it was something he couldn't help but feel.

Dragons are awesome.

Honestly, it *was* cool. Creatures like this existed. In a way, it was perfect. Now it may not be clear what way that was, but it was awesome.

Dragon.

The fire dragon opened its maw, twisted its neck, and inhaled. Was it taking a breath? He didn't know what was happening, but Haruhiro watched it intently. He was honestly entranced by it. There were little lights flickering in the back of the fire dragon's throat.

What are those? he wondered. That was all he thought.

"Uwahhhhhhhhhhhhhhh!" When he heard Ranta's scream, he began to suspect he was lacking the proper sense of crisis here. He looked and saw his comrades making a mad dash to get away. They were like herbivores fleeing from a pack of wolves. Of course, Ranta and the others were no herbivores, and there were no wolves on this mountain. There were only salamanders and the fire dragon Ranta and the others were trying to get away from.

Well, yeah, of course they're running.

Why was Haruhiro just standing there? That was strange.

The fire dragon inhaled, and inhaled, and inhaled. Finally, it exhaled. No, it wasn't breathing out, or was that what the fire dragon's breath was like?

Haruhiro rolled backward. The hot mass that assaulted him left him unable to stand.

Fire. True, honest flames. The fire dragon spewed fire. He thought he might have been burned. It was hot enough he wouldn't have been surprised if he melted away.

How much time had passed? A few seconds? A few minutes? More than that? He didn't know.

Haruhiro lay on his side like a dried-out caterpillar. Literally. Steam rose from all over his body, his skin cracked and dried until it was quite honestly crispy and crunchy. His eyes, his nose, and his mouth were all dry. His skin looked ready to crack apart. He was scared to even blink, if he didn't blink or work out some tears, something seriously bad would happen to his eyes. He knew it.

The same went for his mouth and nose. His body needed to use all its remaining water to moisten them, or he was in serious trouble.

He didn't seem to be on fire. That flame breath hadn't burned him. Probably because he hadn't taken a direct hit. Haruhiro had gotten hit by the aftereffects. But even that had been enough to leave him like this. If he'd taken it head-on, he would have been reduced to ash in an instant.

That meant the fire dragon hadn't been aiming for Haruhiro. Then where had it aimed? What was its target?

He could feel the tremors that came with the fire dragon's footsteps. The fire dragon was on the move.

"Ranta and...the others. Merry... Yume... Shihoru... Kuzaku..."

His comrades were trying to run. From the fire dragon, and probably its fire breath. Was the fire dragon aiming for them? Not for Haruhiro, but his comrades? Had it spat fire at them? Was that why Haruhiro had been spared? Because his comrades?

What was happening?

"I have...to look for them."

That was right. What happened wasn't the issue. He had to find them.

Haruhiro used a rocky outcropping on the mountainside to pull himself to his feet. His heel hurt so badly, he thought it might crumble. The pain was what saved him. He was glad for it, even as he wished he could faint. No such luck. He had to search.

When he went in the direction his comrades had fled, he saw the fire dragon's back. The area where the flame breath hit had caved in; there was a quagmire of molten rock at the bottom of the hole. It was a display of the flame's pure destructive power. That would have done more than turn him to ash. If he'd taken a direct hit, there wouldn't have been anything left of him.

Maybe...maybe he wouldn't find his comrades at all.

Don't think that, he told himself. *Don't think stupid things. You can't think. Move. Make yourself move. Get your body moving. It all starts with that.*

He couldn't convince himself to follow right behind the fire dragon. That was much too dangerous. Haruhiro decided to take the long way around. The fire dragon might be looking for something, or it might be chasing his comrades. Maybe they had gotten away. If he circled around in front of the fire dragon, he might meet up with them.

That was right. There was hope. It wasn't hopeless.

While keeping the fire dragon in sight, making sure not to get too close or too far from it, he plotted his course. The terrain was his enemy. It was rough and bumpy. Lava peeked out from the sunken places that looked like they might be paths he could use. There were always salamanders in the lava.

Whenever he lost sight of the fire dragon, he fell into a sudden panic. In his feverish haste, he got burns.

I should jump into the lava and end it all. He often caught himself thinking things like that.

When he caught a glimpse of the fire dragon in the distance, it gave him courage. The fire dragon was there. That relieved him, and he couldn't help but laugh.

"They're alive, right? All of them," he mumbled to himself.

Don't doubt it. If you doubt it, you've lost. Lost? Lost to what?

To myself, probably.

To the weakness of my own heart.

He didn't think he was strong, but had he been this frail all along? He didn't know how much he'd thought he'd grown, but what the hell was this sad state of affairs? It was beyond awful.

Did I think I'd grown? Did I think I could do it? Did I expect anything from myself? How stupid. In the end, I'm just a small fry. I'm a have-not. I have no talent. I worked hard because there was nothing else I could do. I'd done what I could have. Was it not enough? Maybe it isn't a matter of enough or not enough. It's hopeless either way. No matter how hard I worked, no matter what I did, there were always going to be limits.

What, did I think I would be able to do something? Maybe? That's hilarious. Look at me. I knew it from the very beginning. I can't be anyone but me. I can't be anything more than myself. Endlessly weak, and frail. I haven't changed who I am. In the end, I can't be changed. There's no way to change.

I'm small and miserable, pathetically clinging, and while I may be alive for now, it won't last long.

This is me.

I've had enough, it's time to end it.

Look, the fire dragon is so far away. Get ahead of it? Like I could. It hurts. Not just my heel. I hurt all over. I don't want to walk. I can't move.

I'll just stay here.

Sit down and stay put.

In fact, Haruhiro sat down and held his knees for quite a long time.

"Man, I'm pathetic..." he mumbled.

What a laugh. If I've given up on myself, why don't I just give up entirely? Can't I do that? No, of course not. I'm not that graceful. It makes me think this is just how things are. I'm so pathetic, it makes me hate myself.

I wanted to be someone special. That's the truth, you know? I hoped I could be. Like the people I admire. Soma and Kemuri, or

Akira-san and Miho. Even Tokimune and his team. Renji. They're incredible. It makes me think, "If only I could have been like that." I try to think about it, but it's impossible. What can I do about the gap between us? Nothing. Nothing I can do. There's nothing to be done about it. I know that, but I'm just going to die without ever, not even once, being someone special. What is a life like that? It feels lonely and sad. Well, I'm fine with it.

No matter what sort of life you have, it's the only one you'll get, so it's special and irreplaceable, right?

There's no need to compare myself to others. When you're comparing yourself to others, there's only one standard. In the end, it's how you feel about yourself, right?

I can see where this is going, you know. It feels like it's all about to end, so, at the very least, I should give my own blessings to this insignificant life.

"Like you could, idiot," he muttered.

I wanted to lead a life I could boast about to anyone. I wanted to be someone I could be proud of. I grew timid, thinking I couldn't do things, and that's why I ended up like this. But then I used that as an excuse. I acted like I was doing my best, and I tried to be satisfied with that, but in the end, you know what, it was pathetic. I haven't done everything I could have. I half-assed it, and that's no good at all. And now the curtain's probably going to fall with me still feeling dissatisfied about it.

It wasn't like he thought, *I'll give it my all,* and tried to look forward. It was just too painful to stay the way he was. He couldn't sit still. He stood up because he had no other choice. That was the truth.

He couldn't say he'd honed his senses at the time, but he felt a presence. Without turning, he did a forward roll. Something fell right behind him.

To avoid using his right heel, he used his left leg as an axis to turn around, drawing his stiletto as he did. His enemy had a long machete-like weapon that he'd swung at Haruhiro.

It wasn't that Haruhiro thought he'd get taken out if he tried to dodge. His body reacted on its own. Haruhiro plunged head first into his enemy's lower body.

When he tried to stab the enemy, he jumped back and evaded it. Haruhiro charged in, not stopping to wonder who the enemy was or why this was happening. At some point, he found himself holding not just his stiletto, but also his knife with the hilt guard.

His heel hurt. He'd be lying if he said he didn't feel the pain, but he didn't let it bother him. He attacked.

He was on the attack.

The enemy's blade was about one-and-a-half meters long, meaning it had far more reach than Haruhiro's weapons. The enemy was larger than he was too, so he wasn't going to be able to fend him off with Swat for long. Haruhiro didn't eventually come to that conclusion; he knew it instinctively. He had to close the gap and attack.

All the enemy did was run around. He had a weapon, but he was half naked. From the look of him, he seemed to be an orc. He was slender compared to the orcs of Waluandin. But he wasn't just thin. His body reminded Haruhiro of a bowstring pulled to its limits. His skin lacked its customary green smoothness. It was raised in some places, twisted in others.

Maybe those were burn scars. They covered his whole body. And his eyes. Both were muddy and white. Could he even see Haruhiro?

Whether the orc could or not, even when he backed away, he never went near the lava. His movements were elegant, like a master martial artist. Haruhiro, even as he pressed the attack and put the orc on the defensive, didn't have the orc on the ropes. He had leeway to work with. Plenty of it, probably.

Haruhiro might be being forced to attack, but if he didn't attack, he'd be attacked. And if he was attacked, he wouldn't be able to defend himself. If his heel wasn't wounded, he might have risked running, but there was no chance of escaping when he couldn't run properly. He wished he could talk his way out of it, but that wasn't possible, either. Even if he didn't think he could win, he had to.

It was kill or be killed.

It was no time to calculate odds. Even without him considering them, countless thoughts raced through his head at high speed.

His enemy's footwork was unique. He was standing on his tiptoes, which seemed to sink into the ground.

The orc was awfully flexible. He controlled his machete with just his right hand. His left hand wasn't even on it.

That machete didn't seem metallic. It looked like it had been carved out of stone. A long machete made of stone might have been handmade.

Did he live here? How did he eat and drink? Was this a livable environment?

He'd be attacking soon.

See, here it comes.

The orc twisted his body, pulling it diagonally. The long stone machete thrust forward.

Haruhiro didn't fall back. He couldn't avoid it. Instead, he put all his strength into a Swat with his knife with the hilt guard. He couldn't handle a combo, but if it was just one strike...

The machete was heavy.

The orc's strength was immense, but Haruhiro pulled it off. He deflected the blow and immediately went in to attack. The orc slipped back and away from him, scrunching up his face.

Was that a smile? Fine. Smile away. Haruhiro wouldn't smile. He'd attack.

He got in close, striking with his stiletto and always taking aim with his knife. He knew. He didn't need to think about it, he just knew. The orc was *enjoying* this. He might have been crazy, even by orc standards. He was enjoying the fight and trying to savor it.

The orc probably intended to force Haruhiro to give everything he had, and then once he was satisfied, he'd kill him. That being the case, Haruhiro had one small chance for victory.

He was already giving his all. He couldn't move any faster or swing his stiletto any harder. This was his limit. Just keeping it up was tiring, and he'd only degrade from here. He couldn't turn this into a drawn-out battle. The more time that passed, the fewer chances he would have to attack. The orc knew that, too. If they fought, and fought until they were through, then luck, situation, and a variety of other factors would gradually drop off until, in the end, the strongest was guaranteed to win.

And, in this case, it wouldn't be Haruhiro. It would be the orc.

That was why, before it came to that, Haruhiro threw everything he had into one desperate gambit. Of course, the orc knew that. He was egging him on.

Bring it on, he seemed to say. *Come on, bring it.*

The line was nowhere to be seen. Haruhiro saw an invisible, narrow bridge laid out in front of him, and he had no choice but to cross it. The orc was on the other side of the bridge. He knew Haruhiro was coming and was eagerly awaiting his chance to demolish him. Haruhiro's odds of pulling this off might not be zero, but they were close to it. Even so, Haruhiro would cross the bridge.

Because he had no choice? Because he had to?

No.

Because I want to live. I don't want to die. I can't let myself die. I'll kill him, and live. Live. Live. Live for all I'm worth. I'll beat him. I'm gonna win. Now, cross the bridge.

Assault.

He had thought he was giving his all before, but maybe he had been wrong. Haruhiro surprised himself. He hadn't known he could move so fast.

In a turn of good fortune, he overshot the orc's expectations for him. Haruhiro easily got in too close for him to reach. From there, all he had to do was stab like crazy with his stiletto and slash away with his knife.

The orc quickly brought his knee up to defend himself. Haruhiro stabbed the hell out of it, slashed it up, and pushed in.

The orc reached out with his left hand. He tried to pull Haruhiro in to seal his attacks.

Haruhiro didn't worry about it, instead poking his stiletto through the orc's belly and gouging him. His knife slammed in to the orc's right armpit. He pushed the orc down.

The orc wrapped both of his legs around Haruhiro and squeezed, grabbing Haruhiro's hair with his left hand. Then he slammed the hilt of his long stone machete into Haruhiro's head.

Even so, Haruhiro continued twisting his stiletto inside the orc's guts. Moving his knife vigorously, he tried to cut the orc's right arm off at the shoulder. He bit the orc's neck, tearing into skin, meat, and blood vessels. Blood flowed. It wasn't just warm, it was hot.

Haruhiro bit into that open wound even more. The orc screamed. Haruhiro didn't let out so much as a grunt.

Destroy, destroy, I'll destroy you, destroy you, destroy you until you can't move. Live, live, I'll live, I'm gonna live. Win, I'll win and live, I'll survive. It's kill or be killed, live or die. I'm not the one who's gonna die, it's you.

Oh, wait, maybe I can stop now?

No, not yet. He needed to do more. Haruhiro didn't stop until the blood coming out went cool. When he was completely, absolutely certain the orc was dead, all the strength drained from his body. Haruhiro burst into tears.

He'd won. Haruhiro had won.

His opponent had been strong. In terms of pure strength, probably stronger than Haruhiro. Far stronger, maybe.

Why had Haruhiro been able to win?

He didn't think his opponent had been arrogant. The orc had never let his guard down. If his enemy's strength had been a ten, he'd probably assumed Haruhiro's was a five. Maybe a four. But at the last moment, he'd been able to add just a little extra to that five-maybe-four. That was all he had needed to decide the battle. Indeed, Haruhiro had been gambling. It had gone as planned. In that sense, it had been a perfect victory. The weak overcame the strong. By himself, with only his own strength and ability, he had seized this victory.

Haruhiro looked down at the remains of the defeated. He wanted to learn what he could about his foe.

The orc was two meters and twenty centimeters tall. There was no way to weigh him, but he had to be over one hundred kilograms. He could be two, maybe even three hundred kilos. That was huge. He'd looked slender, but he was still massive.

Burn marks covered his entire body, scars traveling down all the way to the tips of his toes. This had to be deliberate. He must have burned himself. There was an intricate design carved into his exposed fangs. A dragon, he realized.

Haruhiro went through the orc's possessions. He had a belt around his waist, with pockets for items and a sheath. He had a golden ring, four blackish scalelike objects, and a small knife. Haruhiro took it all.

The orc's eyes were open, so he closed them, and put his hands together because that seemed like the right thing to do. It was a strange thing to think, but Haruhiro felt this orc had shared his life with him. It was thanks to him Haruhiro was alive now. At least, that was how he felt.

Haruhiro was bruised all over, and in such bad shape it would be hard to find a part of him that didn't ache. The life the orc had given him might burn out eventually. Even so, he was living on now. Since he was alive, there were things to do, or rather things he wanted to do and things he had to do.

He wanted to see his comrades.

He didn't think for a second, *I'm sure they're all fine,* or, *I'm sure we'll meet again*. He had no high hopes of it happening, but he wanted it to. He decided to continue the search. Until his life ran out, he would keep on looking.

Leaving the orc behind, Haruhiro walked off. When he turned back after a short distance, he saw the salamanders were already swarming over the corpse. Without a hint of irony or sarcasm, Haruhiro thought it was the second most fitting end he could have received. The most fitting would have been him challenging the fire dragon and being incinerated or devoured.

Haruhiro had no leads. Not even a direction to go in.

Whenever he saw the fire dragon off in the distance, he found it strangely encouraging, and broke into a smile.

When the pain and exhaustion made it too hard to walk,

Haruhiro accepted it and sat down to rest. He lay down sometimes, too. If he couldn't get up again, that would be that. He could accept it. However, that wasn't likely to happen. If he lost consciousness, well, there would be no helping that. However, until the time came, his wish would not fade.

I want to see my comrades.

After all I've been through, I'm not going to think that's pathetic.

Really, I don't want to be left all by myself. It's lonely.

There were times when he not so much fell asleep as passed out. When he came to his senses, he was happy.

He was still alive. He could search again.

You know, like this, it feels like I've gone everywhere. When was the last time I thought about that?

I was riding a bicycle. Wait... Bicycle?

I dunno what that is, but I thought I could go anywhere on it.

I felt like I could go everywhere. What was it that got me out there? Oh, right. One of those things you see all the time. The rainbow. It was after the rain. I saw a rainbow. Where did the rainbow start, and where did it end? I thought I'd go and see. I swore I'd find it.

I gave up along the way. Now, I wouldn't give up. I'd go as far as I could, and even if the rainbow vanished, I would wait for it to appear again.

When I close my eyes...ah, I can see it clearly.

The rainbow.

The bow of seven colors beyond the sky.

I'll head toward the rainbow. I'll head for the rainbow, and never stop going.

He sensed a tremor. Haruhiro opened his eyes to find the fire dragon close by. Close enough that he could look up at it. He went to shake its hand, then stopped.

He decided to stay put. He worried he might get stomped. If it happened, it happened. There was nothing he could do about it.

He closed his eyes and watched the rainbow.

At some point, the fire dragon left.

He was alive. Still alive. But his body felt heavy, or rather sluggish.

I guess I can rest. Yeah. I'll take a rest.

He'd found a good place. There was a depression. For some reason, it was a little cool. No, it was really cool. It was a wonder how the ground could be cool in a place like there. It was hot everywhere.

He slowly came to the realization that he was crawling. Walking was hard, after all. Crawling wasn't much easier, but it was better than walking.

How far did this depression go? It seemed to go on for quite a while. But here was good, he thought. *Here was good.*

Suddenly, he was engulfed by total darkness.

On the verge of it, he had a vague memory of thinking, *Maybe I'm done for.* And then, his eyes snapped open.

It looked like he was alive. Stubborn, wasn't he?

To live was to not die, after all.

He couldn't move so much as a finger. He was having a hard time just breathing. He went on like that for a long time. He had no real hope of recovering, but suddenly, it occurred to him he *could* get up. You never know until you try, after all. So, he did, and he could.

If this kept up, dying might take him a while. Did he have to keep living until then? Well, if that was the case, live on he would.

Even so, when he sat with his back against the rock wall, all the muscles in his body relaxed, as if some vital core had slipped free.

I can't see the rainbow.

It sure is dark, huh? This place is dark.

Wait, where is this place...?

A depression.

A cool depression?

He turned to face it.

That's a hole, isn't it?

"...Seriously?" he whispered.

It was dark. His vision was hazy, and he couldn't see very well, but it was a hole. In the bottom of the depression, there was a hole about two meters across. It wasn't vertical; it was on a diagonal slant. He couldn't imagine it was any old cave. Not with this coolness.

It was abnormal. He was on a mountaintop covered with lava, after all. Haruhiro was right in front of the hole.

It had to be the tunnel.

That hole led through to Grimgar.

"This...can't be happening..." he whispered.

He could go back.

To Grimgar.

"This is...the rainbow's..."

A moan escaped from deep in his throat.

How?

How is this the beginning of the rainbow? It's the end of the rainbow. There is no rainbow. There never was. It's an illusion.

It was always going to be impossible. I mean, at this point, I really can't move anymore. Besides, what am I going to do if I make it back alone? That's no good. I need my comrades with me.

Even if I search on my own, and I happen to come across the place we were looking for, it's meaningless, isn't it?

Is this the end that's been waiting for me?

Is this how it ends?

How worthless.

But if even a little of my strength returned, and I was able to move, I'd search for them. My comrades. Then, at the end of it all, I'd die alone. Even if it's pointless, painful, and unpleasant, I'll live for something until I die. I'll keep living on.

I still don't know if I'll be able to wake up again or not. I can't bring myself to think "I hope I wake up", but if I do, I'm sure I'll keep struggling on.

For now, I'll sleep.

I wish I had someone to sing me a lullaby.

I don't like being alone.

Someone, be with me.

Someone.

...Please.

All I need is for you to be here.

"Awaken."

A dream. It must have been a dream.

That voice. He'd heard it before.

It was a man's voice. Who was that? But he didn't hear it now. That was why he must have been dreaming.

His eyes were shut tight with some kind of film. He struggled to open them. What did he think about that? *I'm still alive,* maybe? It was a wonder that he was. But was he truly alive? Wasn't this the world after death? It was hard not to be a little doubtful.

He heard something. Footsteps, if it wasn't some auditory illusion. He was still a thief, even if he wasn't much of one, so he could tell it was footsteps.

They were approaching. Multiple sources. Probably five people.

"Ah!"

He heard a voice. Haruhiro forced himself to raise his head and turn his eyes toward the voice.

I'm alive.

"Haru!" Merry came running. She hugged him and touched his face all over.

Merry. She sure is beautiful, huh? I'm realizing that all over again. Yeah. I dunno. What can I say? I have no words.

Haruhiro tried to smile. He wasn't sure if he managed it. He wasn't confident.

"Haru-kun, Haru-kun!" Yume cried.

"Haruhiro-kun!" Shihoru.

"Haruhiro!" Kuzaku shouted.

"No way, damn it! Seriously, you piece of crap." And Ranta.

Don't call me a piece of crap, man, Haruhiro thought. *Whatever, it's fine.*

Well, no, it isn't fine.

Not really.

"I'll heal you right away! Haru! Can you hear me?! Hang in there! It's going to be okay! Everyone's here!"

Haruhiro nodded, then closed his eyes.

He could see the rainbow.

I'M NOT GREAT WITH ACTION GAMES. The reason is that I can't handle doing the same thing over and over.

While I'm playing, I start to see, *Oh, this is what I should be doing here.* I can play through once or twice, but I have trouble doing any more. I start feeling mischievous and do something differently.

No, you may be thinking, *that's just a lack of practice.* I could do it right if I just kept playing again and again. That might be true, but the truth is, I'm not great at folding my laundry either, and for some reason I can never fold it all the same way. Unless I really focus on getting them all folded the same and pour all my attention into it. *Huh, that's weird, I have ten similar-looking T-shirts all folded in completely different ways.* That's what happens.

With T-shirts, if they're not all folded the same way, it's inconvenient when I go to put them in my dresser. It's the same for socks and underwear. As a result, my dresser is always a chaotic mess.

Now, I think this is a matter of personality, or maybe the way my brain is structured. My brain was made that way for some reason. I like action RPGs, but I'm terrible at them. It's sad.

Now, there's still a bit of time between November 24th when I'm writing this afterword and when the anime *Grimgar of Fantasy and Ash* begins broadcasting, but it's just around the corner. The other day, I sat in on a dubbing session. It's shaping up to be a wonderful anime, and I'm looking forward to it. It's been an educational experience, too.

The manga version of *Grimgar of Fantasy and Ash* Ms. Mutsumi Okubashi has been serializing in *Gangan Joker* also follows the same fundamental outline as the novel, but the details and flavor are slightly different, making it stimulating for me.

I must work harder as a novelist. *Grimgar* is just getting started, after all.

Haruhiro and the others can never move forward more than a step at a time, if that. The way things are going, I'm not entirely confident where they will go and whether they'll arrive wherever they're going. But if they keep moving forward, the road will surely go on.

I will say, I do have some idea in my head of where I want things to end up. It's all up to them, though, so it's possible they may arrive somewhere else entirely. If that happens, it happens. For the people who haven't had the chance to show up much yet, I plan for them to make appearances little by little, so look forward to that.

I've run out of pages.

To my editor, K, to Eiri Shirai, to the designers of KOMEWORKS among others, to everyone involved in the production and sale of this book, and finally to all of you now holding this book, I offer my heartfelt appreciation and all of my love. Now, I lay down my pen for today.

I hope we will meet again.